GUERRILLA WARFARE—NOMAD STYLE

A guardroom stood to one side, occupied by two lounging lizards. The Nomad slipped past them quietly. He stopped at the next room, lifted the latch, and eased open the heavy door. He ducked into the darkness.

When his eyes adjusted to the gloom, he saw that the apartment was tenanted by a lone dragon lying in the sunken pit that served as a berth. Death Wind drew his knife.

Crouching low, he flowed across the room. Every sense was alive, every muscle attuned. The knife rose in the air. Death Wind balanced on the balls of his feet as he lowered himself to within striking range. His nostrils flared and his chest expanded as he forced air into his lungs.

Scaled lids fluttered, the squat body stirred.

Moonlight glinted briefly off the steel blade as it plunged downward with all the force Death Wind's muscles could bring to bear. The dragon lurched in slowly dawning awareness. The knife sheared off the breast bone at the same time that the long tail whipped around and caught the Nomad in the head. He was flung backward by the force of the blow. He crashed noisily over a stool and into the hard wall . . .

DRAGONS PAST

GARY GENTILE

ACE BOOKS, NEW YORK

DRAGONS PAST

An Ace Book / published by arrangement with
the author

PRINTING HISTORY
Ace edition / March 1990

ISBN: 0-441-16652-0

Ace Books are published by The Berkley Publishing Group,
200 Madison Avenue, New York, New York 10016.
The name "ACE" and the "A" logo are trademarks
belonging to Charter Communications, Inc.

PRINTED IN THE UNITED STATES OF AMERICA

10 9 8 7 6 5 4 3 2 1

DRAGONS PAST

CHAPTER 1

Scott dragged the heavy power cable across the floor, dropped it behind the computer console, and pulled off the access panel. He reached into the maze of wires, felt along the gray insulation. It took him a minute to find the wire he wanted. He worked his fingers to the terminal, stabbed it with an arc welder, and pulled it free. He scraped the insulation off the power cable, applied the arc welder, and attached the new leads to the still-hot terminal.

"There, that should do it."

Rusty flexed long fingers. "Are you sure? I can't keep having power failures in the middle of a program. I have enough trouble as it is."

"I'm never sure when I work with dragon hardware." Scott moved around the console, behind his friend, and thumbed the power switch. "But if my deductions are correct, we should be on a different circuit, and I don't think we'll have any more overloads. Give it a try."

The annunciator board glittered with yellow, incandescent lights. Some shone for a moment, then winked off. Others flashed sequentially, each with its own tone. The viewscreen brightened.

Rusty took a deep breath and sighed. He pulled on a pair of thin hide gloves that had sharpened wooden pegs protruding from the fingertips. "Okay, here goes."

With deft manipulations Rusty flicked toggles along the side of the alien keyboard, inserted pegged fingers into pointed depressions, and palmed plastic levers. Strange, indecipherable symbols ranged across the screen, and a speaker emitted discordant intonations. Rusty played the input valves with practiced ease.

"That is quite a display of talent for so young a lad."

Scott spun around. "Oh, hello, Doc. I didn't hear you come in."

"Stealth is a faculty I still retain, although my bones do

1

creak a mite if I bend too much." Doc hobbled closer, leaned against his wooden cane. "What kind of chicanery are you performing now? I thought this machine broke down yesterday."

Rusty's eyes kept their focus on the foreign calligraphy appearing on the screen.

"No, it just uses so much power it was causing a voltage drop." Scott fanned the room with a large bronzed hand. "What with all the peripheral devices going at the same time, the main distribution circuit couldn't handle the load. The computer kept glitching on us."

Doc watched the proceedings, absently playing with his long white beard. "I'm still amazed at what you boys have been able to learn about dragon technology, as abstruse as it is."

"No technology is incomprehensible once you understand the basics. Look at it this way. Last week you set Helen's broken leg which, to me, is an absolutely incredible accomplishment."

Doc rubbed his own bent extremity. "I hope I did a better job on hers than I did on my own."

"But you had medical training and experience that made the job a simple one—for you. And I'll bet you could just have easily set a dragon's leg."

"Yes, well, the physiology is essentially the same despite evolutionary variations. A bone is a bone, and a leg is a leg. They all grow alike, and they all heal according to established biological precepts."

Scott grinned. "Exactly! And the same holds true for technology. Granted the dragons built things differently, partly because of the materials at hand, partly because of their physical differences, and partly because of their lizard way of looking at things. They didn't have large oil and coal deposits, so they had to reach atomic energy directly before they could form a centralized power network."

Rusty stabbed a kill switch that cleared the screen. "And they designed their tools and machines to suit their own anatomical dimensions." He held up his gloved hands. "Sandra sewed extensions into the fingers that approximate their clawed digits. Now, I can run the computer as fast as a dragon technician."

"Faster," Scott said.

"I can poke all these indented buttons with fake talons, and snap switches with the curled ends. It took a little getting use to."

Scott picked up a coil of wire. "And look at this. Dragons are color blind, so it would be senseless to color code their electrical leads. Instead, they have a notching system similar to Roman numerals. That way they can *feel* the ciphers without having to look at them. And under the insulation is plain old copper wire, just like we use. Doc, electrons don't care who manufactured the filaments, they flow just the same."

"Yes, well, I guess you've got something there."

Rusty started up the computer again. "I can even get their computer to work. I can load programs, I can enter the data banks, and I can print a hard copy on that laser printer over there. But I can't make it *do* anything."

Scott laughed, long blond hair shaking. "He can even get it to sing, if you can call that noise a song."

Rusty squirmed on the uncomfortable alien stool. "More like a funeral dirge if you ask me."

Doc watched the computer light up. The beeping tones followed a simple monotonous routine. "How do you know what you're doing?"

Rusty's fingers danced across the complicated keyboard. "I've learned certain functions that lead to the same results. Watch." For several seconds he flicked switches and punched buttons.

"I do declare," Doc said slowly. "Have you memorized an entire twenty-two character sequence?"

"Twenty-three. But all I'm doing is defining parameters. I don't understand what any of it says."

Lights flashed on and off, the speaker twanged in cadence up and down the music scale. Unfamiliar symbols appeared fleetingly on the screen. The laser printer clattered, then started humming as a lamina of white plastic spit out the left side.

Scott took a few steps, waited for the machine to stop, and ripped off the finished copy. "The printer doesn't use ink, it burns holes through the material. To see the figures you have to lay it down on a black surface. This board is a reader." He placed the sheet on the movable panel. "It doesn't need lights because the black shows through the holes."

"Ingenious." Doc took the reader and ran a crooked finger

across the odd figures. "Do you read it from left to right, or right to left."

Rusty switched the computer to a different mode. It emitted lights and tones. "Who knows? Maybe they read from the bottom up."

Scott humphed. "It's all pterodactyl scratch to me."

Rusty pressed a lever. A clear cube, each facet an inch across, popped out of a hidden recess. He opened a compartment that held identical cubes lined up like eggs in a carton, each slot padded with soft cloth. He exchanged the cube in his hand for another, held it up.

"This is how they store information. It's a crystal matrix that can be inserted into this receptacle with any one of the sides facing the scanner on the bottom. Each facet is notched with a specific symbol, and each side loads a different program. So far, I've been able to figure out how to count to six."

Rusty dropped the cube into the aperture, ran through another sequence on the keyboard. More dragon hieroglyphics filled the screen. "I'm still looking for a computerized Rosetta Stone. Now, I can convert this into a series of dots and dashes, but, of course, I can't read that either."

"Incredible."

The computer went into its song and dance, the printer clattered, then began humming. As the plasticized laminations appeared, the pitch changed from a uniform hum to a Dopplering whine.

Rusty's eyes pinched. "Hmmn. I've never heard it make *that* sound before."

Scott froze with his hand on the printout. He bent over, put his ear close to the fluctuating dials. "It's not coming from here."

Doc turned ever so slightly, faced the doorway. "If I didn't know better, I'd say that sounded like a—"

"Mother, please." Sandra jerked her head away, but her long tresses stayed with the comb. "Ouch."

"Well, if you would stay still for a moment and let me get the witches out, it wouldn't hurt at all. You have such fine silky hair, why do you let it get knotted up like this."

"I already brushed it once today."

Helen cleaned black strands from between wooden teeth.

"Stop it. If you make me break this comb Death Wind will be awfully mad. It took him half a day to whittle it for you."

"*He's* the one who likes my hair smooth, not me. I don't care if it gets a little rustled."

"Sandra, at least show some appreciation for his effort." Helen held her daughter close. She twisted the long hair into a simple braid that would keep the loose strands from flying in the breeze. "You can't start letting yourself go just because—"

"Mother, stop treating me like a child."

"I'm treating you like you deserve. You'll understand when you have children of your own."

"Ha! Not in *this* world. I've got better things to do than pamper some little brat—"

"You said it." Helen stuck the comb in the back pocket of Sandra's shorts and patted her on the rump. "And I'm still your mother, no matter what he is to you. There, you're all done. Now go outside and play."

Sandra scowled, but headed for the door. Outside, she leaned against a blobbed plastic railing. From the uppermost roost, once occupied by dragon officials, she had a view of the entire city: low-roofed structures, open courtyards, flyer landing pads, the hatchery, slave quarters, all stitched together by rolling, narrow streets. Much of the city was amorphous orange plastic, melted by fire and flame, now caught running and solidified in a permanent blackened mass.

"I'm glad they're dead. Every last one of them. I never want to see another dragon."

Bending her splinted leg and moving awkwardly on crutches, Helen stepped out into the sunshine. The radiant rays softened the lines of hardship on her face. "They were only slaves, dear."

"I don't care. If they're dragons, I don't like them."

"They weren't responsible for anything." Helen leaned up against her daughter. She was a head taller than Sandra. "They couldn't help what they were."

Sandra pressed against the warm touch. "So what did they die from?"

Helen shrugged. A light breeze played with her tawny hair. "Loneliness? Homesickness? I don't know. The Nomads fed them, and took care of them, just as they would any wounded animal. But they just withered away. Slaves are never healthy, because they don't have a purpose, or any real reason for living. When you live by doing the bidding of others, your own life doesn't have much meaning. You have no reason to care."

"Mother, did—did they torture you much?"

"The technicians?" Helen stood up on her good leg, placed the crutches in front of her. "Yes, but it wasn't done cruelly, as you might think. It was—well, it was kind of how they communicated what they wanted done. The dragons don't have vocal cords, so they can't speak. What they did was shoot us with stinging rays that made us move. And if they wanted us to do something, they just kept stinging us until we figured out what it was they wanted us to do. Then, they stopped stinging. Unless someone got out of line. After a while, you learn to get up and start moving as soon as they arrive. You anticipate what they want, and you get hurt less."

"They treated you like animals, like beasts of burden. The dirty—"

"Sandra, I told you to stop using those words."

Sandra grimaced. "I didn't say anything bad."

"But you were going to."

"So what? I couldn't say anything bad about the dragons that isn't true. They're lousy bastards, every one of 'em. And I'd never knuckle under 'em, no matter what they did to me."

"Sometimes, dear, even if you don't want to, it's easier to just go along with things. To stay alive is the primary motivation. You can always plot. And we did. We were working on schemes when you rescued us. But they would have cost lives. There would have been sacrifices."

"You know, sometimes you sound just like Pop."

"Well, he *is* my father."

"Yeah, he's a neat guy. I wish—*DW!*"

Death Wind, tall and dark, walked along the parapet. His bulky musculature was overtly visible since he wore only moccasins and a loincloth. Long shaggy hair hung down to his broad shoulders.

Sandra ran to him, threw her arms around his back, lay her head for a moment upon his chest. "Where've you been all day? I thought you were going to help me make the bed."

"We make it—we *will* make it—tomorrow. I will get more padding from the nursery, and cut the legs from a workbench. Today I helped Scott move machinery. He shows me how to make electrical connections."

"Oh, *him*." Sandra drew away, jumped backward onto the flat-topped railing. The courtyard was at least fifty feet below. "He's always working on *something*."

"Honey, get down from there before you fall." Helen placed her crutches under her arms, limped to her daughter, pulled her off by the arm. "Death Wind, you're going to have to watch her. She tends to be *so* impetuous."

The savage's expression did not change. "That is Sandra."

Helen laughed. "I know, but she can afford to change."

"Mother! I'm a grown-up now. I proved it a month ago."

"I didn't say you weren't, and I said nothing about growing up. All I said was there was room for growth. We all grow, throughout our lives. The day we stop growing, we die."

"Nomads learn always: about their people, about their land. It is the only way." Death Wind raised a thickly veined arm, gestured toward the jungle beyond the city limits. "My people must work together, and learn together. It is the only way to survive. We collect wisdom always, even without need. If it has no use, we pass it on to our children. Maybe they need."

Helen leaned on her crutches, formed a triangle with the two youngsters. She placed a hand softly on his shoulder. "Death Wind, do you miss your people, your mother and father? They've been gone over a week."

His forehead furrowed, his eyebrows pinched. "They go home, where they belong. They cannot stay in one spot, for it is in their blood to move. And now that the land is free from dragons, they roam in peace. Later, I will visit." He raised his fist and thumped his breast. "I carry them with me always, whether they live or die."

"A good attitude." Helen pursed her lips, nodding slowly. Her dark eyes dropped. "I wish I could adopt it. I will always miss . . ."

"Hey, whaddaya say we go get some chow? I'm so hungry I could eat a dinosaur." Sandra dragged Death Wind by the arm, indicated with her chin for her mother to follow. "They killed a fresh one from the pens this morning."

Death Wind placed one hand on his sheathed knife; with the other he patted his belly. "I have tasted it already." Slowly, his stern features relaxed. "But, I can eat more."

"You can always eat more." Sandra laughed. "Come on. Let's go."

Helen's eyes widened. She peered over her daughter's shoulder. "Why—why is the sun—moving." Both Sandra and Death Wind followed her gaze. The golden globe shimmered, grew larger, veered slantwise. Then Helen twisted on her crutches and looked at the *real* sun. "Oh, my god."

CHAPTER 2

Heart pounding, Scott charged for the doorway. The sky was clear and blue, with only a few scattered puffy clouds coasting along the horizon. He spun toward the thrumming sound, southward. A golden object hung in the sky, riding on a column of heat waves.

His stomach twisted into a knot. "It's a dragon flyer!"

Rusty was suddenly next to him, technician's vest flapping. "Where the heck—"

"Not from Shangri-la, that's for sure."

Doc poked his cane between the two, pried them apart, and stepped out the opening and onto the portico. "I do say, this is rather unexpected. I thought we had seen the last of them. I'm afraid this is going to pose quite a problem."

"Problem, hell. It's going to start a war. Let's go!"

Scott took off, with Rusty on his heels.

"But where—"

Doc's question was cut off as a large object crashed into the ground. Death Wind landed on his feet, legs bending to take up the shock of the fifteen-foot drop from the lowest level.

"Armory," the Nomad said. "Quick."

"I'll race you," Scott shouted.

As the three of them ran off Sandra screamed down from the penthouse, "Wait for me."

But no one waited. They bolted into the street and along the narrow corridor of orange plastic. They cut through an alley that emerged on the walled lane leading to the weapons storage building. Others, captives the dragons had collected during their rampaging sojourns into the wilderness, were there ahead of them.

The huge doors were already open, and anxious people were inside the armory passing out power packs and laser pistols. The three warriors joined the melee donning weapons that were kept constantly charged. Men and women dashed madly about,

9

shouting orders and observations. There was no confusion:
they were all warriors, trained by a lifetime of fighting.

Scott adjusted the straps across his chest, as he had done so
many times before. "Let's get back to Computer Central."

"What are we going to do?" Rusty said.

"I don't know. I guess we defend ourselves."

Rusty straggled out of the armory, the backpack slung over
one rounded shoulder. "But what's our plan?"

Scott was already in the street. "Stay alive."

Death Wind wore one power pack, carried another by the
straps. "This not good. Could be other death machines
coming."

"Let's hope not." Scott weaved through the crowd. People
crisscrossed along the street, heading back the way they had
come, back to their dwellings, their families. "We'll have our
hands full with just one."

The dragon saucer stopped at the perimeter of the city. The
shimmering force field was a pylon that kept it high in the air.
It hovered over the revetments, but made no attempt to lose
altitude. It seemed to be watching—and waiting.

Rusty gasped under the weight of the pack. "Is it my eyes,
or is that flyer bigger than the others?"

Scott glanced aloft as he ran, trying to keep up with Death
Wind. "I'd swear it's twice the size. Look how much wider it
is than a landing pen."

"It is moving," Death Wind observed. He skidded around an
intersection and down a side street. Apartments lined both
sides, vacant now that the dragon contingent had died off. "It
comes to the tower."

"They're staying high, though." Scott pulled the pistol out
of the pack-mounted holster, felt the weight in his hand. "They
don't want to vaporize the central computer with their force
field."

"If they're afraid of doing damage, maybe they won't land
in the city," Rusty said.

"Look, someone's shooting."

Laser beams flashed up from the ground. With sharp
intensity the penciled lights cleaved the air, reaching out for the
cone-shaped energy funnelers on the saucer's undercarriage.

"It's too high. They're not doing any damage."

The dragon flyer thrummed, moving over the city but still
out of range. Its shadow crept over the streets and low

structures. A port split the curved edge, a circular bank of nozzles poked out and down.

"It's about time you guys got here." Sandra's voice trembled as she dashed out of the portico. "Whaddaya do, stop for tea on the way?"

Scott was breathing hard, but controlled. He stayed out from under the canopy and kept an eye on the approaching flyer. "They had a fresh batch brewing. Rusty, hurry it up. It's starting to come down."

Rusty trudged in from the street, leaned his scrawny body against a plastic column. "This thing—is so—heavy."

Sandra turned around, arms behind her, back to Death Wind. He slung the power pack over her shoulders. She humped it up high, cinched down the straps, reached behind and pulled the firing mechanism out of its holster. "Yeah, but it'll blow 'em to kingdom come if they get close enough."

"Pardon me for interrupting your bandying conversation, but I think you should realize that you're up against an adversary without true remorse. If that is a troop flyer, the soldiers may not be aware of the intrinsic value this humble structure has to their more informed superiors. I suggest that when dealing with an unknown quantity, one seek conceal-ment."

"Go stick your head in a hole, Pop." Sandra held the laser pistol out under his nose. "This is the only quantity I need to know."

"My dear—"

The top of the portico exploded in a shower of molten plastic. Hot, searing blobs flew outward like drops of water splashing from a stomped puddle. Scott felt tiny pinpoints of acid stinging his face, his hands, his bare legs. The explosions kept coming in a continuous line, arcing around them, blowing open the top of the portico, scything through the supporting colonnades. The roof sagged.

"Inside, everyone!" Scott grabbed Rusty by the arm, shoved Doc ahead of him through the doorway. Death Wind and Sandra piled in behind them. "They've got a laser machine gun."

Sandra crouched inside the opening. "I hate it when he's right."

The portico was eaten up in a series of blasts. Then the wall started to melt as fire was redirected. Several beams pierced the doorway, hitting a charging generator and igniting an electrical cabinet. Sparks spit out of the plastic casing as high-voltage leads shorted. The air smelled of ozone and burnt insulation.

The enemy machine dropped lower, the flaring tip of its multitudinous dischargers touching the roof of an adjacent building. The entire structure metamorphosed: doorways and window openings became drooling stalactites of plastic. Orange turned to black. Like a cube of chocolate in the hot sun, the building softened, sagged, poured into rivulets of molten polymers.

"Help! Help!"

"Mother!" Sandra leaped into the doorway.

"Don't—" Scott's warning was ignored. He charged out after her. Death Wind held a piece of her blouse in his hand, the material ripped free when she broke from his grasp.

From half a dozen different directions laser beams shot upward at the descending flyer. People were converging and concentrating their fire on the needlelike power cones. The laser gatling gun swiveled, returning blast for blast. Small explosions followed in the wake of its rotating barrels.

Scott jumped back for cover, his moccasins singed from the molten puddles. He crouched half outside. Helen crutched down the outer ramp. Scott aimed his pistol at the flyer.

Death Wind firmly pushed his hand down. "Do not attract fire."

Scott realized that the flyer's attention was occupied by the flanking attacks. "Good idea."

Sandra reached her mother, jammed a shoulder under her armpit, and hopped with her along the still-smoking floor. "Come on." She yanked the crutch that kept getting in the way. Together they hobbled down the ramp. Death Wind and Scott, guns holstered, rushed to meet them.

Street defenders continued to pour laser beams into the hull of the flyer. Three more gun turrets opened, and with the firepower of four concentric gatling lasers the surrounding structures were swept with awesome and death-dealing energy. Explosions blew holes in thermoplastic barricades, routing the attacking garrisons.

Lasers raked the demolished portico, stitching a seam through the hobbling foursome. Scott screamed and fell, clutching his right leg. Death Wind bundled the women through the door, turned to help his fallen companion. With laser discharges all around them, he picked Scott up and half dragged him to safety.

The air smelled of acid. Doc threw another glass bomb at the electrical panel. The ruptured casing spat gaseous fumes that quelched the fire. Fanning the air, he receded on his cane. "I had to use carbon tetrachloride to put out the fire. Lucky the dragons thought of such safety devices."

Scott grimaced with pain. "Yes, well, right now they're not being so thoughtful."

"Helen, are you all right?"

"Yes, but I can't run with this cast."

Doc nodded, bent to examine Scott's wound. "Let me see that leg."

An ugly hole, still smoking, cut through his calf. Scott gritted his teeth. "Forget it. Let's just get out of here."

"We'd better hurry, too." Rusty held a cloth up to his face as he chucked another firebomb at the front wall. "They're going to melt their way in at any moment."

The staccato report of hits on the outer rampart was followed by bulging panels. A hole appeared next to the doorway. Energy continued to pour in with unerring accuracy. Outside, the oversized flyer settled down on the remains of the building opposite the courtyard, cut off its engines, and stood like a giant toadstool. As the plastic around its base resolidified, a ramp was let down from the central column. The wall of the building dissolved under the constant fire, and beams of light shot across the unprotected room.

"Out the back way!" Rusty pawed at his face, wiping away tears, as he headed for the doorway.

Injured and wounded, they limped and staggered out the other entrance, into a courtyard bounded on all sides by high plastic walls. Dragon furniture lay strewn about, and abandoned eating stations stood idle.

Scott leaned heavily against Death Wind as the savage pulled him across the orange pavement. "Into the mechanical room."

They veered toward the wide opening as the sky brightened with a flood of laser beams. Rusty's power pack was hit, and the casing bored. Shorted contacts arced and smoked, and he shrugged it off and tossed it down a garbage scuttle just as its pent-up energy let loose. Expanding gases and molten plastic blew out of the hole like an erupting volcano.

One of Helen's crutches was burned in half; she fell in a

heap. Sandra stopped and grabbed her arm. Another heat beam seared the back of her head, lopping off the twisted braid and singeing the rest of her hair. "I'm on fire!"

Death Wind fell on top of her, rolled her head against his belly, put out the blaze. The air stank of burning skin and hair. All six crawled through the opening as the gatling gun fired sizzling laser beams all around them.

"It looks as if they temporarily have the best of us," Doc said.

Sandra's eyes flared red. "Brilliant deduction, Sherlock."

"I thought so, myself." Turning, "Scott, does this room have another exit?"

"Directly into the street. That's why I picked it. They used it to get heavy equipment in without going through the command center."

"Who the hell cares," Sandra screeched. "Let's get our own equipment out of here."

"A less than prophetic statement, but a useful suggestion. Helen, can you manage on your own?"

"I don't think so, Daddy. Not on one leg."

"I will carry." Death Wind scooped her up.

Scott got to his knees; his body was covered with blisters, and blood dripped down his injured leg. "I can't handle the gun." He shrugged off the backpack. The wall behind him was slammed with energy bolts. "Back between those transformers. Quick!"

The wall facing the courtyard suddenly blew in. Storage cabinets, mounted junction boxes, motors, and cable trays vaulted across the room in wild disarray. Through the gap Scott saw dragon soldiers marching robotlike out of the ruined computer center, spraying deadly energy beams ahead of them.

Scott led the way, tumbled through the wide opening into the street. "It's all clear."

Doc thrust his cane out first, followed it with sharp glances both ways. "The proximity of dragon soldiers demands a propitious retreat."

"I ain't hightailin' it." Sandra poked her head, hair still smoking, into the street. "I haven't even gotten off a shot."

"You always were a hothead," Scott said, managing a weak grin.

"Shut up, you!"

"Can we continue this exchange of ideas in a different

location?" Doc stepped aside to let Rusty, Death Wind, and Helen out of the shambles of the mechanical room. Another explosion roiled behind them, showering sparks and metallic debris through the tepid air. "I have a suspicion that that gatling gun can be set to fire all its barrels simultaneously with a largely inevitable result, the object of which I would not like to be."

Rusty ran across the street, ducked into another opening. "In here."

The battered squad followed him. Scott limped badly, dragging the foot of his injured leg. He was the last to reach the doorway. As he spun around, he saw the flyer lift off the crushed building, rotate its turrets, move toward him on its power beams. Ramps, walls, and barriers melted under the concentrated energy. The thrumming crescendoed as the focusing needles heterodyned. Death Wind set Helen down on a pile of matting.

"Can we get into the sewers from here?" Scott shouted above the shooting and thrumming. He searched eagerly for an exit.

"Not unless you've got a pick and shovel." Rusty surveyed their surroundings. "Hey, there's no door into the next court-yard. This is a dead end."

Doc peered out the opening. "We've got patrols coming from both directions—and through the mechanical room. And the flyer is circling Computer Central high enough so as not to destroy it."

"Nice going, redhead." Sandra dashed around the darkened room, kicking aside brooms and pushcarts. "You've got us into a fine pickle."

"How was I to know it was a street maintenance storage facility?"

"You look before you leap."

"I didn't have time for a detailed inspection."

"This is most strange," Doc said softly. "The soldiers have stopped their advance, and the flyer is hovering directly overtop of us. I should think if they meant to kill us—"

"If anyone's interested, here's a trash chute." Helen scrab-bled along on her knees, dragging the calf-length cast. "Maybe we can—"

"It's clogged," shouted Scott. He dug frantically in the rubble, trying to clear an opening. The flyer's engine whine rose in pitch. The sonic vibration pierced his eardrums, knifed through his skull, and bulged his eyes.

Loose gear rattled. Shelving peeled off the walls. Storage containers crashed down and splattered their contents. Helen was crushed under an electric street melter. Blood ran from her head.

Scott put his hands to his ears, felt icy cold fingers caressing his brain. A heaviness built up inside his skull that could only be let out by screaming. He did his best to relieve the pressure. He let out a long, painful yell that was absorbed by the freezing thrumming. His head was going to explode.

He continued to cry in his dreams long after he passed out.

CHAPTER 3

When Scott came to, his whole body ached: not just the muscles, or the joints, or the skin, but everything. He felt as if he had been run over by a tank and then caught in a rocket blast. His eyes were painful blobs of fire, radiating outward. When he went to rub them, he found his elbows were clamped to a bar behind his back, which was part of a waist band shackled to a bulkhead.

He squeezed and squinted, fighting off red-hot needles. He saw his legs stretched out in front of him, and knew that he was sitting. The room was dark, lit only by annunciator lights on the far wall. In the faint yellow glow he could make out his companions: Doc to his right, Rusty, Death Wind, and Sandra to his left. None of them moved; they huddled in contorted positions on the smooth floor, heads lolling, cuffed by wires.

"Anybody awake?" His throat scratched in agony, the words came out barely a grated whisper. His lips were dry and cracked.

"I am, but I'm afraid to open my eyes." The voice sounded like no one he ever knew, but from the direction it was Rusty's. "Did we get crushed in a sandblaster?"

"My powers of perception are somewhat limited, but I do believe I have returned to some form of consciousness." Doc groaned, and drew his knees up to his chin. "This unnatural sleeping position has not done my back any good."

Sandra kicked spastically. "Are my teeth still in my mouth? I feel as if my gums have been rubbed over an electrified washboard."

"You look okay to me," Scott said.

"Then why do I feel so awful?"

"Sensitivity to light, as dim as it is. We all appear to be physically intact, with no more injuries than we had before that bone-rattling vibration." Doc ran a practiced eye over his body. "Other than a bent fingernail, I'm relatively unscathed."

17

"Goody for you. I've lost five years' worth of hair. DW, move or say something, so I'll know you're alive."

The Nomad shuffled. "I am here."

"I can see that, you big lunk." Sandra stretched out a leg, wrapped it around the bronzed calf of the savage's. "Are you hurt?"

Death Wind stared at her expressionlessly. "Yes."

"Where?"

"Body."

Sandra scowled. "DW, where on the body?"

"Body."

Rusty grimaced as he changed position. "I'm a little better off. I only hurt from the ankles up. My feet are numb."

"You've probably cut off the circulation," Doc said. "Try flexing your muscles."

"Doc, how can my hair hurt?" Scott wanted to know.

"That tingling sensation is in the scalp, but the pain sensors transmit the information to the brain where its interpretation is suspect due to overload. If my suppositions are correct, we were engulfed in a sonic field phased to trick the synapses into believing they felt pain—a kind of direct neural stimulation. A very sophisticated cattle prod that is effective in its goal, but otherwise not harmful."

"I feel a lot better now, Pop." Sandra squirmed in her trammels, inched closer to Death Wind. "DW, how's your tummy?"

Death Wind did not bother to look at the singed hair and skin on his abdomen. Strands of Sandra's hair, where he had put out her flaming brand, mixed with his own belly pelt. He shrugged.

Scott struggled, stretching and testing the strength of his bonds. He felt the slick surface of wristlets, bound together by several inches of wire. Behind him, a joint connected the combination waist band and arm bar to the wall by two feet of thick cable. He could move his body slightly, as well as his hands, but not his arms. As the general pain eased off, he became more aware of the sharp stinging in his right thigh.

"Doc, is there something wrong with my leg?"

Doc leaned as close as he could. "It's rather dark to be sure, but I think you've got a nasty welt from that laser blast. Probably another one where it came out: right through the muscle of the calf, but it looks as if it missed the bone."

"I swear I can still feel the burning."

"They drilled you, huhn?" Sandra said. "And I never got a chance to squeeze my trigger. That's what makes me so mad."

"Have you given any thought to the demise of your mother?" Doc said calmly.

Sandra perked up, her face dropped. "Hey, where is she? I can't see anything in this damn dungeon. Mother!" A silent moment later, she screamed, *"Mother!"*

The door swung open, bright ceiling lights flared on. A dragon soldier stood in the opening, gun in hand. The prison was devoid of furnishings, and Helen was nowhere in sight.

"What have you done with—!"

The squat dragon body lurched into the room on taloned feet, fat tail swinging. The leering head peered down from the stalklike neck. The soldier took a post to the side while a technician came in behind it. It fumbled through the pockets of its equipment vest, brought out a metallic instrument, scanned the prisoners with it. It stepped to the other side of the doorway, the instrument still panning.

A gaudily caparisoned dragon swept slowly into the room, golden cape flowing. It moved with a grace not normally attributed to the awkward-moving reptiles. Its claws wrinkled and clutched at the air. Long talons clicked across the hard plastic floor. It stopped in front of Sandra.

Sandra was goggle-eyed, her jaw slack.

When the dragon leader worked its fingers in front of her face, she jerked back. Burnt strands of hair dropped off the back of her head where it banged against the wall. She drew her legs away from the scaly reptilian feet.

The dragon reached out, clutching. It passed its paws by her as if to grab, but kept out of her reach. It sidestepped, stopped in front of Death Wind. The savage returned its leering gaze, neck arched upward at the eight-foot-tall creature. The dragon feinted with its hands, but the Nomad did not flinch.

Rusty shrank back when the reptile stepped in front of him, but made no other movement. The dragon moved sideways. Scott could smell the fetid breath, feel the foul air blowing against his face, hear the rasping of hot air grating through pointed teeth. A long, daggerlike tongue darted in and out of grim lips. The eyes were red beads with tiny round pupils.

Scott steeled himself for the clutching feint, refused to respond or be intimidated when the dragon reached out for him. Clawed fingers worked in front of his eyes with quick, hypnotic movement. Several scales dropped off on Scott's outstretched legs.

The creature moved on, paused in front of Doc. Its fingers jerked epileptically. Doc swallowed, but made no other outward motion. The dragon finally turned toward the door, still keeping up its senile activity.

The waiting technician stowed the shiny device in a vest pocket, took out a small stringed instrument, like a miniature harp. It played its claws across the tightened gut. The sound was deep, bass, discordant. If it was a tune, it was a completely alien one. Scott could find no rhyme or repetition in the chords.

The caped dragon again faced the captives, glared at each one. The long tongue stuck out, and it hissed like a snake.

"The same to you, pal."

The creature blinked, its head curling back at the sound of Sandra's voice, like a cobra preparing to strike. It approached her, reached out with long fingers wriggling.

Sandra let out a startled yell.

The guard fired its weapon. A jagged, lightninglike bolt sparkled across the room, crackling and engulfing her in a momentary display of shooting stars. Sandra writhed, her mouth open, but no sound emerged. She flopped on her side, straining at her bonds, and vomited violently on the floor.

The dragon leader eyed her silently, tongue darting.

Sandra curled into a fetal position and opened her eyes. She gasped as she looked up at the dragon. "You'll get yours, buddy. You'll get yours."

Again the guard fired upon her. The dazzling fireworks flared around her like a glowing spiderweb. Her body was outlined in brilliant white pinpoints, like a child's connect-the-dots drawing. Her body spasmed, and her arms and legs flopped about as if driven by hidden springs. She coughed and gagged, vomited again.

"Shut up! They don't want you to talk."

Scott barely got out the words when he saw the pyrotechnics billowing out of the needlelike gun barrel, like a ball of scintillating water. When it hit him, he felt his skin burning as if it were on fire. Deep icepicks of pain stabbed into his muscles, he jerked and twitched involuntarily. His insides revolted. A bomb exploded in his stomach, singeing the lining with acid. Hot, stinging fluid exploded up his throat, out his mouth, through his nostrils. Long seconds passed before he could breathe; then, each breath was fire.

The dragon gathered in its cape, turned, and trundled through the door. The technician played a few more notes on the harp, then left. The lights went out as the guard closed the door.

In a hushed voice, Doc said soothingly, "Are you two all right?"

Scott was still coughing, but he managed a nod and a groan.

Sandra groaned, "About as all right as you can be after swallowing a volcano."

"The dragons have a curious array of weapons, and I think it is less than wise to offer overt resistance when they can retaliate with such impunity."

"The power pack was the same as the laser guns, just the output nozzle was different."

"Shut up, redhead. This isn't the time for technical observations." Sandra cleared her throat, spat on the floor. "I've just had my guts ripped out."

"Even a fish would stay out of trouble," Scott croaked. "If he kept his mouth shut."

"Shut up, you. I don't need any of your witticism." She coughed again, slithered away from the malodorous puddle. "I've got enough troubles with one dragon wiggling his fingers under my nose while another one plays the harp. The next thing you know they'll start singing to us."

"If they do," Doc observed calmly, "I hope you will be more attentive to their musical inclinations. I don't think they'd enjoy being booed off the stage by a pugnacious lower life form."

"Pop, I can live without the platitudes."

"My dear, I'm just trying to point out that a prisoner must act in accordance with convention."

"And I'm not going to be humiliated by a bunch of lizards. If they—"

The room took a sudden lurch. Scott felt his stomach rise up into his throat. The floor buffeted sickeningly, then straightened out.

"What the heck . . ."

Rusty said, "We're in the air. We must be inside a flyer."

The old man stroked the bottom of his long white beard, the

part he could reach with his arms bound. "Yes, lad, I agree. The dragons are obviously taking us somewhere."

"But where?"

"I will be very interested to find out," Doc said. "However, I do not suppose we will know until we get there."

"And what did they do with my mother?" Sandra wailed.

"The last thing I remember," Scott said, "was the shelving collapsing on top of her. Maybe she got buried and the dragons didn't see her . . ."

Sandra's shoulders slumped. "I just hope . . . she's . . . all right." She straightened, and threw back her shoulders. "'Cause if she's not I'm gonna kill somebody—"

The lights flared into brilliance, the door swung open. An armed soldier entered the room, gun at the ready.

Death Wind kicked Sandra hard. He whispered, "Do not speak."

Right behind the guard came a slave, carrying two plastic pails. The dragon worker shuffled across the room, set the pails in front of Sandra, retreated backward until it reached the doorway, then turned and left. The guard backed out, gun nozzle pointing. The lights doused with the closing of the door.

Rusty broke the long silence. "What was that all about?"

Sandra reached out with her feet, hooked a bucket between two petite but dirty ankles, and pulled it up between her legs. She bent her head and sniffed. "It's pig slop." She kicked it aside.

Death Wind stretched out a moccasined foot and deftly maneuvered the pail in front of him. With his elbow bound he could not reach his hands into the bucket, so he dropped his face right inside the circular rim. He slurped for a moment, then straightened. "Food." His head dropped again, and he sucked the ingredients into his mouth like a snorting swine.

Sandra dragged the other pail across the floor. "Hog wash."

Death Wind pushed the first bucket to Rusty, dragged over the second one. He bent and slurped. "Water. Funny water."

"Funny! The stuff's got enough iron in it to attract a magnet."

"Give me some of that," Scott said.

Rusty's head came up out of the bucket, lips covered with gray ash. "It doesn't taste too bad, but it won't win any contests." He pushed the slop jar toward Scott.

The blond tasted the broth, coughed, and sucked in great

mouthfuls. "This isn't exactly dining at the Ritz." He shoved
the pail to Doc.

Doc ducked his chin so as to keep his beard out of the mess.
"Hmmn, it tastes rather like some form of grain, although
oddly tainted. It's probably highly nutritious."

"Hey, let me have some of that porridge," Sandra said.
"Before you guys finish it all."

"I thought you didn't want any," Scott taunted. He took
another couple mouthfuls when Doc passed it back to him, then
nudged it toward Rusty. The other bucket came his way, and he
swallowed great quantities of foul-tasting water, soothing his
cracked lips and parched throat. He offered it to Doc. "The
stuff is dilute iron oxide. With a slightly higher mineral content
it'd be solid."

Doc sampled the brew. "Well, at least we know they're not
going to starve us to death."

Sandra brought her head out of the food bucket. "No,
they're gonna poison us." Despite her protests, she continued
to suck in the slop. The buckets passed back and forth among
the prisoners until the nearly empty food pail wound up in front
of Sandra. She managed to tilt the rim with her fingers, work
it onto her lap, and pour the remaining contents into her mouth.
She licked her lips of the remaining fodder. "Is there any more
of that liquid ore?"

Scott leaned back against the wall, staring off into the
darkness. He salivated so as to clean his mouth and lips, then
spat into the pile of dried vomit. His stomach churned. "I
wonder what's for dessert."

The door opened again, and light filled the room. Two
guards entered, took opposite stations. Two technicians lumbered through the opening, each carrying an eight-foot-long
pole with a lighted box near one end and a yawning, two-
pronged claw on the other. One dragon posted itself by the
annunciator panel. From a distance the other poked Sandra in
the stomach with the mechanical grab, withdrew the pole, and
released a spring which snapped the clamp on the wire binding
the wristlets.

The other technician stabbed a flared button with its paw.
The cable attached to the waist band retracted into the wall.
The dragon pulled Sandra forward by the wrist shackles.

"Hey, whaddaya think you're—"

A scaled finger pushed a lever on the lighted box. A

coruscating ring traveled down the eight-foot length, burst like a bubble on Sandra's fingertips. She screamed. The dragon dragged her to her feet, backed toward the door.

"You bastards. Wait till I—"

Another circle of light raced toward her balled fists, enveloped her fingers, shot up her arms. She shrieked again, louder. She ran forward on the pole, kicking, but could not reach the dragon with her feet. She fell, got up, and kicked again.

This time the ball of light reached her shoulders. Sandra gasped, but no sound emerged. Her eyes widened. After a moment, she gulped in air like a beached flounder. She was drawn slowly out the door. The first technician stepped around behind her, attached the other pole to the back of the waist band and elbow clamp. Together they prodded her out of the room.

Sandra was not struggling when the door closed behind them.

CHAPTER 4

"Uh-oh. I have to do something unpleasant. I don't think I can hold it in any longer."

Doc hunched his shoulders, stifling a groan. "Don't worry about it, Rusty. I've been doing it all along. There's no way to stop nature from taking its course."

Scott retreated from his own puddle, but could not shut off the nauseating smell of his own vomit. His skin was hot and clammy, his arms ached from their unnatural position. He struggled in his bonds. The plastic rod binding his elbows would bend, but not break, and the attaching cables were beyond his strength. He lay hunched over on one side, exhausted and sickened.

"How's that leg, my lad?"

Scott did not raise his head from the floor. "Sore."

"You're lucky. It appears to have missed the bone. What we would call a 'flesh wound' in the field."

"Terrific."

"Did you know that your skin is blistered?"

"Yes, I can feel it."

"Death Wind, how's everything with you?"

"Okay."

"Do you know what happened to Helen? Back there in the city?"

"I put her down. The roof caved in. I did not see."

"Ah." The sibilant sound was Doc's only epithet.

The lights came on, the door opened, two guards shuffled in. A technician pulled on a long pole attached to Sandra's wrists, while another pushed at the small of her back from the end of another. Both held tightly onto the insulated grips. A subdued Sandra, whimpering, clothes torn to shreds, allowed herself to be uncoupled from behind and reshackled to the bulkhead. She continued to cry softly.

Bloody gashes streaked her legs, her back, her chest, as if she had been mauled with a garden trowel—or a dragon's sharpened claws. She made no attempt to cover her exposed breasts.

As soon as the forward clamp released its hold, Scott heard a loud snap. Death Wind's hands suddenly shot out, grabbed the end of the electric prod, wrenched it out of the unsuspecting dragon's paws. The savage brought his feet under his haunches and bounded sharply. The rear cable ripped out of the already broken waist band, and he launched himself straight at the offending technician.

The glowing end of the rod rapped the dragon in the jaw and caught the extended tongue in mid dart. Before it could hiss, Death Wind swung the pole around like a pugil stick and slammed the clamp end alongside the dragon's narrow skull. The head lolled over on the long neck.

The two guards fired almost simultaneously, but Death Wind was protected from their blasts by the bulk of the technician that was slowly falling over. It took the brunt of the static discharge.

"Go get 'em, DW."

Wielding the prod like a sword, the Nomad charged the other technician, parried, and flicked the pole out of its grasp. He jammed the clamp around its neck and shoved the lever forward as far as it would go. The light ring burst into the dragon's face, coruscated over its head and down its slender, snakelike neck.

As the dragon began to collapse Death Wind swung his weapon, but was caught first in one blast, then in another. He was flung backward by spasming muscles; he skittered across the floor.

Scott reached out with his good leg and hooked his heel over the glowing prod. A lightning zigzag caught him on the calf. His leg reacted galvanically, and twitched painfully. He fell back with a cry of pain. A guard lurched on powerful hind legs and scooped up the fallen pole.

Death Wind lay inert.

A guard backed against the opposite bulkhead, stabbed a mushroom button. A yellow light came on, flashing, and harplike tones played out of a speaker. In moments a squad of soldiers charged sluggishly into the cell, spread out with gun nozzles aimed. A contingent of technicians followed them, paws flying as they gathered up their fallen comrades and dragged out their still bodies.

Rusty's whisper was barely audible. "Don't say a word."

To the tune of music, a technician brought in a new waist band and attached it to the unconscious savage. By the legs he was hauled across the floor to his former location. Rusty and Sandra cringed away from the lumbering dragons while Death Wind was reshackled to the wall mount. Slowly, the dragons retreated, first the technicians, then the soldiers. The music stopped. The lights went out.

Sandra could barely reach Death Wind's outstretched leg. She touched him tenderly. "DW. DW. Are you all right?"

Rusty bent over as far as he could and picked up the limp hand extended his way. "He's still got a pulse."

"Those lousy bastards." Tears ran down Sandra's face. "Those lousy, no-good lizards. I'll burn 'em all, down to the last scale."

"My dear, squeeze his calf for muscle response. Rusty, chafe his wrists if you can. I don't know what crisscrossing beams might do to the circulatory system."

"He's still breathing," Rusty said.

"How about his eyes? Can you see that far? Are his pupils dilated?"

Rusty struggled against his bonds. "No, I can't get any closer. It's too dark anyway."

"Why don't you—"

The lights came on, and every eye turned toward the door. It opened slowly, and a lone dragon duckwalked ponderously into the room. The naked soldier cradled a nozzle that was ten times the diameter of the lasers and stunners. An enormously fat connecting cable trailed into the corridor.

Scott gulped, flattened against the wall. He was looking right into the mouth of the tube. With the other paw the dragon pulled a foot-long lever. Scott saw a sparkling bubble emerge, soar across the cell, growing larger, expanding, attacking, engulfing. He closed his eyes just as the force hit him, dousing him with cold, stifling his breath. His body was jerked around to the limit of the shackle, washing him back and forth with awful power. His body tingled with icy stabs of pain. He sputtered for air.

Then the awful feeling was gone, and Doc was deluged with the spray. He was buffeted around like a feather in a gale, his body flopping unmercifully. After several seconds the spray washed over Scott's head, then concentrated its power on

Rusty. He was totally inundated until the nozzle drenched Death Wind's motionless form, making his body dance like a mannikin. Only Sandra screamed when she was hit.

The power died down, the nozzle ceased its effluence, the soldier backed out of the cell, the door closed.

Scott sloshed around on the floor, pushed wet hair out of his face. He felt amazingly refreshed. "The next time they decide to give us a bath, I hope they use fresh water."

Death Wind shuddered. Slowly, he contracted his limbs and crawled up to a sitting position. He shook his head like a wet hound, then stared at his companions. "Doc is right. Resistance is no good."

"Oh, DW, are you all right? I thought they hurt you badly."

"Hurt, yes." The Nomad ran his hands over his body. "No damage. You?"

Sandra shrugged. "I got a little rough handling when they tried to pin me down, but once I stopped resisting they let up on me. The scratches aren't deep, but rubbing salt in the wounds doesn't make me feel any better." She extended a hand, managed to touch his fingertips. "Thanks for what you did."

Death Wind gave a slight nod.

Scott rung out his shorts. "Well, now that we're all cleaned up, I guess we're ready for round two."

"They've already won by a technical KO." Rusty pushed puddles away with the flat of his hand, clearing a dry spot around him. The bulk of the water drained through a grill in the middle of the floor. "Boy, when I heard that music I thought for sure the angels were coming to take me away."

"Yes, the dragons appear to have eccentric behavioral patterns of which I was not previously aware," Doc said. "I'm sure there is some significance to the playing of the harp, something outside my experience."

"Kinda like the cavalry blowing the trumpet during the charge," Sandra offered.

"Possibly, although I did not know the dragon intellect was musically or artistically inclined. I thought their only method of expression was the stick symbolism of their writing."

Sandra scowled. "Pop, can we stop studying them long enough to hate their guts?"

"My dear, knowledge of one's enemy is the most important weapon in the arsenal. Previously, we have fought only against military forces and soldier mentality. Now, we have a unique opportunity to study the dragons from the inside, and to learn more about how their leaders operate."

"*Pop,* I hate to burst your bubble, but—we're prisoners of war. Get the aitch two oh out of your noggin."

Doc laughed whimsically. "No, my dear, the human mind is never made prisoner by a cage alone. It is the failure of the will that makes one a captive of enemy forces. We have more freedom now to study dragon hierarchy than we ever had before, and we must take advantage of our position. The fate of the world may rest upon it."

"Pop, I don't think I'm getting through to you—"

"No, he's right," Rusty interrupted. "Don't you see. We thought we had conquered the dragons, but we didn't. We haven't won the war, only the first battle. If there are more dragons alive—anywhere—or anywhen—we've got to annihilate them. We've got to make sure there's no chance of future retaliation."

"Yes, we must resolve ourselves to see it through." Doc wagged an extended digit. "We must learn everything we can about their world, their society, their culture. Before, I was able to study them only from the outside, or from the rare and clandestine excursions into their stronghold. And you saw how valuable that intelligence turned out to be. But if there are more of them, if there are other outposts, we must continue the fight. The only difference is that now we wage war from the inside."

Sandra was quiet for a long moment. "You know, sometimes I don't think I understand you. Other times, I know I don't."

Doc laughed again. "Then you must learn to think as a warrior, not as a woman."

"And you'd better stay on his heels," Scott said, "or he'll always be one step ahead of you."

"Well, has it ever occurred to you that we may be in danger? Dragons don't show much compunction about wasting human lives."

"In the wild, that's true. They treat us like vermin. But think of all the prisoners kept alive at the city. It seems that a human, once captured, takes on a different role and instead of being exterminated is somewhat pampered—in a POW sense, of course. And I don't believe they would have harmed you if you

had not talked out of turn, or fought their guards. No, I think
they have plans for us."

Rusty shuddered. "Maybe they want to torture us because
we took over their turf."

Doc shook his head. "Again, no. To my knowledge dragons
do not waste time on revenge. They are, as far as I have been
able to ascertain, totally without emotion. They respond to
logic, killing when necessary to attain their goals. What we
must do, in order to thwart them, is to discover those goals.
And if we do not show any overt resistance, I think we can do
some useful underground work."

"Yeah, well, all I want to do is discover my way outa here."
Sandra folded the shreds of her blouse as best she could, tying
knots in some of the loose strands. "Without a scaled escort."

Seven feeds and two hosings later, and to the tinkling of
bells, a horde of guards and technicians filed into the jail cell.
Prods were clamped to all the prisoners, front and rear, and
they were marched out wordlessly and unprotestingly.

Scott was truly amazed at the sheer size and inner convolu-
tions of the flyer. The corridors seemed to curve on forever,
with ramps connecting various levels. He saw scores of
hatches; those that were open led to cubicles similar to the
prison cell.

Machinery and exposed wiring crowded the corridor. Hundreds of battery packs lined the walls, some connected to
cables that led directly to massive charging generators. He
recognized a coolant system that could feed only a nuclear
reactor. Except for copper conductors and terminal points,
almost everything else was constructed of synthetic resins
bonded by epoxy compounds.

They approached a spacious balcony, overlooking the central exit chamber. The retractable core was extended and open,
and cooler air found its way inside. Dragon slaves were hauling
gear and pulling hand carts down the massive ramp and out into
the sun. Their shadows were long.

Scott made as many observations as he could, wishing he
could reach into his pocket for the pencil and notepad that for
some reason had not been taken from him. He exchanged
glances with Doc and Rusty whenever he saw something
interesting, and pointed with his eyes.

Three gurneys trundled out of a recess, scraping on plastic

wheels. The slaves paid no attention to their cargoes. But Scott took special notice of the stiff technician, still wearing its vest, lying under the clear plastic wrap. The second gurney carried another vested dragon.

"Mother!"

Sandra struggled, but was held firmly in place by her jailers. Each pushed the stunning lever, and she was caught in twin coruscating balls of light. Her back arched forward, and she fell to her knees, sobbing.

"Stay still, my dear. There's nothing you can do."

"They've got her covered in plastic. She can't breathe."

"She doesn't have to. Don't you see the rigidity of her limbs."

Scott clenched his jaw, staring at the passing parade. Helen lay partly on her side, one leg drawn up, and one arm bent and held upward against the force of gravity, frozen. "Rigor mortis," he breathed.

Sandra was hit with another pair of bolts. She collapsed to the floor, gasping from electric shock overload. Death Wind jumped toward her, but took only a step before his rear guard zapped him in the small of the back. The waist band glowed for an instant, but he stayed on his feet. He stopped wrestling.

"My dear, you are only making it worse."

"Those *bastards!*"

Every guard, every technician, stopped in their tracks. The only sound was that of Sandra's wailing. The gold-caped leader, neck bobbing and forelegs working, clicked across the balcony toward the prisoners. It waved its paws ominously, clutchingly, as if it wanted to strangle them.

Death Wind remained perfectly still. "Sandra, you must not resist."

Chest heaving, Sandra slowly climbed to her feet. She stared at her mother's body, then at the chief dragon. It hissed, tongue darting.

"All right—for now. We play it Pop's way. As long as I get to kill that one."

The caped dragon waved its paws, the funeral procession began again. Behind it, the five prisoners marched solemnly, resignedly, into a sun-scorched dragon land.

CHAPTER 5

"Out of the flyer and into the flying pan."

"Shut up, you."

Scott tilted his head. "I was just trying to keep up morale."

With the back of her arm Sandra wiped sweat off her brow. "Yeah, well, you're not doing a very good job."

"After all, we're not all wearing air-conditioned clothing."

"I said, shut up!"

Rusty paced the floor of their cell, four steps up and four steps back. "Doc, if you're cooking up a plan, you'd better get on with the recipe. With the sun shining through that transparent dome, we'll be well done in a matter of minutes."

Doc folded his body into a corner. "I do not believe the dragons found any humor in Sandra's rejoinders about their incestuous parental activities."

"What was I supposed to say when that guard goosed me with the prod?"

"My dear—"

Sandra held out her hands. "Okay, I'm cool. From here on out I promise not to lose my head—unless somebody tries to take it. I just wish one of them dragons would bend over in front of me, 'cause I'd love to do some kicking."

Doc slumped into his own lap, breathing hard. "Right now, my dear, I could do with a little less hot air."

Scott took off his tunic, crouched in front of Doc, and fanned the older man. "They didn't bring us all this way to knock us off. I think they just want to soften us up."

"If I get any softer I'm going to melt away. I need water."

"Hang in there while I call room service."

Doc's laugh was barely audible, but his smile was there for all to see. "I like it, Scott. Despite what my granddaughter says, I enjoy your wit."

"I'm glad someone appreciates me."

Rusty used his own tunic and took over the fanning. "I need

the exercise. My arms are still stiff from being locked into that brace. Doc, where do you think we are?"

He shook his head weakly. "I forgot to bring my compass."

Scott dabbed the doctor's forehead, dried his damp hair. "Have you ever heard rumors of other—dragon outposts?"

"Not in the North American continent."

"South. We are south." All eyes turned toward Death Wind. The savage sat calmly against an orange plastic wall. "I watch the sun. It is higher."

"That's because it's noontime, silly," Sandra said.

Doc looked up at the sky. "No, he is quite right, although I had not taken particular notice. The inclination above the horizon is much higher here. Nomads have a constant awareness of stellar activities, since it guides them on their migrations. Now that I think about it—" He paused and rubbed his chin. "The sun is nearly perfectly overhead, almost as if we were . . ."

"On the equator," Rusty finished.

Scott wiped his own freely flowing forehead. "Then, unless we crossed the Atlantic Ocean, we must be in South America."

"So this is Montezuma's revenge," Sandra said slowly.

Scott pounded on the thick door. "Hey, out there, let us out of this oven." He heard harps, and backed away immediately. "Uh-oh. Here comes another serenade."

The door swung open. Two squads of guards, armed with stunners, created a gauntlet. The gold-caped leader blocked the end of the double column, while behind him stood a technician strumming a bass harp.

With Rusty's help, Doc struggled to his feet. "I guess this means they want us to come out. And remember, my dear, no more aspersions about their unwed ancestral heritage."

"Don't worry. I've been zapped enough." She stabbed a stiff finger at the leader. "But I still want him."

"All in due time. Scott, I'm afraid I'm going to need someone under my other arm. That's good. Thank you." The doctor led with his chin. "Shall we?"

Sandra held onto Death Wind's hand, followed the trio out of the heated cubicle. "Easy on the trigger digits, fellas."

Scott looked up at those leering faces mounted on stalklike necks. Some of the soldiers hissed, flecking outward with vibrating tongues; others revealed rows of sharpened teeth; all exuded foul breath. There were never less than two stunner nozzles aimed at his midriff. Scott gulped.

The gold-caped leader waved them on with wriggling fingers. Doc hung heavily between Scott and Rusty, his game leg made worse by dehydration. The twin files of soldiers kept up the slow pace along the broad corridor. A hot breeze flowed in through glassless windows.

Scott whispered into Doc's ear. "Can you see those plowed fields out there? I didn't know dragons went in for gardening."

"I'm at a loss for an explanation. Even the slaves at the city ate ground dinosaur meat."

Rusty squinted his eyes in the glare. "Looks like mostly soybean, but there's also corn, peas, and carrots."

"And lettuce and spinach, too," Scott added.

Doc's head struck back, his cheeks pinched. "You can differentiate the vegetation this far away?"

Rusty humphed. "Of course. We grew all that stuff in our hydroponic gardens. The foliage patterns are distinct, although I can't see the leaves from here. Might be romaine lettuce."

"Aren't those peanuts—"

The gold-caped dragon turned around slowly, cocking his head.

Sandra poked Scott in the rib cage. "Pipe down, you. You wanna get us all electrocuted?"

The dragon waved its paws, resumed its course.

Scott whispered over his shoulder, "You're stunning enough to get even with them."

The cortege wound up a great circular ramp. The orange plastic motif was unchanging and unadorned. Dusty sunbeams filtered down through a louvered dome of clear material, similar to the roof of their prison cubicle. Vertical slots in the wall admitted light as well as air.

The ramp leveled off at the end of a great hall with a high flat ceiling. A throng of dragons, wearing capes of various color schemes, milled throughout the unfurnished chamber. They were in constant movement, chugging along pigeonlike, heads bobbing, and working their arms and paws nervously. Some hissed as the humans passed.

Technicians mingled among the dragon leaders. The vested lizards carried small harps and strummed tuneless chords on them. Scott thought he discerned a repetitive measure being played, although the deep sound had no tonal qualities to it.

"Just what we need, a symphony orchestra."

Sandra punched him in the ribs again. "I'm warning you."

Dragons shuffled out of their way. A canopied area appeared, occupied by a lone dragon wearing a silvery, reflective cape. It hunched forward on a plain plastic stool with a notch in the backrest for the thick tail. The point of the tapering appendage flicked slowly from side to side. The scaled breast heaved sonorously.

"The head honcho."

Scott turned his head, gave Sandra an expression of horror. Guiltily, she covered her face with her hands.

The gold-caped dragon stepped aside for a vested technician, which played its harp with irregular strains. The silver-caped leader waved it aside with gnarled claws, then reached out clutching for the band of people. By watching its dextrous motions, Scott had the impression that it wanted to strangle them.

He watched the flailing arms, the curving digits, the drooling, bloodless lips, the beady red eyes, the sagging scaled skin. This lizard was old. It stuck out its tongue, red and darting, and hissed. The head sagged on the long, slender neck, and it was forced to look up from the downward curve.

Another technician neared its side. It played a stringed instrument directly into the head dragon's external ear opening. After a few notes it was fanned away by the drooling leader. With short jabbing motions, the silver-caped dragon punched the air. The half-closed lids gave it an odd sleepy appearance.

More harps came into play. The gold-caped leader walked sluggishly up to the five people. Scott cringed as the dragon reached out and grasped Doc's free hands. The eight-foot-tall beast lifted Doc's stark white fingers, squeezed them, let them go. Doc did not move, but kept his arms at half mast.

The dragon swung around at its leader. The silver-caped oldster punched the air again; the harp played by its side. Scott saw the paw reach out for him, felt the dry, leathery touch, the gentle pressure on his knuckles. When the dragon let him go, he was shaking. The technician plucked strings, the gold-caped dragon stabbed the air in front of Scott's face with threatening, daggerlike claws. Scott pulled his hands to his sides.

As the older leader made more punching motions, the harp by its side sang discordantly. The gold-caped dragon hissed, then walked past Scott and grabbed Sandra by the shoulder.

She cringed, but allowed herself to be dragged aside. She remained perfectly silent.

The dragon feinted at her face, missing her by a hair. She stood her ground. The dragon hissed, turned toward its leader. Claws reached out. Then, the gold-caped dragon released Sandra, marched past her and between the columns of soldiers. It turned once, cape swaying, stabbed with a crooked paw, then continued on its way.

"My interpretation of the action is that the interview is terminated," Doc whispered. "It has shown off its captives. I suggest that we follow Goldie out of the presence of his eminence."

They all swung around, Sandra and Death Wind leading. The guards did not fire, but moved along with them at the gold-caped leader's pace. They left the hall to the accompaniment of hissing dragons, paraded down the circular ramp, then along a narrow corridor away from their previous prison.

The procession angled down ramp after ramp until it passed out of the sun and into the cooler air of a subbasement. Angled mirrors funneled meager reflections into dark corners and shone weakly through the grill of the door that closed behind them. Overhead, inlaid crystals let light in through the ceiling.

"Let me sit. Please." Doc faded from Scott's grip, fell into a heap on the plastic flooring. "I'm just about done in."

"Damn it, they didn't give us any water," Sandra shouted. She went back to the door and banged on it with her fists. "Hey, you lizards. How about some refreshments."

Death Wind checked out the walls of their cell, reached into a trough at the far end. Scott heard crinkling sounds, saw the savage pull something up to his nose and sniff.

Sandra joined him. "Hey, DW. Whatcha got?"

"Food." The Nomad took a bite, crunched it slowly. "Fresh."

"What? Let me at it." Sandra dug into the trough, pulled out some leaves. "Ugh, what is this stuff?"

Rusty tasted a leaf of green foliage. "Hmmn. It's lettuce. And good, too." He took a handful to Scott and Doc. "In fact, this may be the best lettuce I've ever had."

Doc crunched it greedily. "It's even wet."

"Water in bottom of trough," Death Wind said.

"Come on, Doc, let's get you a drink." Scott shoved a handful of lettuce into his mouth, and chewed as he helped the old man to his feet. "You're right, Rusty. This stuff is great. Better than any we ever grew at home."

"Salad," Sandra spat. "There's nothing in here but rabbit food."

Doc dug his hands into the vegetation and brought cupped water to his lips. "As long as it's edible, my dear, that's all that counts."

Rusty rummaged through the torn lettuce leaves. "There are beans floating in the water." He chomped down on a mouthful. "They're hard, and uncooked, but very nourishing." He passed them around.

Scott heard a scraping sound from the wall in front of him, then a dull thud. In the dim light he saw several intersecting creases in the plastic. He felt a ridge along the wall. "Hey, there's something here. A trapdoor, or something. But I can't get it open."

"Let me try." Death Wind ran his fingers across the top of the trough, traced out a one-foot-square panel. He took his knife out of its sheath and dug it into a crevice.

"Hey," Sandra shouted. "Where'd you get that knife."

The Nomad was taken aback. "From Father."

"But, how come you have it with you?"

"Always carry."

"I mean, didn't the dragons take it away from you? They took our guns."

"I still have."

"Then why didn't you pull it out sooner?"

"No need. I kept it under loincloth. Now I need."

Sandra sighed, her exhaled air blowing singed hair off her forehead. "DW, sometimes I don't know what to do with you."

"You should know by now," Scott said.

"Shut up, you."

The Nomad pried the panel open, got his fingers inside, and pulled. The small door popped out, swung on a top hinge, and a flood of vegetable matter flowed down a chute and into the trough.

"Wow, look at all the food!" Rusty exclaimed. He ran his hands through the fresh vegetables. "Look at this! Tomatoes. And bananas."

"And oranges."

"And pears."

"And—what the hell's this spiked thing?"

Scott took the strange fruit from Sandra. "Rusty! Look! It's a pineapple. I've only seen these on tape." He lifted the unstuck lid and shouted up the chute. "Hey, you have any pomegranates up there?"

"Scott, this is a cornucopia." Rusty stuffed his mouth with the various foodstuffs. "I haven't eaten like this since . . ." His voice trailed off distantly.

"Don't start thinking of home, now," Scott said, enjoying the feast. "This isn't the time for nostalgia."

"Excuse me, but could I get over there where the water is a little deeper. I sorely need another drink."

"Sorry, Doc." Scott sank his teeth into an orange as he moved out of the way. "I can't believe the dragons are treating us to a banquet. This stuff is delicious."

Sandra nibbled on a pear. "Don't get too excited. They're probably fattening us for the slaughter."

Scott stopped in midbite. "Hey, you don't think—"

The dungeon door creaked open, a broad shaft of light spread across the floor. A dragon guard, stunner in paw, stepped back. Two people were shoved into the room. The door clanged shut, the bolt shot into place.

The girl's only article of clothing was a G-string. Long, tangled dirty blond hair cascaded across bobbing pink breasts. Under the dirt-smeared face were the bright blue eyes of a teenager. Thin brows pinched as she studied each of the five prisoners.

The man was of medium height, well built, and wore a loincloth that was made of only slightly more material than that of the girl's. He, too, was barefoot. Straight, jet-black hair reached down below his ears, blended with the curly beard. He took a couple steps forward, tilting his head and pinching his dark eyes. He looked at each of them in turn, then spoke in a guttural, throaty voice.

"Well I'll be a son of a bitch. What the hell do we have here?"

Sandra fell back between Scott and Death Wind, clung to them both. Scott put a hand on her back, felt her heart racing. She was breathing hard. Suddenly she pulled away, stepped hesitantly toward the bearded newcomer. She stared at him hard, peering up in the dim light. Then she screamed and jumped at him.

"*Daddy!*"

CHAPTER 6

"Toad?" The bearded man bent down, peered deeply into her eyes. "Is that you, Sandy?"

"Oh, Daddy." Sandra threw her arms around him, buried her face in his chest, sobbed softly. The top of her head just reached his chin. "Daddy, I don't believe it."

The man blinked. "Well, I'm not too sure myself this is really happening. It's—it's unbelievable."

Doc limped closer to the entwined pair. He stretched out a gnarled hand and placed it on Sandra's back, in the tatters of her blouse. "Hello, Sam. Fancy meeting you here."

The man's jaw dropped, was snapped back in place by Sandra's bobbing head. He seemed not to notice. "Henry? What the hell is going on? Am I dreaming?"

"If so, we all are."

Sam reached out over Sandra's still heaving body, wrapped his fingers around Doc's neck, pulled him closer. "Henry, I just can't believe this. Of all the godforsaken places to meet, this is the damnedest. And after all these years—"

"Fifteen or twenty, I reckon. Before she was born."

Sam pulled Doc into his other arm, and the three of them hugged and cried for several minutes.

"I thought you were dead," Sandra said when they broke free. "When you didn't come back—"

"I know. I know how it must have been. I thought about how you must think I failed you. I'm sorry. There was nothing I could do about it. They killed—the others. Somehow I survived—knocked unconscious, I guess. When I woke up, I was here, in this city. A prisoner. I've thought of escaping, even made plans. But I can't do it alone. I need help. I—Henry, who are your friends?"

"Ah, many pardons. I suppose I should introduce you. Scott, here, is our mechanical genius. Rusty is a computer wizard. And Death Wind—"

"A Nomad, isn't he?"

39

"Yes, and somewhat related—"

Sandra went to the savage, melted into his side, under his brawny arm. "DW's my—that is, we—uh, I mean—"

"They got hitched, Nomad style," Scott supplied.

"Shut up, you!"

Scott smiled, held up his palms. "Just trying to help."

"My god, you mean you're married?" Sam breathed. "You found someone strong enough to tame you?"

"Daddy!"

Sam ran a hand through thick hair. "Sorry, Toad. But I guess—I just never thought it would happen. Not in my lifetime, anyway. Well, congratulations, uh, Death Wind. You sure have your hands full."

The savage nodded, showing white, even teeth.

Sandra pounded him on the chest. "Hey, you don't have to agree with him."

"Oh, I almost forgot." Sam turned around, held out his hand. The young girl came forward hesitantly, into the light. "This is Jane. Or, at least, that's what I call her. She didn't have a name until I gave her one. She lives here. A native. Say hello, Jane."

Her mouth worked silently for a moment, as if her lips were trying to wrap around the words. "Hel . . . lo."

"Tell them who you are."

"I . . . am . . ." She looked up at Sam, her face twitching. He nodded. ". . . Jane."

Sandra sneered. "What's wrong? Is she retarded?"

"No, she just doesn't speak. None of them do."

"Whom do you mean by 'them'?" Doc asked.

"The people who live here, in this city."

"You mean, with the dragons?" Rusty practically shouted.

Sam nodded slowly. "Yes, they've been here for generations. Ever since the takeover. Henry, I've learned so much about the invasion—"

"Yes, we've had some rather intimate contact with the details, too. We'll have to compare notes. But, why can't they speak? Is it congenital, or do the dragons perform laryngectomies?"

"Nothing so drastic. No, they're just not allowed to talk. Any vocal noise other than a hiccup has historically been treated with electric shock: a great deterrent. So, today's generation has lost the knowledge of speech." He pulled Jane close, hugged her tightly. "I've taken her under my wing, like my own daughter. We met in this very dungeon, right after I got here. This is where they put people caught making noise, like humming. The dragons think this is torture—the dampness, the cold. They don't realize we like it here, that we come here to escape the work details, so we can study, and learn. I'm teaching her English, poor tutor that I am."

"She hasn't made much progress," Sandra huffed.

"On the contrary, I think she's done pretty good. A lot better than I have learning dragon."

"Do you mean to say the dragons have the faculty of speech?" Doc said.

"No, but they do have a language, and an amazingly complex one, at that. They talk with hand signals. The placement of each digit—"

"So that's why they kept waving their dirty paws in front of my face," Sandra exclaimed.

"Yes. And have you heard their strings?"

Scott laughed. "Sure. They just treated us to some of their chamber music."

"It's not music. The notes correspond to codes that the dragons learn from egghood. Jane can interpret that code, just as easily as you can read a book. And she knows dragon sign like the back of her hand. She's a natural linguist, and picking up more from me every day."

Rusty was enthusiastic. "Can she make sense out of their calligraphy, too?"

"Yes, she's a keen observer, apparently with total recall. I just wonder what she could have accomplished by now if she had had an education."

"Doc, this is great. If she can read their computer lingo I can figure out how to work their programs."

"That's assuming we can gain access to a terminal. We don't exactly have the run of the house." Doc made exaggerated motions of feeling his clothing. "And I forgot my keys."

"Getting out of here is no problem." Scott walked over to the food trough. "The way they restock the salad bar is our highway to heaven. Someone thin, like Rusty or Sandra, can shinny up the chute, then come around and slip the bolt on the door."

"You're not getting *me* in that rat hole," Sandra said.

"Scott, I think you've got something—"

Sam cut Rusty off. "Wait a minute. We don't want to leave now. We just got here."

"An unusual way for a prisoner to speak about his cage. Excuse me, but do you mind if I sit down. This leg has had about all it can stand." Doc squatted on the floor, and the others crouched or sat in front of him. "Now, Sam, I believe you mentioned several escape routes you've been working on. Would you care to elucidate on them?"

"Well, sure, but like I said, I'm going to need help. I'm pretty sure we can get out of here, especially since the dragons are so short-pawed. For some reason they've been leaving in herds, so there's only a small contingent left behind."

"Have you any idea where they're going?"

"Sure. Right here." Sam snickered at the upraised eyebrows. "The question is *when* are they going. No, that doesn't sound right either. I never was too good in grammar. Anyhow, the warp field's been working overtime. Or maybe undertime. I don't know. Whatever the case, they're going somewhere in time—and not coming back. Jane says it started about the time I got here. They're migrating somewhen else."

"Now what do you suppose they have on their minds?" Doc said.

"Scales," Scott chuckled.

Sam jerked a thumb at his daughter. "You've been hanging around this one too long. She used to drive me and her mother crazy with her wisecracking." His eyes widened, his face fell. "You know, I've been so overwhelmed by recent events I plumb forgot to ask about your mother."

Sandra drew in her breath, put her fingers to her mouth.

"What—what is it?"

Doc cast his eyes down, fidgeting. He took a deep breath, raised his bushy white eyebrows, and stared straight at his son-in-law. "Sam, I don't quite know how to tell you this, but—"

"She's dead, isn't she?"

"Sam, she was with us. She—"

"Is she dead, or not? Don't beat around the bush, just tell me."

"She was wrapped in plastic when they took her off the flyer. She had hit her head, and—"

"That's enough!" Sam held up his hands. "Spare me the gory details. I— She's— The bastards. I'll kill 'em all. She's the only reason— It's just that—she's so—she's—the only— woman I've ever loved . . ." Great, quivering tears streamed down his cheeks, dropped off his angular jaw, onto his hairy, heaving chest. The confident, muscular stature drooped, deflated like a punctured balloon.

Sandra sucked in her breath, coughed back her own tears. She kept her hands tucked into her lap. Death Wind jabbed her with his elbow, made motions with his hand. Sandra sobbed louder, but reached out and placed her trembling fingers on her father's bare leg, squeezing. He grappled with her hand, brought it to his breast, hugged it, then raised it to his lips and kissed her palm.

"I love—you too—Sandy. It's just—"

"I know, Daddy. I know. But I'll take care of you now. You can count on me."

Father and daughter fell into each other's arms, crying openly. Scott gulped, found tears rolling down his own cheeks. He could hardly swallow. And he was afraid the others would hear him sniffing.

Doc's soft hand reached out again, to comfort. "I know it's difficult for you, Sam."

"My thoughts for her were the only thing that kept me going. Now—"

"I understand. Helen was my own flesh and blood. I raised her from an infant. I will miss her, too. But life goes on, and so must we. She will be alive within our hearts as long as we live, and we will carry her with us always. Helen was one who touched everyone she met, helped everyone she knew, giving of herself unselfishly. But at least her suffering in this world is at an end. And we must carry on her tradition, as she would expect us to. We can't give up now. She wouldn't allow it."

Sam ran his fingers through his daughter's singed, shortened hair. He clutched her tightly against his chest. "I know you're right, Henry. You always are. And I don't intend to give up now. Not by a long shot. We're gonna blow this dragon land to kingdom come."

"You said it, Daddy."

"We still need a plan. We must have your ideas, and Jane's intimate knowledge of her community. And the people. We must free the people."

"That's not going to be easy. The people don't want to be free. Not the natives, anyway."

"Slaves enjoying their condition? That is contrary to the human psyche. Surely they are not so well off that they would accept domination."

"No, it's—well, it's hard to explain. You see, Jane's people have been here since this place was put together. In fact, they helped build it. Most of them were miners, caught underground. Because of their breeding, because they've never been allowed to talk, they have—retrogressed. They have the intellect, but not the—will. No desire. They're—pardon me for saying this, Jane—but they're mostly just dumb animals. Draft animals. Some of them till the fields, plant food, raise crops, reap fruits, grains, and vegetables. But most work for the dragons as either laborers or personal servants. You see, our dexterity is something the dragon slaves don't have. So, humans are treated like trainable monkeys."

"They ain't gonna treat me that way!" Sandra said vehemently.

"You see, Henry, the problem isn't that they don't want freedom. It's that they have no idea what freedom is. They've been kept in total ignorance. They don't know any other way of life. They're like living automatons, sleeping, eating, and doing what they're told. Trying to get them to revolt is like trying to convince cattle to stop giving milk.

"Now, the captives are different. There are others, like me, who've been—collected—most of them quite recently. We're a small but growing faction, whispering to each other when the dragons aren't paying attention, making plans at night, purposely hindering any employment we happen to be included in. If we get sent out in a work party, we try to sabotage the native workers' construction. Not enough to be obvious—we don't want to get anyone sent to the pens. But we carry out subversive operations, chinking away at their armor." Sam shrugged. "It's not much, but we do what we can."

"Do you, or your people, know the layout of the city?" Rusty said.

"Every inch of it. Our duties carry us everywhere. And since the dragons look upon us as inferior animals, because they're so used to dealing with the native population, they don't think we have the capacity for learning—or revolt. What we really need in order to overthrow the bastards is a guiding influence." Sam stared hard at Doc. "Henry, you can provide that. You haven't lost any of your charm over the years, so I doubt if your political talents have faded. You got us together once before, you taught us how to fight."

Sam stabbed a finger into the plastic deck. "You can do it. You can spark us where no one else can. And the natives have potential. Jane is proof of that. They don't lack intelligence, just initiative. If we can only get through to them . . ."

Doc rubbed his bearded chin. "Your praise fills me with intrepidation. However, as far as reaching into their souls, cultivating their repressed inhibitions, liberating their true potential as thinking, self-aware beings, that's going to require some tangible powers of which I am not possessed. How can I reach them when they cannot speak, or understand speech?"

Sam hugged the native girl. "Through Jane. She's a natural messenger. She's been trying to communicate her whole life, but until recently she's been stifled by her environment. She can talk to the people in sign—"

"You mean, all the natives understand dragon finger speak?" Scott said.

"Sure. How do you think they receive orders? The main problem is in teaching Jane to vocalize."

Doc placed a professional hand on the girl's throat, ran it up and down the tiny Adam's apple. "Say ah." He turned Jane's open mouth toward the light coming through the door grill. "Her larynx appears to be in good shape, although possibly underused. However, it's not a muscle, so it can't atrophy. It does not require constant exercise. Increased use may cause soreness, nothing else."

"Well, I guess I'll continue my lessons," Sam said.

"Scott is better." All heads turned to Death Wind. Sitting cross-legged, he pounded the blond on the back. "He is a good teacher. I learn from him better English. He teach Jane very well."

"Scott, what do you say? I admit I'm not too good at it." Sam smiled at Jane, while pointing a finger at Scott. "Would you like to have a new instructor? I'm sure he can teach you more than I ever could."

Jane looked at Scott. He blinked back at her. Slowly, she let her full lips part, revealed the glimmer of a smile. She held out her hand. "We are . . . friends?"

A huge grin spread across Scott's face. "You bet."

Jane arched an eyebrow.

Scott realized he spoke in the vernacular. "Yes, we are

friends." He gestured widely with his hands. "We are all friends."

"Take good care of her," Sam said. "She means a lot to me."

"I'll do my best."

CHAPTER 7

Sam winced as he plucked a flea out of his beard. He rubbed it between thumb and forefinger, then placed it on his thumbnail and quickly rolled his other thumbnail over it. The small snap was a satisfying sound. "That's an amazing story, Henry."

Doc scratched leathery skin under his tunic. "Only the highlights, of course. I wouldn't want to bore you with details."

"You haven't lost your grand flair for adventure, that's for sure. And this private army you've recruited seems like it can tackle anything you throw at them. I'm sure if we put our heads together, we can break out of this place. Although, getting home across two continents presents quite a problem."

"We don't have any home," Rusty lamented.

"That's not true," Doc countered. "Wherever you are is home."

"Pop, come back to reality. A prison is not a home. Hanging curtains on the walls and carpeting the floor will never make it home. It'll always be a prison."

"Whatever happened to 'grandfather'?"

"It was two syllables too long. And stop trying to change the subject. I'm for breaking out of this berg and heading for the hills. Once we're on the outside, we can figure a way to blow the place up. You wanna play spy, you stay here with the rest of the retards."

"My dear, please be fair. Jane is the product of a disadvantaged community. She lacks education and opportunity, not intelligence. If we can get through to her, we can get through to her people. You can help by showing some respect for her situation. We are all human beings, and we are all in this together."

"And I say forget the local yokels. Let's stir up the captured outsiders and make a run for it. They'll fight, at least."

Sam plucked another flea from his beard. "Toad, I thought your mother and I raised you better than that."

Sandra turned on him with a sneer. "You raised me to be a survivor. All right, I'll do whatever I have to do to save me and mine, but I won't risk my neck for a bunch of domestic sheep following the herd to slaughter. If they won't do anything to save themselves, I don't wanna have any part in doing it for them."

Death Wind placed a hand on Sandra's shoulder. "These people need help. Their minds are crippled, but can be healed. We can heal them."

"They can heal themselves. Why do we have to do it for them?"

"Men help men. It is code."

Sandra jerked back as if struck. Death Wind's statement was not only the Nomad code, it was part of the Nomad marriage vow. Clenching her teeth tightly, she stared at him with dark, penetrating eyes. Death Wind did not stare down. Sandra climbed to her feet, and stalked two paces into a corner where she stood facing the plastic wall.

The silence in the cell brought a strident whistle to Scott's ear, a ghostly monotone that seemed to emanate from his head. He squinted with pain as he drew his wounded leg close to his chest, with knee to chin. After a long moment, he said, "Okay, folks, let's try to plan for the future and figure where we go from here."

"Not where, but when," Doc said distantly.

"Whatever, as long as—" Scott drew in his breath as a new wave of pain hit him. "Doc, all of a sudden it's hurting a lot. Could it be infected?"

"Not this soon." Doc bent forward, took Scott's foot, and stretched out the leg so it rested in his lap. He inspected the wound. "It takes longer than a few days for infection to set in. No, I suspect that in the healing process the blood is gorging the injured vessels. Let's try elevating the leg so that gravity draws the blood away from the extremity."

"Doc, I don't want to lose it. Is there anything we can put on it to prevent infection? Some kind of salve. We used to have medicines in Maccam City that—"

"Antibacterial ointments merely cover up the wound; once applied, they then become a bed of infection. All we have to do is keep the scab sterile. Under these conditions, clean will have to do. The bleeding is actually to your advantage. Perhaps . . ."

Jane dipped her hand into the trough and brought out a wad of crispy lettuce. "I . . . help." She knelt by Scott's side, swung his leg around so that it lay in her own lap, and rubbed the lettuce leaves delicately over the burn holes. Scott flinched at first, until he felt the coolness. Jane used the crinkled leaves as a washcloth; she patiently cleaned away the dirt, and debrided the wound.

Doc pursed his lips and nodded slowly. "Exactly what I would have done. This girl knows much more than we give her credit for. Simply because she cannot communicate her knowledge, and her feelings, does not mean that she is devoid of such intangibles."

"The natives know how to shift for themselves," Sam said. "They have no other choice."

When Jane finished cleansing the holes in Scott's calf, she ran the fingers of both hands along the back of his thigh. He felt a strange tingling sensation that was not confined to the area she was touching. Her long hair swung outward, and he could not help but stare at her bare breasts: they reminded him of firm, ripe pears. Jane did not look up at him; one hand stopped at a spot halfway up his thigh, and squeezed, while with the other she raked her long nails over his skin. Gradually, the pain in his leg faded until it was little more than a dull throb.

Scott covered his lap with his hands. "Hey, that's really great. You've got the magic touch. The pain's almost gone."

Doc murmured, "She is obviously expert in the art of pressure points. A valuable asset, under the circumstances. I think we have much to learn from this backward and unsophisticated young lady. Sam?"

Sam crushed another flea between his thumbnails. "Yes."

"In your contact with these people, have they ever exhibited any special talents? Any—habits, or seemingly primitive proficiencies—that we may put to our advantage?"

"Well, I haven't been with them that long, but they do seem to have a natural acumen for anticipating dragon movements or demands. I mean, they seem to know exactly what's expected of them, and act without direct instruction. Almost like an innate ability to read dragon minds."

"Telepathy?"

"No, nothing like that. No, they just—well, I guess they've lived with dragons so long they know how the lizards think. They understand dragon psychology. Some of it is reading dragon methods of communication, of course, but it seems like they can interpret dragon body language—not just individual dragons, but overall patterns. They know intuitively what is expected of them, and they do it. It prevents them from getting zapped, or ending up in the pens."

Doc nodded thoughtfully. "A valuable survival skill."

"Excuse me, Sam." Rusty leaned forward over folded, lanky legs. "What are these 'pens' you keep referring to? Are they some kind of outside prison cells?"

"No, they're—they're not." Sam stared down at the floor. "They're where bad people are sent. People who do not conform, or who become sick and can't work. It's where old people go, and babies who die in childbirth, or infancy. It's where the dead are taken."

Rusty squinted in the dim light. "Is this a real place, or an allegorical heaven."

"Oh, it's real all right. And it's anything but heaven. No one who goes there ever comes back."

A long silence ensued, broken eventually by Jane's gasp and retreat. She dropped Scott's leg as she backed against the wall and covered her mouth with her hands. Her eyes blazed with abject fear.

Sam slithered to Jane's side and put his arms around her slender shoulders. "It's okay, honey. It's okay. Try to put it out of your mind."

The girl broke into uncontrollable sobs. She buried her face in Sam's chest.

"She doesn't understand everything we say, but she knows about the—" Sam broke off with gritted teeth. He covered her ears with his hands and continued in a whisper. "Her mother was taken to the pens. Her father died a long time ago. She's an orphan."

"Her sensitivity to the subject is understandable." Doc patted the girl on the leg. To Sam, "Do you think we can reach these people through her? Can we open a line of communication? Do we have a chance of breaking them free of their Pavlovian training? Can we foment revolt?"

Sam slowly released Jane from his grasp. She eased back to

a sitting position, wiping tears from her cheeks with callused palms.

Sam sighed. "Henry, I don't know. I haven't seen much initiative here, at least among the native population. Other captives, like myself, will jump to the cause—given the slimmest chance of success. Most of them would rather die fighting than live cowering. But there aren't that many of us—certainly not enough to carry off a revolution. We have no weapons, no tools, no outside allies . . ."

Doc nodded. "Other than Death Wind's knife, the only weapon we possess is our collective intellect. Psychological warfare notwithstanding, mental prowess is the best armament in any conflict. And solidarity, of course."

"We can get the captives to stick together, no problem, but we're only a couple dozen strong. They're real scrappers, like you: brought up fighting the dragons, and suffering losses. But our only hope of reaching the natives is through Jane. We need an interpreter so we can talk to these people."

Scott moved his injured leg into a more comfortable position. "I don't know how well I can pick up tone talk or finger speak, but I'm sure I can teach English to Jane so she can translate for us."

"And I want to learn dragon scratch," Rusty added. "Once I figure out what those squiggles mean, I can crack their input codes. You let me loose inside their computer and I can do some real damage."

Sam shook his head. "You people are incredible. Listening to you, I'd believe we were winning this war, and only stamping out pockets of resistance, instead of jailbirds with a life sentence."

"One must always maintain a positive outlook," Doc said.

"But you're halfway between inspiration and the absurd. Why, if I didn't know you better, I'd think you were insane."

"A modicum of madness is what keeps the dragons guessing." A quixotic smile touched Doc's lips. "I've always relied upon the irrational in order to keep them off balance. If we're going to win this time, we must strike when they least expect it. This girl, and her people, may be the key to victory."

"All right, I'm sorry." All eyes turned to Sandra. She stepped out of her corner and through the middle of the powwow, then knelt by Jane's side. She held out her hand. "Maybe I flew off the handle."

Jane stared at the outstretched palm.

"She doesn't understand what you mean," Sam said. "Her people don't greet that way."

Sandra looked nonplussed. "How do they demonstrate friendship?"

"They groom each other."

"Huhn?"

"They go through their hair, picking out fleas, ticks, and lice."

"How barbaric. What do they think they are, a bunch of chimpanzees?"

Sam took his time before answering, then spoke slowly with exaggerated enunciation. "Sandra, these people do not live in a style of choice. The dragons keep them rigidly controlled. They work in the fields, they live in a corral, and they have no bathing facilities. Once a week the dragons irrigate the stalls with high-pressure hoses. They are surrounded by vermin of every kind. Prisoners of war are forced to act according to their jailers' bidding—or suffer the consequences. The natives have simply developed a mode of living that fits the conditions forced upon them."

Sandra said in a huff, "Look, I just felt sorry for her. Okay? I didn't ask for a sermon." She plopped down next to Jane, extracted the comb from her back pocket, and ran it through the native girl's long tresses. The hair was tangled in knots that pulled sharply, but Jane gave no sign of minding painfulness. Sandra pulled the curly locks over the other girl's tanned shoulders. "As long as we're cooped up together in this cell, we may as well make the best of it."

Sam grimaced at Doc, who winked back with a quirky smile.

Scott dragged his eyes away from Jane's bared breasts. "Sam, tell us about this place. What's the layout? What do we need to know to stay alive?"

"The most important thing is to do as you're told. Dragons tolerate no disobedience. All the guards have pain guns, and even if they have two brains they don't think twice about using them. They—"

"Excuse me, Sam, but the enlarged sacral plexus, where the spinal cord passes through the pelvis, is used for motor control of the hindquarters rather than for expanded cognitive processes. It is not even an afterthought."

"Henry, I'm not a vertebrate anatomist, or an animal physiologist. I was just speaking colloquially."

Doc spread his hands. "Please go on."

"Thank you. Well, like I was saying, dragons may be slow on the draw, but the guards have a real itchy trigger finger. Sometimes, if you sense it coming, you can avoid the pain shot by jumping out of the way. You act as if you'd been hit, and they don't know any better. But the best thing to do is follow instructions. When they call, you come. When they tell you to get to work, you do it."

"That'll be hard for us," Rusty commented. "We don't know their lingo."

Sam nodded. "Yes, I had some trouble at first, and got zapped a few times because of it. But I learned to do what everyone else was doing. If they were picking fruit, I picked fruit. If they were digging holes, I dug holes. If they were hauling trash, I hauled trash. If they were called upon to pick parasites off the dragons' backs, that's what I did. I've picked up some of the tone commands, so I can understand the simpler orders like get up, walk, run, and come here."

"Picking parasites?" Scott said with disgust.

"That's our greatest occupation. Human fingers are nimble enough to pluck out the insects that infest their scales, something they find impossible to do themselves. It's easy work."

"Yuck." Sandra stopped combing in midstroke. "It sounds nauseating. You ain't gonna get me to touch one of those slant-eyed lizards, unless it's to slip a knife in its throat."

"My dear, I completely understand your revulsion," Doc said sympathetically. "I would sooner swim in raw sewage than pet a dragon, but the alternative for resistance is less desirable. You would be well advised to curb your antagonistic attitude in favor of survival."

"And maybe you should butt out—" Sandra thrust the comb onto her lap. After a few seconds of thoughtful silence, she picked it up and resumed dressing Jane's hair. "Well, you may have something there."

"As usual, your grandfather is infallibly correct," said Sam. "Oh, we're all used to being zapped with the pain guns. They keep them on low power so no one gets incapacitated: crippled slaves don't work well, and too many high-power hits does permanent damage to the central nervous system. The guards strike at random just often enough to invoke their might, and as a reminder of their authority."

"So we go with the flow," Scott said. "What about the city? How big is it, and what keeps people from getting out of it?"

"It's about five miles across and designed like the cross section of a tree, with a central core surrounded by concentric rings. Right in the middle is the time transport structure: a clear plastic dome embedded with power nodules aimed inward. It looks like a transparent porcupine turned inside out. It's the tallest structure in the city, so you can see it from everywhere: especially at night, because of the coruscating focusing nodes—is that what you call them?"

Doc nodded, and Sam went on. "Anyway, encompassing that are a couple of nuclear generating plants, mechanical spaces, transformer stations, and guard shacks. The next ring is administrative. All the bigwigs live and work in a girdle of two-story houses interconnected with courtyards. The Silo, as I call it, where you met the head cheese, is in the northern quadrant. There are alleyways that pass through the living quarters to let technicians reach their work stations.

"Outside that you've got a separation zone filled with storage sheds, soup vats, vegetable hoppers, granaries, freezers, meat larders, and miscellaneous warehouses. Beyond that are the slave quarters, both dragon and human, then come the cultivated fields and the dinosaur kennels. I call them dinosties; they smell worse than pigs. Oh, and the landing platforms are at the extreme perimeter. That's where the rampart takes over. Looks like the Great Wall of China, only the parapets are thicker. And the battlements are heavily defended with casemated laser guns. It beats me who they think they're going to fight off. The range is full of dinosaur herds, but they're not going to attack. It's just dragon offensive psychology, I guess."

"Or offensive dragon psychology," Scott quipped.

"Do they have communication links?" Rusty wanted to know.

Sam nodded vigorously. "Hard wire. And slave-drawn carts for transportation. This whole place is a weird mix of primitive encampment and futuristic technology."

"If the walls are slick plastic, we'll never storm them," Scott said. "Are there external stairs, or ramps, or do we have to break in through armored doors?"

"Doors that hinge open from the bottom, but without the moats. I've only seen them from a dis—"

"None of that matters," Doc interrupted with a wave of a gnarled hand. He stretched out his bad leg and kneaded it absently. "The outer barricade is the least of our problems. What is important is getting back in time."

"In time for what?"

"Oh, we'll get back," Sandra interjected. "If we have to crawl, walk, or skip to ma Lou. No walls ever held me in before, they ain't gonna stop me now. I'll get outa here if I have to huff, and puff, and—"

"This is not the time for fairy tales," Doc said abruptly. "That time is past. And that's our way out of here—through the middle."

Scott placed a hand on the old man's forehead. "Doc, are you feeling all right? Can I get you some more water?"

"Dehydration must be affecting—" Rusty started.

"No, no, no. I'm all right." Doc gently pushed Scott's hand away. He stroked his long white beard. "Listen to me for a moment. Hear me out. Now, tell me, where do you fight a fire?"

"Huhn?" said Sandra.

"I said—"

"At base," Death Wind intoned.

"Right. And how do you beat an enemy?"

"Cut off head."

"Exactly. You don't squirt water on licking flames, and you don't conquer a foe by slashing away at his arms. Every Nomad knows that."

Sandra said in frustration, "Quit talking in parables and spit it out. What the hell are you trying to say?"

"I'm saying that we do not want to escape. Not yet. We have come a long way to get here, but we have further to go before our war is won. We have worsted our opponent in only one battle. In so doing, we have learned that our adversary has more extensive holdings. That means that we must strike again—not just at this stronghold, but at the origin of evil."

Doc paused, and stared each one in the eye. "We must fight the dragons when and where they come from. Their present is our past, and unless we destroy them then, we will have no future. Our plan of attack is clear: we must go back in time."

CHAPTER 8

Doc surveyed the crowded barn with professional interest. Nearly naked natives lay strewn about the plastic floor like a crateful of rag dolls dropped through a chute; they were dazed by torpor. The heat in the auditorium-sized room was unbearable, the stench even worse. The slaves were crammed together under the shade of the roof, preferring the torridity of bodily contact to the near combustion temperature of the adjacent, sun-baked corral.

"So, what do you think?"

Doc mopped his expansive forehead with a dirty piece of hide. "Are they always like this?"

"What? Lifeless? Thoughtless? Moving like automatons?" Sam shrugged his shoulders. "Can you expect anything more?"

"I don't know. I've never encountered a condition such as this. They lie about like sated sloths. It's frightening. I had no idea what we were up against."

"You can understand how exceptional Jane is among this bunch."

"Even the children do not move about. They do not play."

"They're not allowed to play. They're not allowed to learn. They're not allowed anything but a food allottment and a place to sleep."

Doc gulped. "It is a truly pathetic human condition."

"Now you understand how getting them to fight for their freedom is as useless as convincing a rock to walk uphill. The captives show a little more spirit—the more recent ones, anyway. Eventually, after they're here long enough, they lose their will, their incentive; they become like the rest. Maybe we can cure some of them—those that still retain the power of speech and the capacity of independent thought."

Doc sighed. He knelt by a woman whose skin was shriveled with age, whose body was wasted through overuse. Tiny breasts like sagging prunes quivered as she panted like a dog in an overwarm cage. Her stare was vacant, her eyes sunken into her skull. Doc held her wrist and counted her pulse.

"She's not far from the pens," Sam said sadly. "She hasn't moved in three days. The work load has been light, and they haven't needed every available hand. But if she's still comatose the next time they clear out the barn, she'll take a one-way stretcher ride."

Doc stood up slowly, his eyes riveted on the pitiful package of humanity. "The dragons do not care for the sick, or the aged, or the infirm, or the insane. That is what separates them from humanity."

"You're right. They dispose of the useless. I guess they figure there are more where they came from."

"And the pens? Where they bury the bodies. Is that where the mercy killings take place."

Sam jumped, as if his whole body had been struck with spasm. "Who said anything about mercy killings?"

"Why, I thought you said . . ."

"I said . . . I said . . ." Sam's face sagged like melted plastic. "Uh, Henry, can we step over to the side?" Without waiting for an answer, he picked his way through the insensate forms. Doc hobbled along behind him. They stopped at the edge of the barn. Sam stared out into the blazing sunshine and the dirt-filled corral. In the distance, the fortress wall dominated the landscape. "Henry, I . . ."

"What is it, son?"

"Henry, I—" Sam gulped in several deep breaths of fetid air. "I killed an old woman the other day—just like that one." He jerked a thumb over his shoulder. "Two of them, in fact."

Doc's voice was craggy. "What do you mean? Were you treating them?"

"I had been, yes. But they were too far gone. Even a cursory examination must have shown you that there's not much we can do to cure disease, or relieve their suffering. I have no instruments, no drugs. The dragons would have taken them to the pens . . ."

"I don't understand." Doc's bushy white eyebrows pinched sharply. "If they died under your care, that is not the same as killing them. Every doctor, when he takes the Hippocratic Oath, swears to attend people to the best of his ability. But sometimes, a patient's condition is beyond human attention. You mustn't blame yourself—"

"No, Henry. I strangled them. With my bare hands. I—I couldn't stand to see them dragged off to the pens for—extermination. I . . ." Great, glowing tears rolled down Sam's sweat-covered face and were soaked up by the black beard. His smooth features convulsed into a caricature of Sardonicus. His chest heaved. "I had to do it."

Doc leaned against his son-in-law and placed a fatherly arm around the taller man's shoulders. "Sam, what is it about the pens that is so awful. What do the dragons do to people there? Do they use them for—food?"

"Worse. Much worse." Sam wiped the tears off his cheeks. He broke Doc's embrace and turned to face him. "They have these vats—like giant mixers—with sharpened cross grates that are pulled back and forth manually. Dragon slaves operate the machine. All leftover organic material is dumped into the hopper. The grates slice it all up, very slowly."

Sam took a deep breath. "Garbage, bones, domesticated dinosaur meat, dead dragons and humans. Nothing is wasted. And if the people are still alive when they are dropped in—you can hear them scream as their flesh is macerated, and piece by piece they are ground into—fertilizer."

"How's the leg, Scott?" Rusty whispered.

"Could be worse." Scott crawled into the shade and massaged his sore calf. "It itches like crazy, though."

Rusty folded his lanky form into an imitation chain link. "Remember what Doc said. Don't scratch it."

"Don't worry. I'm scared to death it'll have to be amputated."

Jane sidled up against the orange plastic wall, out of the direct rays of the sun, and stretched Scott's wounded leg into her lap. Gently she kneaded the flesh. "Better?"

"Yes, much better." He pointed a finger at her and smiled. "Hey, that's another new word for you."

"I—speak—learn—English?"

Scott pronounced his words with care. "Yes, you are learning to speak English very well."

"Well?" Jane spelled out a dragon equivalent with her fingers. "Water—ground."

"No, not that kind of well. This well is like good. The word that better is the superlative of—I mean, it's like—"

"You're confusing her with syntax," Rusty said.

"Then help me.

"Well, you're the teacher."

"Well?" Jane said again, frowning.

"Now you've confused her more." Scott shook his head. "Jane, forget it. Just—we'll start over. When I say—"

Jane abruptly let go of his leg and stood up. She motioned with her hands for the boys to follow suit.

"There are no dragons around—"

Rusty grabbed Scott by the armpits and hoisted him to his feet. "I don't see any either, but she hasn't been wrong yet."

"Great, the only break of the day, and the first time we get to talk, and they have to cut it short. I wish we could get back into solitary confinement. It was cool there, and nobody bothered us."

Jane silently shuffled off along the roadway.

"Shut up, Scott." Rusty dragged Scott after the girl. "I got zapped twice this morning, and I don't relish another dose of nerve juice."

"What's the matter with us, Rusty? We never talk anymore."

Rusty jabbed him in the rib cage. "Quiet." Now he heard the faint strumming of a harp, plucking a tune that was indecipherable to him. Slaves marched in from all quadrants. Rusty was hot enough without the press of bodies closing in on him. Worse than the confined heat was the mindless stare of the native slaves: bleak, inanimate eyes glimmered slightly less than chunks of burnt-out coal. Human slaves went about their assigned chores as sluggishly as their dragon counterparts.

Scott whispered out of the corner of his mouth. "I've seen vegetable soup with more life than these folks."

A dragon guard pivoted ponderously on stalklike legs. Its tongue darted out with a hiss. If half drew its stun gun, but replaced it when the twang of a harp-commanded movement. Jane, Scott, and Rusty tagged along with the mob. If Jane knew what their next job was to be, she did not vociferate such privity. She never spoke when dragons were in audible range.

The roadway was bounded on both sides by parapets over which the dragons, whose grotesque heads crowned elongated necks, could see. Rusty, tall as he was, stayed constantly frustrated by the high-walled corridors. The overall city plan was simplistic, but the map he was building in his mind was intended as an aid for eventual overthrow.

"Looks like field work," Scott muttered. "Unless they're taking us home."

Rusty glanced behind him and observed their position in relation to the shimmering time transport structure dominating the foreground. After sweeping foul-smelling private quarters all morning, he would be glad to work in the open air. Although the fruits and vegetables were grown naturally in the ground, instead of in troughs of chemical liquids, the farm work reminded him nostalgically of his youth in Maccam City—now a painfully dim memory.

They were brought up short by a tonal command. For a long time natives milled like cattle in the hot sun, under the baleful stare of dragon guards. Several technicians pushed through the throngs of people. As one passed him by, Rusty studied its equipment vest and made mental notes of the strange instruments it carried. One technician stopped in front of a formless plastic building, with a typical blob facade, and inserted a slender metal rod into a narrow slot. Two guards then pulled back on large handles, sliding open a ten-foot-tall wall panel on greased tracks.

A blast of icy air erupted from the opening. The white mist that touched Rusty's bare arms was a wet condensation that made him shiver. At first, contrasted to the noontime heat, the cold felt good; but soon the frigid temperature became a discomfort. He tried to hang back when the crowd moved forward, but the pressure from behind was too great. He marched with the others into the sanctum of the cold storage locker.

"Get a whiff of that ammonia," Scott muttered. "They could us a little maintenance on those loose solder joints."

"Are you volunteering?"

"Sure. I could fix the refrigeration so it would never work again."

Rusty hugged his chest and rubbed his arms vigorously. Already his teeth were chattering. Beside him, although he saw goose bumps rippling her skin, Jane seemed not to mind. She placed an extended index finger perpendicular to her lips, the way Scott had showed her to indicate silence. Rusty nodded affirmatively.

Ahead of them, natives were piling sides of dinosaur meat onto four-wheeled dollies and pushing them back in fire brigade fashion. Rusty took up a station where all he had to do was give each cart a shove toward the door; the next person in line did the same.

The building was actually a catacomb of separate freezers, each with a different type of stores. Thickly cloaked technicians directed the work force using a combination of tone talk and finger speak. They were clearly in a rush. The guards wore long ponchos, but carried the power packs and stun guns on the outside where the armament was immediately accessible. There was no cause for a show of force, for the natives, not afforded the luxury of extra clothing, labored with feverish abandon.

With the clattering of wheels, the drone of machinery, and the hubbub of activity, Scott and Rusty had little difficulty making observations and exchanging a few words. Scott forged ahead and entered one of the side chambers with part of the native crew. He stepped out a few moments later, after the room was emptied of its supply of flesh, and joined Rusty in loading the frozen slabs on a three-tiered cart.

"Quite an assembly line they have here."

Rusty's teeth were chattering so hard it was all he could do to nod.

Scott finished packing the lower tray and pushed the cart on its way. "Come on, let's check out this place."

Jane shook her head vigorously when she saw Scott and Rusty mix with the throng of natives and work their way deeper into the freezer complex. Rusty desperately wanted to run outside where the sun was hot enough to fry eggs. He was afraid he would shake apart like a motor with an unbalanced flywheel. His curiosity was tempered by the biting pain of cold. Only Scott's decisive conduct forced Rusty onward.

"Let's see if there's a way of sabotaging this place," Scott said. He squeezed through the crowd of uncomplaining natives, pulling Rusty along by the hand. "Maybe we can break a few pipes and spoil some meat."

A guard took notice of their surreptitious movements. Its hiss was lost in the clamor of activity, but Rusty saw the pink tongue dart out a warning. He and Scott joined a group that was unstacking collapsible stretchers. They grabbed one of the flattened litters and, following the direction of the others, unfolded the wheels from the undercarriage. When they were done, they had a waist-high gurney.

"I wonder what they use these for?" Scott said.

Rusty clamped his mouth shut; his teeth hurt from chattering so hard. He saw another gurney being pushed along toward an oblong doorway, so he followed suit. He waited next to a distracted guard, suffering from the cold worse than Scott, until an opening appeared in the line entering the room. He pushed his cart inside right behind another. The nearly naked native stumbled suddenly, fell to his knees, then crashed to the floor with a dull thud. Rusty jumped to his aid.

As he rolled the old man over, a searing pain bolt engulfed him from behind. He had only one glimpse of the old man's face, the rough craggy beard, the cracked and withered skin, the gaping mouth that tried to suck in air, the purpling cheeks that was a sure sign of cyanosis; then he was flung back by reflex action as his muscles went into painful spasms. He rolled aside, an instinctive reaction to avoid a follow-up shot. He came to rest against a frozen shank.

Every nerve ending in Rusty's body screamed for mercy. The cold was temporarily forgotten. He looked up quickly at the leering guard; it was making no attempt to fire again. It simply stared down at him, working the fingers of its free paw. Rusty nodded and got halfway up. His legs were frost-nipped; his muscles responded grudgingly. He fell back down, on top of the rock-hard slab of meat.

For a moment his eyes closed. He swallowed as a wave of nausea threw his stomach contents into a maelstrom. The pain ebbed. Slowly, he became aware of his surroundings. The cold hammered at him again. He pushed himself off the frozen steak. Partway up he stopped, immobilized.

After a long moment, the urge to vomit was rekindled. Fear galvanized his legs like those of Volta's experimental frogs. He kicked away until he came up hard against the thick tail of a dragon guard. He leaned back on the lizard for support, unable to take his eyes off the grisly scene before him.

Cold eyes stared sightlessly back at him. This was not just another dinosaur steak sliced for the stew pot. It was a frozen human corpse.

Sandra glared at the technician who had just finished waving its paws at her. All morning she and Death Wind had picked cotton with a group of natives: work they learned easily. The afternoon had been spent weaving thread in a mill; neither had ever seen a loom before, requiring them to team up with natives who knew the job by rote. Now, the couple had been singled out from the crowd.

When he saw Sandra's mouth open, Death Wind took her by the arm and pushed her forward. Together they approached the finger-speaking technician. Out of the corner of his eye, the Nomad saw a dragon guard reach for its stun gun; the reptile paused with its paw on the handle, the weapon undrawn, when the human pair stopped and looked up at the lizard in charge.

The technician turned on its clawed feet and clicked on the plastic flooring out of the building. Death Wind pushed Sandra along. The guard followed.

"What do they want?" Sandra said in a barely audible voice.

"Follow."

Sandra shrugged out of Death Wind's grasp. "I don't need two bosses."

Death Wind hung back far enough to miss tripping over the dragon's swinging tail. They were marched at a slow pace out of the factory. The sun was low on the western horizon, the temperature was not uncomfortably hot. They were led along a narrow roadway to a main thoroughfare where other people joined in the exodus toward the center of town.

The blue coruscations of the time transport structure were hypnotic. An azure ring of energy started at the base of each cone-shaped focusing node, ran along its narrowing length, and burst with a snap at the pinpoint tip. The cycle repeated itself with increasing speed and intensity. The ball of potential energy grew brighter with each coruscation. Multiplied by a thousand times, the clear plastic dome was a mind-boggling aura of pure power.

Death Wind was looking at the mountain-sized transporter when it discharged its pent-up static charge in one huge explosion: like a sharp peal of thunder of magnificent proportions. A thousand shooting bolts of electricity directed at the central core left searing lines embedded on his retinas; for several long seconds he was blind. As his sight returned, the eerie coruscations started recycling, and the transport nodule was prepared for the next passage through time.

Sandra and Death Wind were herded into a compound where a throng of natives milled. The Nomad took the opportunity to tank up from a water trough. After a while the people were prodded through a gate, led along a narrow alley, and lined up along the perimeter of the dome. Not a single person spoke.

Death Wind observed his fellow men, and saw none with any curiosity in their eyes about what they were about to experience.

"DW, look at that!"

Death Wind poked Sandra in the rib cage. She shut up immediately.

A long line of gurneys were being wheeled along the streets, two natives to each. The procession stopped at the edge of the dome. Upon each stretcher was laid out a naked human body, stiff with rigor mortis. A technician inspected the grisly cargoes, then waved each team through the arched opening.

"What are they doing?"

Death Wind poked her again. It was easy to see through the thick clear plastic what was going on inside. One by one the gurneys disappeared into the house-sized transfer zone. An opaque, blue effervescent light obscured further observation. The dragon slaves waddled back out. The stretchers kept on coming until a score were swallowed up by the electric curtain. As the discharging nodes whined in their final excitation, Death Wind closed his eyes tightly. The transfer was as loud as an overhead thunderstorm, the brilliant incandescence like a solar prominence. It was over in an instant.

"Something crazy is going on. What the hell do they want with a bunch of dead people?"

Dragon slaves reentered the transfer zone. They exited with crates and boxes and bags, all manufactured from plastic pulp or woven of resinous thread. They dropped their loads at the dome entrance. The natives who had wheeled in the gurneys were ordered to pick up the heavy loads and carry them away. When that work force was depleted, the group of which Sandra and Death Wind were a part was put to the task.

Like automatons the natives lumbered along the roadway. Sandra hoisted a sealed carton to her shoulder and followed wordlessly. Death Wind did the same. A heavily armed escort accompanied the train of laborers through the power generation sphere. The air reverberated with the clatter of machinery and humming transformers. Heat exhausted from the cooling towers made the passage nearly unbearable. Overhead, a sealed, clear plastic tube suspended from a track afforded a comfortable atmosphere for technicians making the trek through the mechanical works. Straight ahead was the Silo, the dragon administrative complex.

Led by an armed guard, the natives filed through a narrow archway. Tone talking, a technician directed them where to pile the goods. A caped administrator appeared when it was Sandra's turn to unship her carton. Its harp twanged shrilly. Sandra froze with the carton waist high. Behind her, Death Wind halted in midstride. He did not understand the signal, but knew that its command overrode that of the technician. Lizard fingers wriggled silently, then the caped dragon turned and waddled off.

"Follow," Death Wind whispered. Already, a guard was pulling out its gun. Death Wind placed a hand on Sandra's back and shoved her forward. "Follow."

The guard tagged along at a discreet distance. Its gun was drawn and aimed. The caped dragon slowly preceded them up a ramp to a second-story balcony. It entered private quarters where two guards stood in waiting. The room was sparsely furnished with utilitarian seats and tables. The eight-foot-tall dragon perched on a stool behind what could have been a workbench. Piercing lizard eyes glared at the human slaves.

Death Wind moved forward and placed his package on the workbench in front of the dragon. Even sitting, the lolling head was a foot higher than the Nomad's. When no stun bolts stabbed out at him, he knew he had made the right interpretation. As he stepped back, he stared silently but meaningfully at Sandra. She deposited her carton next to his.

The dragon leader ripped open the plastic package with curved talons. With a dexterity that Death Wind did not know the dragons possessed, it pulled out a clawful of slender metal tubes. Each was the size of a rifle barrel, one end of which was enlarged to fit the dragon palm. After laying the tubes on the bench top, it deftly picked up one in each claw.

It aimed the narrow end of the instrument at Sandra. The scintillating burst of light caught her in the midriff. She gasped, bent forward at the waist, and fell to the floor in a heap.

Death Wind was caught in midleap by the burst of light from the other instrument. He did not even see the floor hit him in the face.

CHAPTER 9

"Rusty, my boy. Rusty!" Doc shook the lad as hard as he dared. In the dim light of a waning moon he could see little more than a long, writhing form. "Wake up, my boy."

"Wha—what." Eyelids flickered weakly for a moment, then opened sharply. Eyeballs darted in their sockets like bouncing marbles. Rusty shivered with ague. "Doc, is that you?"

"Yes, my boy." Doc placed one hand on Rusty's sweaty forehead, the other on his wrist. He counted Rusty's pulse in relation to his own, a procedure he had perfected after years of practice.

"I'm so cold—and yet I'm hot. My head—"

"You're getting over a fever, my boy. Try to relax—"

"Doc! There's a guard coming in from the corral." Scott scrambled on all fours along the straw-filled floor. Breathing hard, he slid to a stop next to his young companion. "It must have been the noise—"

"Where is Jane?"

"I thought she was here."

"She left right after you. Didn't you—"

A cone of light stabbed through the barn door opening. The dragon guard was illuminated by the backlash of the brilliant searchlight attached to the power pack slung over sloping, scaled shoulders. Another dragon marched in behind it, this one armed with a stun gun. The beam of stark white light passed over the sleeping forms with the intensity of the noonday sun. Awakened by the disturbance, natives squirmed in their straw matting.

Doc threw several handfuls of straw over the top of Rusty. "Quiet, lad. Just rest easy until they pass." He buried himself under a layer of bedding so he could watch the proceedings without showing his eyes to the guards. He lay bare-chested and without his sandals. When the light swung in his direction he closed his eyes tight. The light lingered overlong. He half expected the kick of a clawed foot or a stab of pain from the

66

stun gun. At long last, darkness returned and the dragons continued their inspection of the other prisoners. Many minutes passed before the guards left the barn. Doc realized he had been holding his breath. "I do say, that was a close one."

"What's going on?" Rusty squeaked

"Are you okay," Scott wanted to know. "We've been worried about you."

"Well, I feel a little weak—"

"The fever is broken." Doc examined Rusty's hands and feet as best he could; his eyes had not yet readjusted to the darkness. "You had a touch of hypothermia from your sojourn into the freezers, and a bit of frostbite as well. How do your fingers and toes feel?"

Rusty made exaggerated motions of testing his extremities. "Well, they feel a little funny—kind of numb."

"That will pass. They got you out of there before any permanent damage was done."

"Who did? The last thing I remember—" Rusty winced as he rubbed his temples with his knuckles.

"We stood you up and walked you out. Jane and I—where the heck is she?" Scott twisted around. The rustling of straw attested to minor movement within the barn, but that was nothing more than native folk getting back to sleep. "Doc, are you sure she followed me?"

"Quite sure." Doc reached over Rusty and touched Scott on the arm. "You needn't worry about her. She is quite capable of taking care of herself."

"That's not the point. I just don't like—"

Jane alighted from the air with a stealth that neither made a sound nor moved a stalk of straw. She crouched on the balls of her feet, poised like an animal about to pounce on its prey. "I—am—here."

Scott reached out for her. "Jane."

She took his hand and held it to her breast. "You—okay?"

"Sure, I'm fine."

"You gone?"

"Just for a little while. When Rusty started calling out in his sleep, I ran out to the corral as lookout. Good thing, too. But where did you disappear to?"

Jane pointed toward the ceiling.

"I don't understand."

She made scratching motions with her hands. "I climb."

Scott shook his head. "Doc, do you know what she's talking about?"

"I can think of a possible interpretation, but I prefer not to accept it without a practical demonstration. Jane, would you mind showing us?" He pointed to her with a crooked finger. "You—climb."

In a flash she leaped upward—and did not come down. She clung momentarily to the crude plastic wall, then scampered along the vertical barrier like a nimble mountain goat traversing a rocky ledge. She ascended twenty feet to the ceiling, hung there for a moment, then returned to floor level by a different route.

Scott looked at her, his jaw sagging.

"Ah. Just what I thought. I saw some of the other children playing a similar game the other day—without her awesome agility, of course. She is indeed a person of rare talent."

"You like?"

"Yes, my dear. I do indeed like."

Jane pointed at each of them in turn, including herself, each time extending a finger. She held up her hand with her thumb withdrawn. "Where Sam?"

Doc said, "He went on a scouting mission. He may have gone through the corral into the next barn."

"Dra—gon?"

"I'm sure he will take great care. He is quite an enterprising individual. I am more concerned about Sandra and Death Wind. While we were on KP, they got picked up for some other detail. They have not come back. Hopefully, Sam will bring back some news of their whereabouts. Rusty, exercise your arms and legs for me, please."

The red head stretched and curled and did some sit-ups. "Whew, I'm still a little stiff. Mostly my back. And my memory's a little fuzzy—" He sat still for a moment, head tilted. "I remember the cold—the awful cold. And other people—"

Scott ran his hands along the walls. "The surface is lined with horizontal swellings, as if the plastic extruded through slits in the forms when it was still molten, but I still don't see how she can climb like that. The lips don't stick out more than a quarter inch."

"Scott! Was I seeing things, or were there really people—bodies—in that last freezer compartment?"

"Sorry, Rusty." Scott sat down next to his friend and folded his legs Indian fashion. "It was pretty scary. There were rows and rows of them, all stacked up like books on a shelf. I thought for sure the guards were going to gun us down when we carried you out, but you weren't the only one to drop from the cold. Doc, it wasn't cold like snow, it was—it stung. It burned—like a hot coal, or a soldering iron."

"Yes, it sounds more like dry ice—solid carbon dioxide." Doc squeezed his chin and ran his hand down his long white beard. "It freezes at over a hundred degrees below zero. It is used as a refrigerant in systems—"

"Doc! Forget about dry ice." Rusty leaned forward, shoulders back. "The important thing is, why did they freeze those people? What are they going to do with them? And where were they taking them?"

"Well, uh, Sam had some interesting observations in that vein." Doc glanced at Jane. From the expression on her face, she was painfully aware of what he was saying. "However, there is no need to go into it now. As long as you survived the experience—"

"A lot of others didn't," Scott interjected. "I saw half a dozen natives pass out either from the cold, or from the sudden return to the outside heat. The dragons just dragged them away by the legs, the same as you'd drag dead game."

"I believe we have firmly established that the dragons have no sense of moral obligation where human beings are concerned; perhaps even where they themselves are concerned. They consider us a lower life form to be utilized as they see fit: as draft animals, as food, and as—whatever. Let us accept that. Instead of flinging incriminations of their heinous activities, let us concentrate our energies on circumventing their master plan of extinction of the human race and the dominance of dragons. That is what we should think about."

Rusty sat back on his elbows. "Sure, Doc, I guess you're right."

"And the sooner the better," Scott added. "Let's start by ganging up on the guards the next time they make the rounds. After what I saw in the freezers, I want to spill some blood—lizard blood."

"You are beginning to sound as impetuous as my granddaughter, which alone should warn you that your methods are unsound. Killing a couple of dragons prematurely would jeopardize our chances for success of the overall campaign. I don't want to tip our hand. I think it paramount that we continue to gather intelligence, especially as our position here is fairly stable. No one has ever infiltrated the dragons' ranks as we have."

"We get shot to pieces, bound hand and foot, beat half to death, and you have the audacity to call it a tactical maneuver. Doc, you never cease to amaze me."

"Why, thank you. I accept that as a compliment. On the other hand—"

"Sam!" Jane jumped up and ran toward a loping figure momentarily silhouetted in the broad entranceway. She threw her arms around him and hugged him tight. "Where—go?"

Sam returned the hug. He ran his hands up and down her bare back and kissed her on top of the head. "I was doing a little scouting." The pair walked side by side to the corner that Doc, Scott, and Rusty inhabited. "Rusty, good to see you up and about. How do you feel?"

"Not bad, considering I almost got turned into a block of ice."

"How did the mission go?" Doc asked.

"Pretty good." Sam disentangled himself from Jane, and the two of them squatted on the straw-covered floor. He took a crumpled piece of material from where it was tucked into the back of his G-string and handed it to Doc. "Thanks for the shirt. There was a slight chill in the air. I needed it."

Doc nodded grimly, understanding fully the coded message. At least one old woman would not be carried off to the pens in a stupor. "Think nothing of it. Did you make contact with any more outsiders?"

"Yes, and I've enlisted a few more recruits, too, who are eager to cross swords whenever we're ready to mobilize. I even picked up a few homemade weapons. But the big news is, I got word of Sandra and Death Wind. They were spotted last night in a barn on the other side of town."

"Are they okay?" shouted Scott.

"Are you sure it's them?" said Rusty.

Sam's teeth glistened in the faint orange glow of first light. "The description fits: tall, dark, quiet, broad-shouldered, high forehead, and swept-back ebony hair, mated to a feisty, big-breasted woman with a singed scalp. Those aren't my words," he apologized to Doc. "That's the way I heard it. There's not another couple like them."

"I daresay," said Doc.

"It's as I suspected. They ended the work day in a different quarter, and the dragons took them to the nearest barn. It happens all the time. It's tough when mothers are separated from young children. Days, even weeks, may pass before they're reunited." Sam shook his head slowly. "An egg layer lifestyle doesn't suit a familial culture. The dragons could care less."

"That seems to be tonight's topic of discussion," Doc said.

"Hey, take a look at these." Sam extracted two slender needles from the material of his loincloth and handed them to Doc. Each was nearly a foot long. "A guy named Wendell gave them to me. He likes to be called Windy."

"A simple but formidable weapon." Doc inspected them and passed them on to Scott and Rusty.

"They're plastic stalactites. He broke them off from a poured roof, where the excess plastic had dripped over the edge. You know how tough this stuff is. He spent hours honing the point till it's as sharp as a tack."

Scott touched the point with the tip of his finger and drew blood. "Kind of dangerous to carry around. It'll make a pin cushion out of your leg if you keep it on your belt."

Sam nodded. "I'll bet Jane can weave a sheath for it, out of straw. You'd be surprised what she can do with her fingers."

"Not after seeing her make a monkey out of herself." Scott jerked a thumb over his shoulder. "She climbed that wall like it was a ladder."

"Yes, she's quite agile. She can do things average folks never even thought of." Sam mussed her hair and smiled at her. "Can't you, honey?"

Jane grinned. "If you say so."

Sam laughed raucously. He rocked forward so far that his face brushed straw. "Scott, did you teach her that?"

Grinning, Scott said, "You've got to watch her. She's like a parrot: she mimics whatever we say. And the more she learns, the more that makes sense to her, so she's picking up the language in a geometric progression. The problem I'm having is that she's very easily influenced by what she hears, and she's hearing words and phrases I don't want her to know: slang expressions, improper usage, and colloquial grammar. It would make my job a whole lot easier if you people would mind your p's and q's; then I wouldn't have so much to unteach her."

"English was never my strong point, but I'll try to contain my penchant for the vernacular." Still smiling, Sam continued, "You know, I haven't laughed, or even smiled, in months—ever since I was captured. Being a prisoner hasn't been nearly as bad as being separated from my family. Becoming united with my daughter, and my long-lost father-in-law, and meeting you boys has meant a lot to me. I—I wanted you to know that in case—well, in case everything doesn't go the way we plan. I mean, if we get separated for some reason."

"We will have to ensure that that eventuality does not occur." Doc kneaded the cramps out of his bad leg. "Let us remember, however, that the group objective has greater importance than individual caprice. There can be no peace while dragons live, and no security for the future—indeed, for the future of mankind—until we eradicate from the earth every vestige of dragon influence. Personal sacrifice is our watchword, survival of the species our goal. And lest you think I am being heroic, or histrionic, understand that my will is governed by my genes. We are what we are because that is the pattern of our evolution. If we were any different, we would have died out long ago—or perhaps we never would have originated. The question that remains to be answered is—can we live up to our potential?"

CHAPTER 10

"I haven't done this much doctoring in a turtle's age."

Sam humphed. "I've been making rounds ever since I got here. Why, in two months I'll bet I've treated half the community for one thing or another. Usually, all I can prescribe is a poultice, or barn rest. The natives are good that way: when one of their number is sick, the others hide him like they do the elderly. At reveille, when the guards come in to make up work crews, the strong, healthy adults stand out in front."

"Traditional herd instinct." Doc finished touching up the bruise above Death Wind's eye. "There you are, my boy. The next time you faint, try throwing your arms out in front of you."

"He didn't faint," Sandra said belligerently. "And neither did I. We were shot by some new kind of self-contained gun."

"Please excuse my metaphorical reference; humor is part of my bedside manner. I did not mean to be imprecise."

Sandra sneered, but did not comment further.

"What worries me is the implication of rearmament." Scott tucked his thumbs in the front of his shorts and perambulated around the corner of the barn that the squad had appropriated. "Why do they think they need more weapons? Could they possibly know about our plans for insurrection?"

"Maybe they're just playing it safe," Rusty offered. "Because so many dragons are going back in time, the natives now outnumber the local dragon population ten to one. This small firearm is the perfect defense for a technician that can't carry a power pack to operate the larger unit. It'll tuck right into a spare vest pocket."

Doc sat down and hunched over his knees. "Perhaps it is part of an ongoing plan. Sam, you said they've been sending personnel back at an ever-increasing rate?"

"Yes, but it had nothing to do with your arrival. The activity began soon after I got here, although I'm not paranoid enough to believe that my presence posed such a threat to them. If anything, it seems to coincide more with your destruction of the North American outpost. Toad, how many cartons of these self-contained stun guns came through the transporter?"

"Must have been a dozen, at least, Daddy. And it looked like each box held ten or fifteen."

Sam shook his head. "One gross of guns compared to three or four thousand natives and outsiders is negligible. Besides, there's no history of rebellion to cause such a change in tactics."

"It might have been only the first shipment."

"That's not right. It *may* have been the first shipment," Scott said.

"That's what I said."

"No, you said, 'might have been.' Might is the past tense of may. I'm trying to teach Jane correct conjugation. Your jargon keeps confusing her."

"Who gives a damn?" Sandra shouted, hands on hips.

"Listen, Toad, I'm just trying to help her—"

Sandra lunged at Scott and slammed him up against the wall. She scrunched up the folds of his shirt and pinned it against his throat. "Nobody calls me that except my daddy. Got that?"

Scott glared down at her, hands at his sides. "I got it without the body language. I can still hear, you know."

"Then don't forget it." She released him and stalked off toward the barn entrance.

Scott tugged his shirt back down to his waist. He cleared his throat and called out to her retreating form. "I'm sorry. Okay?"

Sandra did not reply.

Scott glanced at Death Wind; the Nomad winked at him. "Anyway, the guns are the least of our worries. They've already got enough armament to kill everyone in this compound three times over. All we've got is one steel-bladed knife and two plastic needles."

"Garrote?"

Scott looked down at Jane, sitting on the floor weaving straw into rope. "Yes, although I think dragon necks are too strong to strangle. But that lasso may come in handy. Doc, now that we're all together, I think we should start formulating our plans. A week and a half in this place and already I'm going stir crazy."

Doc snorted. "That is quite a statement, coming from a lad

who has spent most of his existence hermetically sealed in an underground chamber whose largest open space was a closet."

"That was different, Doc. I didn't feel cooped up then because I didn't know any other way of life. What I don't like is being penned in against my will."

"The real prison, then, is not these walls of plastic, but the barriers of your mind."

"That may be true, but it doesn't make the feeling any less genuine."

"Mere orthodoxy. You have free will; you can always change the way you think."

"Doc, you are amazing. You could find a silk lining in a pile of manure. If I had your—"

"Hey! Cut the philosophy session and let's talk about getting the hell outa here." Sandra stood with legs spread wide and hands on hips; except for her stature and her thoracic bulges, she could have passed for the Colossus of Rhodes. "I've been zapped one too many times by these living fossils. Let's revolt before the revolting lizards get on to us."

"A sensible suggestion," Doc said. "Rusty, would you mind removing your lanky limbs from our sketch?"

Rusty stood up and kicked away the straw that covered the plastic flooring and the map of the city that was carved into it. "I've added a little more detail since last night. Windy's been collecting data from everyone who talks, and Jane has interviewed as many natives who will finger speak with her."

"Excellent."

"My people not dumb. They not understand spoken language." Jane enunciated each word precisely. "Some will help."

"I thought as much. You see, Sam. There are subversive elements in every tyrannized colony. They merely need a directing, cohesive force to channel their energies."

"It took a man like you to get the ball rolling," Sam said.

Doc waved him off. "You were stymied only by lack of communication. Long before our arrival you laid the groundwork by taking this girl under your wing and by spreading discontent among those prisoners who were captured from the outside."

"Can we pat each other on the shoulder later and get on with it?" Sandra knelt by the circular layout. The others gathered around the perimeter of the map. "We've got no time to lose."

"On the contrary," Doc said with his quixotic smirk. "We have a great deal of time to lose: about sixty million years. These aged bones can use the time reversal to good effect. Perhaps by visiting the past I can enjoy a second childhood."

"Pop, sometimes I think you're already in your second childhood. This plan of yours scares me. I'm only going along with it because it's crazy enough to work. Now, I've been all over this burg working for these slave drivers. The way I see it, we've got to slip out under cover of darkness, hightail it through the separation zone, sneak through the dragon quarters, run like hell through the machinery spaces, charge into the transporter arena, and—whammo—look out dragon land, here we come. I'm no mathematician, but I think we've got about one chance in a thousand of making it all the way."

"Your vote of confidence is appreciated, my dear. But I've got another idea that I think is more viable."

"Forget it, Pop. I'm not crawling through two miles of sewer pipe. Besides, if they blow our cover it'll be too easy to gas us. We'll die like—aaagh! What the hell is she doing with that rat?"

Jane sat with her back to the wall. She was facing the circle, but with one hand she fed crumbs to a furry rodent. She looked up in surprise. "Me?"

"Yes, you. Are you looking for a case of rabies?"

Jane raised her eyebrows at Scott. "Rabies?"

Scott shrugged. "Doc, that's your department."

"It is a viral disease transmitted by the bite of infected mammals, via the saliva. I've never seen a case of it. It was effectively wiped out when the mammalian population was exterminated. Besides, rats were not a common carrier. Historically, the fleas that prey on rats were responsible for epidemics of bubonic plague that decimated—"

"I don't need a clinical description. I know all about rats. We had droves of them in the tunnels where I grew up. They're disgusting!"

Sam said, "Sandra was scared by one when she was a toddler. It crawled into her pajamas when she was taking a nap. She's had a morbid fear of them ever since."

"I do not! I'm not afraid of rats any more than I'm afraid of the dark. But I don't feed the damn things, either."

Jane sat, wide-eyed, "Rats are also prisoners."

Sandra placed a hand on her forehead and covered her eyes.

"I don't believe this girl. Okay, that settles it. I'm for getting out of here tonight—moon or no moon."

Jane continued to feed her pet.

"After hearing your and Death Wind's report, I am entertaining a daylight flanking maneuver. Of course, it will mean that we must disguise ourselves—"

"Daylight! Pop, are you completely out of your skull?"

"Audacity often carries off the battle."

"Cut the military aphorisms. I—"

Scott said, "I didn't know you knew such words."

"Shut up, you! Pop, what are we gonna disguise ourselves as—a bunch of cabbages?"

"I had in mind—natives."

"What do I look like—an eight-foot-tall lizard?"

"No. You look like an outsider."

"Pop, we all look the same—to a dragon. One lizard face looks like any other to me, I'm sure all people look the same to them."

"Can you tell the difference between an administrator and a technician?"

"Of course. The administrators wear capes and the technicians wear vests. What's that got to do with it?"

"I believe our clothes have been giving us away and attracting undue attention. I do not think it was mere coincidence that you and Death Wind were selected as subjects for experimentation. I have noticed a subtle disparity in the treatment of outsiders, almost as if the dragons do not trust us as they do the natives. Our clothing gives us away. Ergo, we go native."

"Now, wait just a minute." In a huff Sandra jumped up to her knees. She held out her arm and pointed a rigid index finger at Jane. "If you think I'm going to wear nothing by a few grains of straw like that—like that hussy, then you've got another think coming."

Jane looked inquisitively at Scott; he held out his hand and quelled her question.

"And you keep out of this," Sandra shouted at Scott.

Nonplussed, Scott said defensively, "I didn't say a word. All I—"

"I know what you were thinking."

"My dear, there is more at stake here than vanity. We must

use all the wiles at our disposal. I am less proud of the condition of my body than you are of yours—"

"*Who's* not proud?"

"—but we must do what is necessary in order to achieve our goals. I am sure that if we divest ourselves of our rather ostentatious attire, we can travel through the city with less notice than we have been attracting. It is paramount to my plan that we join the daily food delivery unit." Doc ruffled his fingers through his beard, scratched his chin, and deftly extracted a tiny black flea. "You see, I thought we were going to have to escape into the past. Instead, the dragons are going to take us there of their own volition. We are going to escort some of those bodies through time."

CHAPTER 11

The native work force gathered in front of the ice house, awaiting further orders. People milled aimlessly while bored dragon guards leered down from the sidelines. No guns were drawn. The seven warriors huddled together in the middle of the crowd.

Scott said, "Well, getting in the right labor party was easy enough. It's a good thing Windy tipped us off."

"Pop, what'll we do if they don't want anything but meat?"

"Patience, my dear. Patience. Our strategy is sound, but the time for its execution must be appropriate."

"Does that mean we wait?"

Doc nodded slowly. "If necessary."

"Well, I can think of some executions I'd like to perform in the meantime."

"I'm sure you can, but please try to curb your appetite."

Sandra suddenly turned on Scott. "What're you looking at, mister?"

"Who? Me?" Wearing nothing but a G-string, Scott's entire body turned visibly red. "I was just—"

"I saw you staring." Sandra positioned the long dark tresses in front of her bare breasts. For the hundredth time that day she checked the makeshift clips that kept the slender strands fastened to her own foreshortened locks. "You look at me once more, and you'll be wearing that smile on the other side of your face."

Ever watchful, Death Wind stoically ignored them.

Jane fluffed out her hair. So selectively had Death Wind cut the individual strands from her head that she seemed to still have a full-bodied coiffure. She pulled the braids back from her chest. "You like?"

Scott rolled his eyes. He felt terribly exposed in his brief apparel. "Don't these people have any inhibitions?"

Sam laughed. "Hang-ups are a cultural trait, something of which these people are totally naive. When I first got here—"

"Pipe down!" Rusty whispered harshly. "We're on the move."

Harps played on both sides. The horde of natives lurched forward like the sections of a caterpillar. The tall ice-house doors opened outward, and a mist of cold air rolled over the front ranks. The natives entered the building without hesitation.

"Remember, linger in the back until they finish loading the meat and vegetables. Jane, keep translating for us."

"Yes, Doc. Dragons give the signal enter. Pick up. Carry out. Follow."

The frigid air caressed Doc's skin like a midwinter snowstorm. Goose bumps rose instantly. As the pack surged ahead, he was thankful for the warm touch of their bodies. He tried to stifle his limp, but without a cane his game leg ached constantly. In the handling room the people spread out as they marched into the various cubicles to gather their loads. "Let's mill a bit."

They kept moving, but in such an ineffective way that they each described small circles that kept them in the same area. Enough unused prisoners were left that the dragon guards noticed nothing unusual.

"It's at the other end of the hall," Rusty breathed. "On the right."

The natives were quick to work: the sooner they grabbed a haunch of steak or a basket of vegetables, the sooner they could leave the freezing confines of the ice house. They did not need to be tone talked into working fast.

"Harp say go that way." Jane pointed with her eyes.

"Okay, here we go," Scott said enthusiastically. "Look out yesterday, here we come."

Natives gathered around the stack of gurneys. Working quickly, they teamed up in taking one down from the pile, unfolding the legs, and pushing it into the freezer compartment, where they picked up a frozen corpse and gratefully trundled it out of the building and into the heat of the sun. Due to the arctic conditions, only three dragon guards oversaw the work; they merely stood and looked threatening. The natives needed no further encouragement.

Sam shoved through the throng. "This is the first time I've ever seen these people work with a will."

Death Wind was the first of the group to reach the gurneys.

With muscular arms he easily pulled down one in each hand, passed them out, and grabbed two more. Several natives tried to take them away, but they were pushed aside. In a few seconds, the four gurneys rolled on plastic wheels toward the corpse-filled freezing unit. Natives were already rushing out with their human cargo.

Just as they got to the door, Doc heard the thrumming of notes from a harp. He looked sharply at Jane. "What are they saying?"

"They say stop."

Rusty wrapped his arms around his shivering body. "Stop? Why?"

"No reason. Stop."

"But, we need to get those bodies," Scott protested. He gave the gurney a shove toward the doorway. "We can't stop now."

Sam held him back. "Don't disobey. It'll only get us in trouble."

"But, it'll ruin the plan. We may never get this opportunity again."

Doc said, "Sam is right. If we act out of order the guards will surely take notice. We cannot—" Doc suddenly looked down at the stretcher before him. His brows knitted in intense concentration. He looked around at the dragon guards, saw that their attention was otherwise occupied. With scores of bustling natives in the handling room, no one was paying particular mind to their activities. Doc tugged the knot holding his G-string in place. As it fell away he rolled over onto the stretcher, and tucked the puny piece of material under the small of his back. "Death Wind!"

Scott said, "Doc, what're you doing?"

The Nomad needed no explanation. He slipped out of his loincloth and jumped onto the plastic padding.

Sandra stared down at his naked body. "DW, what the hell—"

"Start pushing, folks," Doc urged in his calm, quiet voice. "Before they notice that we did not get these bodies from the freezers."

Rusty and Sam nudged the gurney forward. Doc, lying flat on his back, winked up at them. "That leg was beginning to bother me, anyway."

"Come on, Jane. Let's go." Scott abandoned the gurney he was pushing, and took his side by the one on which Death

Wind lay. "And, Death Wind, I know this'll be hard for you—but try not to smile."

"Hey, wait for me." Sandra ran a few paces and caught up with them. "This is the craziest—"

"We're committed now. Let's just hope they didn't take a body count. Hey, let's get past those guys."

As they merged into the stream of natives coming out of the meat lockers, the confusion masked their scurrying to bring the gurneys out of the building ahead of the others. Scott banged people out of his way, passed Doc's gurney, and reached the outer door right under the sloe-eyed gaze of two dragon guards. The lizards took no notice of the shuffling for position.

"Henry, if you don't stop shaking you'll give us away."

"Sorry, Sam, but I got a bit chilled in here. My boy, how are you holding up to the cold?"

Rusty's teeth were chattering so hard they sounded like clattering drum sticks. "Another minute and I'd be as cold as those stiffs."

The procession slowed down as it reached the sun-filled courtyard. All around were natives carrying food goods. Harps vibrated with instructions. People were directed along different roadways for destinations yet unknown. The dragons did not give advance information, only orders.

Jane held up two fingers and pointed at each of the counterfeit gurneys. "Scott. Three bad."

Scott's brows beetled for a moment, then he nodded. The dragons may get suspicious of three people pushing a stretcher when only two were prescribed. He bounded through the crowd to the preceding gurney and roughly shoved aside the native holding one side. "Sorry, pal, but this is for your own good." Scott looked back and flashed the okay sign: a fist turned inward with the thumb up.

The two counterfeit gurneys mingled with those headed for the time transport structure. With the strumming of its harp, a technician led the way along the alleys separating the living quarters. Doc got an ant's-eye view as they passed through the machinery spaces. Overhead cable trays carried power from the nuclear generating station to storage accumulators from which the mobile batteries were recharged. Massive motors droned, and transformers hummed monotonous tunes.

"I have to hand it to you, Henry. When a situation doesn't present itself, you make one up." Sam kept a wary eye on their surroundings as he spoke. "You're always three thoughts ahead of everyone else."

Doc carefully peered from side to side. "When expediency is called for it does not pay to hesitate. Audacity often succeeds where temperance fails. Indecision is anathema: any action is better than none."

Rusty murmured, "Doc, do you have a book of these proverbs, or do you make them up as you go along?"

"Hush!" Sam put a forefinger to his lips. "Something fishy is going on."

The funeral procession halted. A squadron of guards and a host of technicians blocked the opening of the plastic dome. Like a herd of draft animals, the natives stood by their gurneys awaiting instructions. Other natives, carrying loads on their shoulders, milled in the courtyard.

"Are any caped—" Doc got his head only an inch off the stretcher pad.

Sam placed a sturdy hand on his father's-in-law forehead. "Don't move a muscle, or you're dead."

Doc relaxed. "Appearances can be deceiving." He let his head loll from side to side so he could observe events.

Scott glanced over his shoulder, and shrugged.

Death Wind lay like a cadaver; he breathed so shallowly that not even his chest moved. But his hawklike eyes watched every movement. Jane and Sandra stood poised for action.

Out of the milling crowd came an outsider, wearing a shirt, shorts, and sandals. He was taller than Sam, but stooped. His wiry beard only partially hid a craggy, rough-hewn face. "Don't know what's happenin', but I seen 'em act this way before."

"Windy," Sam breathed. "What's it mean?"

"Could be some bigwigs comin' through. Got a couple of capers watchin' the proceedin's. An' they been sendin' back all kinds o' slaves. Mus' need a awful lot o' dragon power back then. Frozen carcasses, too. I never see nothin' like it."

"Are any natives going through?"

"A couple. Mostly, it's lizards an' corpses. Right now, the dome's empty."

"Damn. Doc, what'll we do?"

"This two-way transfer procedure complicates things. One never knows whether one is coming or going. Windy, how long has it been since the last transfer?"

"Few hours. The 'pacitors're jus' tabout ready fer another discharge. You kin tell by the cracklin'."

"That must mean that instead of balancing the load by transporting equal amounts from past to future and from present to past, they are sending a big shipment from their time zone to ours." Bushy eyebrows bounced. "Theoretically speaking, of course. That is a calculated guessometry."

"So, what do we do?" Rusty said. "Call it quits and try another day? Or wait for the next transfer and hope we can sneak through?"

Doc pondered the situation for a moment. "We cannot back out. Dragons did not invent time travel by being stupid. When they see the empty stretchers they will know something is wrong. Bodies do not just get up and walk away. On the other hand, if we hang around, they may decide to take the laborers off on another work detail. Death Wind and I may get through, supposing they do not think to check our body temperature."

"Or put you back in the freezers until tomorrow," Rusty added.

"Whatever yer gonna do, do it fast," said Windy. "Now I got the bug, an' got a burr under some o' them deadheads' saddles, I wanna git this kit an' caboodle movin'. Been a POW too long to suit my fancy."

Sam took a firm grasp on Windy's forearm. "Can you make a diversion?"

"Whatcha mean?"

"Draw their attention."

Windy looked over the reptilian overseers. "Sure. It'll cost me a shot with the pain stabbers, an' maybe a coupla days inna clink. Whatcha got in mind?"

"No time to explain. Just do it," Sam fairly shouted. The air smelled of ozone, and the focusing nodes were heterodyning. "And if all goes well, we'll see you back here in about sixty million years."

Windy hesitated for a moment. When resolution caught up with him, he was off in a flash. He ran screaming through the crowd, knocking down natives and spilling their packages. Half a dozen dragon guards drew their guns. They fired into the masses, not bothering to aim. People yelled in pain, fell to the plastic flooring, and writhed in agony.

"Make up a motto, Henry. We're on the move."

Doc felt the gurney lurch. Caught off balance, he had to grab onto the sides to stop from sliding off. "Sam, what are you—"

The gurney mowed down two natives who were thrust aside like billiard balls. Doc hung on for dear life. Rusty shouted and tried to keep up. Doc saw Scott's stunned face among the bystanders. The gurney ricocheted off a pair of dragon knees. The stunned technician rocked back; its thick tail formed a tripod, so it did not fall down, but it hissed in surprise and pain.

Sam shouted over his shoulder, "Come on."

Death Wind was up and running, dragging the girls behind him. A dragon guard swung its stun gun toward the charging brawlers. Before it could squeeze the trigger, the Nomad sliced through the power cable with his knife. The circuit was shorted in a momentary shower of sparks. A split second later the battery pack exploded with a tremendous roar. The dragon disintegrated as the blast tore through its back and ripped muscle from flesh. A volcano of blood and guts erupted into the air, splattering natives, guards, technicians, and visiting dignitaries with a mountain of gore. Death Wind and the girls were knocked down by the blast, but were protected from injury by the mass of the dragon's body: the dismembered parts flew over their heads. A moment later they struggled to their feet and continued running.

All around people screamed, guns fired, and pandemonium reigned.

The gurney raced through the main entrance of the time transport structure. Flanking guards were waddling out into the action as Doc and Sam rolled between them. One guard fired. The shot was way too late; the laser beam bored into the opposite guard's broad belly. The dragon hissed painfully as it teetered sideways. Rusty ducked under the falling neck. Scott jumped over it as it hit the ground. The standing guard fired again, missing altogether. It swung around as Death Wind attacked with his deadly knife. He did not try to cut the connecting cable; they might not survive the blast of another exploding power pack. Instead, he slashed the lizard's forearm and severed its tendons.

Doc stared up at the kaleidoscope of flashing needlepoints: the tips of the focusing nodes coruscated like effervescent haloes. The pitch of the whining capacitor circuits was almost beyond audible range. The air was alive with static electricity; Doc's scalp tingled, and his snowy white hair stood straight out. Only the shimmering blue curtain that surrounded the transfer field stood between them and the Cretaceous.

They passed through the curtain and entered a sphere of eerie soundlessness. Sam dragged his heels on the plastic flooring. The gurney skewered sideways. Doc felt himself slipping off. He held on harder, but the gurney overturned, depositing him on the floor. He went into a controlled tumble and came up against something rough and unyeilding. The silence was palpable, as if all molecular motion had ceased. He blinked his eyes to clear them. Then something wet and slimy splattered on his arm. He rolled back and looked up. A dragon technician leered down at him, tongue lolling.

"Doc!" Rusty screamed.

A huge, clawed hind leg hovered in the air above Doc's chest and descended slowly. Sam scrambled to his knees. Scott entered the sphere at a dead run and never slowed down. He charged right into the fracas. He smacked the drooling dragon mouth with the side of his fist. The technician was knocked off balance by the force of the blow. With its upraised hind leg still in the air, it flailed its forelegs for a pawhold. It executed a short dance step and regained its upright position. Scott jumped up and swung on the neck just behind the head. The added weight was too much for the beast. Its neck twisted around nearly a hundred eighty degrees as its body fell with a thud.

Scott was underneath the elongated neck as it hit the floor. He had a death hold on it, but was losing his grip. "Help!"

Sam was there in an instant. He pulled the plastic needle from the straw sheath tied to his waist, paused for a second until he located the right spot, then plunged the sharpened point into the dragon's ear hole. The needle easily punctured the tympanum and went straight into the brain. The dragon died instantly, although its hindquarters continued to squirm.

Scott crawled out from under the limp neck. "Thanks, Sam. I—"

Another vested dragon stepped into the blue haze. It pulled something long and slender out of a pocket, aimed it at Sam, and—

Death Wind burst through the blue curtain right behind it, vaulted off the thick tail, and leaped onto the dragon's back. Corded thigh muscles bulged as he wrapped his legs around the technician's lower throat. As the leering head lunged upward with a hiss, the Nomad sank his knife into the side of its neck.

Quickly he pulled it out and stabbed again—and again. The dragon dropped its instrument in its struggle to dislodge the savage from its back. Claws raked Death Wind's calves, leaving streaks of blood. The Nomad kept stabbing. The lizard leaned forward and kept right on going. As its face crashed into the floor, Death Wind released his grip and did a somersault over its plated skull; he came up on his feet, knife poised for another attack. The dragon lay in a growing pool of reptilian blood, gasping its last.

"Nice going, Death Wind." Scott crouched with another plastic needle in his hand. His voice was eerily damped, as if the sound waves were absorbed by a partially vacuated medium. "You and Sam must be the first people to ever kill a dragon in hand-to-hand combat."

If the Nomad heard him, he gave no notice.

Sam gawked at the bloodied needle in his hand. "It all happened so fast. I didn't know what I was doing."

Rusty scooped up the technician's fallen instrument, looked it over hastily, and tucked it in the loop of his G-string. "The question is, what do we so now? How do we get this time machine in motion?"

"Actually, I do not believe the support structure moves at all. It merely ruptures the fabric of space-time in such a—"

"Save the physics course for later, Pops. We're surrounded."

"Sorry, my dear. Rusty, do you see any mechanisms that would discharge the capacitor circuits and catapult us into the past?"

Rusty quickly glanced around the pulsating blue sphere. The seven of them stood in varying defensive positions, but nothing else was visible. He shrugged his shoulders and held up his palms. "No."

A long moment of stunned silence ensued.

Sandra put her hand on her hips. "Well, this is just great. Here we are all dressed up and nowhen to go."

"Here, Rusty. Here." Jane waved frantically with one hand and pointed down with the other.

The group circle closed on the spot indicated. Rusty dropped to his knees and examined the clear plastic panel in the floor. Underneath it was an annunciator panel full of flickering lights, an array of gauges both digital and needle, and several rows of throw switches.

Rusty ran his fingers around the perimeter of the panel. "There must be a lock somewhere—"

Doc said, "Locks are superfluous in the dragon hierarchical system. Natural biological stratification keeps unauthorized personnel from—"

"Ah-ha!" Rusty found a circular depression in a corner of the panel, but was unable to get a grip on it with his finger. "It must be a lifting hole, but it's designed to fit a dragon claw. Scott, give me your needle."

Scott handed over the plastic stalactite. "You'd better hurry."

Rusty inserted the point and pried. The clear panel popped open. He pulled it up and over its hinges and laid it down flat. "Now what?"

Jane pointed to a line of scratches above a large circular disk. "This mean—" She hesitated, with one hand wrapped over her eyebrows.

"Come on, girl, what the hell does it mean?" Sandra shouted. "We haven't got all day."

"It mean—it mean—" Jane bit her lower lip. "I think it mean—begin."

Rusty jammed his palm down on the disk. A flash of sparks flew out of the electrical contacts beneath it, and all the indicator lights went out. "Uh-oh. I think I just blew a fuse."

CHAPTER 12

"That's great," Sandra screamed. "That's just great. What the hell do we do now?"

"We're in a time machine," Scott said. "I say we call for time out."

"This is no time for jokes, mister. Any second now a whole dragon army's gonna come pouring through that haze."

"Dragon dragoons, huh?"

Sandra's looks alone could have killed half a battalion.

"Rusty, my boy, is there any chance you can reset that breaker?"

"Maybe. I could also jumper the disconnect switch if I could trace the wiring." Rusty grasped the annunciator board, but it did not move. "I'll need some time—"

"How ironic that we are trapped in a time transport device, yet have no time to spare." Doc pursed his thin lips. "You keep working on it, lad. The rest of us must take the defensive." He glanced up at the others. "I suggest that since neither electromagnetic radiation nor molecular vibration propagates through the force field, we take up stations in adjacent quadrants and prevent physical passage."

"Why don't we take the offensive and attack?" Sandra said.

"We are underarmed for such a military tactic."

"Listen, Pop, if we're going down for the count, I'm gonna take a few of the bastards with me. I don't care if I don't have any weapons. I can lift up a dragon's tail and kick it in the gonads. I may not kill it, but at least it won't spawn any more little lizards."

"My dear, I think it wiser to gang up on them one at a time as they come through the barrier. If we can dispatch an unwary soldier we will be at least one weapon stronger."

Rusty held up the foot-long metal tube he had picked up from the downed technician. "You can always zap one with this." He tossed the instrument to Sandra. "If you can find the firing mechanism."

Doc turned at a clattering sound and saw Death Wind dragging the equipment vest off the technician whose throat he had minced. "Good idea. It may contain something valuable. Sam—"

Sam was already cutting off the straps that held the vest onto the other dragon's chest. "Not only that, but this one's got another one of those miniature zappers." He pulled it out and held it up triumphantly. "Jane, you'd better hang onto this one. I've still got my darning needle."

Jane took the instrument, ran her hand over the smooth plastic surface of the enlarged handle.

"I can't find any trigger," Sandra said.

Jane cautioned her with a splayed palm. "Do this." Several times she made a fist with her free hand. "Dragon tool work."

"What?"

"She says to squeeze it," Scott explained. "The dragons have other tools that work that way."

"But how do I know how hard—" A technician waddling into the time zone forced her hand. Sandra aimed and squeezed. A ring of light burst off the tip of the barrel like an iridescent smoke ring, flashed instantaneously across the intervening space, and engulfed the dragon's ugly head. The beast toppled like an oak tree struck by lightning; it hit the deck with a thud that was absorbed by the eerie acoustics of the temporal sphere. Sandra blew smoke off the end of the tube. "I guess it works."

Sam scampered to where the felled dragon lay. He knelt down and placed his ear against the bulbous abdomen. "It's breathing. It's still alive."

"Gimme that knife, DW. I wanna finish it off."

"No! Wait." Doc hobbled across the sphere and stood between Sandra and the unconscious lizard. "I want it alive."

"What're you, crazy?" Sandra stood with legs spread wide and arms akimbo. "Any millisecond now this place'll be swarming with dragons, more'n we can shake a stick at." She waved the weapon tube in the air. "What if this guy wakes up in the meantime?"

"I understand your concern, and your point is well made. But the validity of your statement is suspect. I think we've got all the time in the world."

"Pop, either the time warp has warped your brain, or you

caught some backlash from this tube." Sandra brandished the barrel in his vicinity.

Doc gently pushed the weapon aside. "My dear, if the dragons proposed to launch an assault, they would not have telegraphed their charge by sending ahead a solitary technician. Dragon psychology does not possess diplomacy; I doubt it came to plea for our surrender."

"You're right, Doc." Scott closed in from the position he was guarding. "Something strange is going on. But what?"

"I suspect we have some advantage of which we are as yet unaware. Perhaps they have no way of knowing that temporarily we cannot trip the transfer switch."

Death Wind and Sam maintained their guard at the far side of the sphere. Doc stared at them. When no one was talking, or moving about, the silence described such total absence of perception that he felt like a fly at the bottom of a glowing vacuum bottle. The Nomad nodded at him from his faraway universe, turned, and stepped through the blue haze. He disappeared from view.

"Death Wind!" Sandra wasted not a moment. She charged across the sphere after her husband. Before she reached the point at which he had vanished, he reappeared. Sandra stopped short. The expression on Death Wind's face was one of puzzlement. "What is it? What did you see?"

"Outside—it is—different."

"Different? Whaddaya mean, different?"

"Dark. No dragons. All still."

Sandra spun on her heel. "Pop, they've cut the power."

"Yes, it could be. Or else . . ." Doc rubbed his beard to a point.

Rusty got his legs under him and assembled his lanky body to its full upright posture. "Or else when I shorted out the switch, the surge passed through the branch circuit breaker so fast it blew the main disconnect. If that's true—"

"You do not understand," Death Wind enunciated slowly. "The sky is dark."

Scott ambled across the sphere. "Hey, Rusty, when you blow a fuse you really do a job on it. Somebody's going to be awfully mad at you when he finds out what you did to the heavens."

Rusty's jaw hung down to his chest. He was speechless.

"I think we had better investigate this, uh, rather incredible phenomenon." Doc favored his bad leg as he walked across the sphere toward Death Wind. He held his hand out like an usher. "Would you care to lead the way?"

Death Wind turned and walked through the hazy blue curtain.

"Hey, wait for—"

Doc did not hear the rest of Sandra's plea because he stepped outside the time transfer zone. An instant later she bounced through the soundproof, sightproof barrier. One by one the others followed.

The focusing nodes imbedded in the inner wall of the time transport structure showed not the faintest scintillation. Through the clear plastic, the visible sky was a purple, star-studded canopy. Nowhere was there a hint of movement, or a trace of sound. Then, from off in the distance, came a hooting the likes of which Doc had never heard before.

"Could it be nighttime already?" Rusty said.

"Maybe time passes quicker inside the shield," Scott offered. "As if we were accelerating. Or maybe our sense of the passage of time slows down."

Doc pursed his lips and stroked his beard. "Even though I do not profess to understand the principle behind the dragons' time transporter, I rather doubt that. It is too illogical."

"So's time travel," Sam said.

"True, but even though time travel is illogical to the finite human mind, it can be proven mathematically. Why, even in the twentieth century, physicists postulated that the neutrino, that evanescent subatomic particle almost impossible to detect, existed in a plane that allowed it to travel through time. That may indeed be the—"

"Pop, get your mind out of the past."

As the small band of humans filed out under the dome's arched entranceway, Doc craned his neck and peered up at the unfamiliar stellar backdrop. Faraway stars twinkled as the light they emitted millions of years previously passed through the heat inversions of earth's lower atmosphere. "For the moment, I do not believe that that is possible. Would you agree, Death Wind?"

All eyes rose to the firmament. The Nomad said, "I agree."

"Doc, where did everyone go?" Sandra said in bewilderment.

"Nowhere, my dear. They are exactly where we left them. It is we who have traveled."

Scott shouted. "Hey, where's the Big Dipper?"

"It does not yet exist, my boy. The stars that form the constellations as we know them will not move into positions we can recognize for another sixty million years. Welcome to the Cretaceous."

CHAPTER 13

"This is not exactly what I had in mind," Doc said. "I wanted to remain in the ranks of the slaves and study from the inside the society of dragons past. Now it looks as if we shall have to become renegades."

"That suits me fine, as long as I get to take it out of their hides."

"My dear, we did not come all this distance in time just to snipe at reptilian flanks. We already know how to destroy. We came here to learn what to destroy. And now that we've consummated an unplanned escape, we will have to fight our way back into the dragon stronghold."

"Hold your eohippus, Pop. This gal ain't going back to prison."

Doc smiled whimsically. "I did not mean to infer that we will allow ourselves to be recaptured, only that if we are to disclose our adversary's weaknesses, we must penetrate their defenses."

"I want to get past their security codes," Rusty said. "With Jane as my cryptographer, I may be able to crash their central computer."

Jane smiled wordlessly.

Scott emerged from the semidarkness, announcing his arrival by tapping a crooked tree limb on the plastic flooring. "You let me loose in their generating station, and I may be able to gum up their power production." He handed the smooth-barked limb to Doc. "Here you go, Doc. I found a cane for you."

"Why, thank you." Doc took the piece of wood and stretched his arms along its length. "Feels like the right size. Where did you get it?"

"There's a forest out that way, a few hundred yards from the perimeter."

Doc sniffed the aromatic wood. "Hmmn, smells like sassafras."

94

"That's what I thought. Some things never change. There seems to be a clearing—"

"Ahoy, there." Sam waved his arms over his head as he returned. "Is Death Wind back yet?"

"No," said Sandra. "And I'm getting worried."

"Don't. He went looking for water. That boy can take care of himself. Doc, we appear to be in a secluded area, surrounded by fields, trees, and shrubbery. There's a road at the bottom of the hill, but I couldn't see anything beyond that. And the whole place is abandoned. No guards—nothing. Only that one technician."

"It was probably left as a caretaker. There is no reason to post guards when there is no enemy to guard against. Sam, I agree with your assessment of the situation. Whatever special dragon contingency was waiting for transportation must have gone forward at the same time we came back. Our streams crossed somewhen in the intervening space-time continuum."

One section of the sky was brightening; tall trees stood silhouetted on the horizon as stars glimmered overhead. The humidity was high, the temperature slightly lower than the comfort range. The world was alive with sounds: the buzzing of flying insects, the faraway calls of animals. The time transport structure glowed faintly as the focusing nodes began to store energy after the recent discharge.

Sam said, "Rusty, what did you find out about operations?"

"It was too dark for me to see much of anything. Other than the dome and a warehouse, the only above-ground building is a control room. I went inside, and by the light of the annunciator panel I could see a keyboard, but I didn't want to touch anything until I know what I'm doing. I heard capacitors recharging under the floor, so my guess is that the machinery and storage batteries are buried. There's probably an access nearby, but we'll have to wait for sunrise before we can spot it."

"It all makes sense to me, Sam." Doc leaned back on his newfound cane. "In our time the dragons built a city from scratch. They necessarily began with the time transport structure, then expanded concentrically around it—a city planned properly from the beginning. But in dragon land, this technological experiment was an outgrowth of previous construction—a laboratory addition which they built away from the mainstream of their civilization. I think we'll find that the electrical energy needed to run this establishment is transmitted from a remote station. By the way, did you take care of the bodies?"

Scott said, "Yes, we dragged them off the plastic and behind a bush, then covered up our tracks afterward."

"That was good thinking."

"Death Wind's idea. The live one is trussed up with some wire we took from its vest. We didn't find much in the pockets—"

"I still think we should waste the bastard." Sandra folded her arms under her breasts. "It'll never talk."

"Not orally, perhaps, since it lacks the vocal chords for true speech. But we cannot overlook the opportunity to interrogate a living dragon; it has never been done before. With Jane as our translator, we may unravel mysteries of dragon aristocracy that we can put to great advantage." Doc shifted his position and stretched out his bad leg. "As far as the dead ones go, the only dragons I have ever examined were soldiers. An autopsy on a technician may provide inestimable information about the structure of the hierarchical dragon brain. How does it differ from that of a soldier. What makes its bearer more intelligent: heredity or education. Does the brain possess Broca's area, that convolution that grants only man among all earth's creations the ability to speak?"

"Spare me the biology lesson. This may be a field trip to you, or a science experiment, but I came here for revenge."

"Not a very admirable quality."

"Maybe not, but it makes me feel good. You can call me shallow if you want, and I won't deny it." Sandra jerked a thumb at her heart. "Your motivations may be pure, old man, but mine are simple—"

"Toad!" Sam angrily confronted his daughter. "I've stood by long enough without saying anything about your behavior, but now you've gone too far. You may be a married woman, but you're still my little girl, and I won't allow you to talk that way—"

Death Wind charged across the plaza with imperative speed. He stopped a few feet in front of the group, breathing normally and showing no strain over his exertions. "Dragons come."

All eyes turned to the Nomad.

"From the road. In a wheelbarrow."

"A what?" Scott said.

Death Wind pinched his brows. "A cart on many wheels that moves by itself."

Scott's hand flew to his temples. "They're coming by bus. We've got to get out of here."

"Bus?" Jane said, perplexed.

"I'll explain later. Come on, people, let's move it." Scott pulled Doc up by the hand. "Do you have any suggestions?"

"Run like hell, as my granddaughter would undoubtedly put it."

Death Wind trotted off in the direction opposite that of the road. The others straggled along at various gaits. The sky was bright enough to light their way across the plaza, around the dome, and to the perimeter of the time transport complex. The Nomad halted as his naked feet hit the dirt under the knee-high grass of the surrounding plain.

Scott stopped next to him. "Yes, what do we do with it?"

Behind a large mulberry bush lay the captured dragon, its legs lashed together like a pig dressed for the spit. The eyelids fluttered, partially exposing the dark orbs beneath. The long tongue lolled out of the half-open mouth like a length of flattened garden hose. A thin stream of saliva collected into a pool below tight-set lips.

"Kill it," Sandra growled.

Doc caught up with the rabble and leaned hard against his cane. "Can we take it with us?"

"It's pretty heavy, Doc," Scott said. "It took two of us to drag it out here."

"Kill it, and let's go," Sandra insisted.

Death Wind knelt by the beast's head. He held his knife limply.

"It knows where we came from," Scott said with more serenity than Sandra. "When we came from."

The knife hovered between the leering lizard head and the foreleg lashings.

"It is already a vanquished enemy," Doc intoned.

Death Wind looked up at Doc with clouded eyes.

Sandra screamed, "Butcher the beast, will you, and get it over with—before we end up on a laser shish kebab."

Doc took in a deep breath and swallowed slowly. "It must be done, Death Wind. Our lives are at stake. Consider it not murder, but a coup de grace."

The Nomad dropped his gaze. The knife slowly rose in the

air—and hesitated. After a long, lingering moment his forearm muscles tightened, and the knife plunged. When the blade entered the throat the dragon lurched and kicked helplessly. Death Wind held down the twitching head as he worked the knife back and forth until the steel blade severed a main artery. Blood spurted out in a thin, sickening stream. Still the dragon struggled. Death Wind withdrew the knife; his hand was covered with the lizard's sticky blood. The dragon's life force gradually departed; finally, it lay still.

Doc placed a warm hand on Death Wind's sagging shoulder. "Come on, son. We have to go."

Death Wind squeezed his eyes tight, waited a long moment, then stood up tall. His hand still dripped blood. "Yes."

The seven renegades raced through the tall grass for the protection of the trees. A gentle breeze rustled through Doc's silvery mane. Despite his barefootedness, he found the going easy; the downward slope made him seem to fly.

"I knew it was too good to be true." Sandra skidded to a halt, almost sliding off the brink into the wretched bog that separated them from the tree line. Stumps and clots of weed poked through a bubbling, sulphurous smelling morass. Bright flowers in hues of crimson and yellow softened the evil-looking appearance. "Anybody bring a raft?"

Gasping for air, Doc caught up with the group. He was thankful to have a cane to lean against. "I guess going around is out of the question?"

Sam shook his head. "It curves back in both directions. The way the banks are cut vertically on both sides, I'd say it's a natural feature artificially extended—to keep out unwanted intruders."

"And I thought man invented the moat to keep out dragons," said Scott.

"I doubt," said Doc, taking his time between breaths, "that man has invented anything that dragons have not already perfected—except for the elements of emotion."

"So, what do we do?" Sandra wanted to know.

"Fortunately, my dear, I brought my wading boots." Doc slid down the embankment and hit the film-covered water with a splash. "Not so bad. It is only ankle deep." He steadied himself with his cane and delicately placed one bare foot in front of the other. "Although there is quite a bit of sharp debris on the bottom."

The others followed his lead.

"Yuck! You didn't say anything about the ooze." Sandra scrunched up her face as she slipped into the swamp. "It feels so slimy."

Scott and Jane held hands as they sloshed through the quagmire. Death Wind took the opportunity to wash his hands and clean the blood from his knife. Sam and Rusty did their best to hop from stump to soggy island to stump. Doc found himself practically groveling as he fought the suction at every step. His cane was useless most of the time; its narrow tip buried itself in the soft mud.

The stars were gone, and the sky was bright enough to dispel the gloom of early morn. Sticks cracked underfoot. Strange chirps and whistles emanated from all sides like a weird stereophonic orchestra. The air hummed with oddly patterned bees seeking the day's first nectar. Extraordinary insects buzzed like bombers—

Sandra's scream pierced the air. She punched frantically at a dragonfly the size of a large bat. The two-foot wingspan enabled it to move with incredible celerity. The prop wash tossed her hair around like autumn leaves in a windstorm. "Help." Sandra stepped into a deep hole and sank in over her head. She came up sputtering words and phrases that, at that day and age, had not yet been coined.

Scott scooped up a floating branch and hurled it at the double-winged monstrosity. The wet clump of wood and attendant moss ricocheted off the dragonfly's extended abdomen, and swept it aside, but appeared to do no other damage. It soared off with an angry droning sound. "Doc, I didn't know they had biplanes in the Cretaceous."

"I have no doubt we will encounter many curious forms of life. This is a time that was—or rather, is—replete with—"

The high-pitched scream that cut him off issued from Jane's larynx. She pointed at a ripple in the water coming her way. The creature's skin tone perfectly mimicked the green scum. Only a pair of wide-set eyes gave it away.

"It's a gator," Scott shouted as he whipped out his plastic needle and pushed Jane behind him.

Sandra yanked free the miniature stun gun, aimed, and squeezed. "It's not working!"

A moment later the swimming beast was enveloped in a momentary electrical display. It writhed only once before it stiffened. Rusty held up his tube weapon like a western gunslinger. "Right between the eyes."

Forward momentum took the creature close to Scott before its gaviallike nose dipped beneath the surface. Death Wind sloshed past Scott, reached underwater, and caught the thing before it sank to the bottom. He held the four-foot-long specimen by the eyeballs.

"A crocodilian of some sort," Doc observed. "A small one."

"You mean, there could be bigger ones?" Rusty said.

"Undoubtedly—perhaps ten times as big." Doc ran his hand over the coarse, knobby exterior. The skin was rough, like sandpaper, and the protrusions were sharp. "Amazingly good camouflage."

"A nice set of dentures, too." Scott took Jane's hand and pulled her along. "And I don't want to be wearing them."

Death Wind trampled after them, dragging the crocodilian through the water. As he climbed up the fern-covered embankment at the edge of the swamp, Sandra said, "What're you gonna do with that?"

"Make breakfast."

Sandra gulped and curled her upper lip. "Yeah. I guess I've eaten worse."

"Food comes in strange packages," Doc said. "And they will probably get stranger."

They headed for the trees. Behind them, high on a hill, the time transport structure glowed brightly as its capacitors recharged. The shrubbery that dotted the field was like none Doc had ever seen before. The landscape was one of dampness and dense foliage, jungle and swamp, patches of high, open ground: an amalgamation of geological features. The sweet scent of flowers mingled with the fetid odor of dank rotting vegetation.

The red sun rose, bringing with it heat, spreading before it the prismatic color borne of a dust-laden atmosphere, and illuminating a primitive, antediluvian world that had never before known the step of man. For the squad of human desperadoes this was the dawn not just of a new day, but of a new era.

CHAPTER 14

Using both plastic needles as darning tools and Death Wind's knife to cut slits in the material, Sandra pleated one of the pilfered vests so it would fit more comfortably around her narrow shoulders. She had lost a hairpiece in the swamp, so her ample left breast was unabashedly exposed. She worked quickly to cover herself. "It it gets any hotter, I'll melt."

"So put on a jacket," Scott said with feigned sarcasm.

"Shut up, you."

Scott shrugged and returned his attention to Jane. She drew squiggles in the dirt: symbols that represented dragon scratch. Scott and Jane continually reversed their roles as teacher and student, each learning from the other.

Rusty looked over Jane's shoulder and memorized the drawings that looked like a cross between Egyptian hieroglyphics and Chinese picture writing. At the same time, he went through the pockets of the three vests and tried to make sense out of the oddly shaped tools and instruments. "How about that? I've just figured out that this is a pad and pen set."

"Hey, that's something we can really use." Scott took one of the rectangular plates that Rusty handed him. "Why are the words smeared?"

"Because I—hello, Doc, Sam. What did you find?"

"An earthworm about six feet long," Sam said, smiling. "I thought it was a python at first. Scared the hell out of me. Some flying beetles the size of boxcars: you need antiaircraft guns to shoot 'em down."

Doc smiled as he crossed his legs under him and slid down his cane like a fireman down a fire pole. "Death Wind is watching the road. At the moment there is no activity in either direction. However, having a highway through the jungle will certainly mitigate our transportation problems, as well as provide a direct route to dragon headquarters. Rusty, what were you saying about stationery supplies?"

"Huhn? Oh, the writing materials." He held up a fat

cylindrical metal dowel with a point at one end. "This is an etching tool, and—Scott." Rusty took the plastic slate back from Scott and demonstrated how the surface could be carved by the etcher. "Then, when you want to start over, you can erase the board with this." The box fit awkwardly in his hand. It hummed after he squeezed it, and when he ran it over the writing surface the scratches disappeared. "It's a low-power, battery-operated heating unit. It wipes the slate clean by melting a coating of thermoplastic—that's a chain-type polymer with no chemical bonding between chains."

"Ingenious."

"And, it's got a hole in the top that matches exactly the hole in the handle of the stun gun. I think it's a charging port."

Scott said, "And neither gun is working. Apparently, the self-contained battery is good for only a single discharge—a one-shot deal. I don't think Sandra's was damaged at all by the water—it had already shot its bolt. Rusty's doesn't work now, either."

Doc nodded and arched his bushy white brows. "I am happy to see that you boys have not been sitting idle."

"I also performed that compass experiment you suggested, and you were right." Scott placed before him a tiny plastic cup filled with water. "These are all things we got from the vests, uses unknown. I shaved off this sliver of iron, pounded it with a blunt instrument—what I call a screwdriver, although the tip is triangular instead of slotted—and—" He dropped the filing into the water. Surface tension prevented it from penetrating and sinking. Slowly, he rotated the cup. The orientation of the iron filing did not change. "Wallah! It points north." Scott aligned his hand with the longitudinal axis of the sliver. His fingers pointed toward the setting sun. "But not the north that we know."

"Further proof—if, indeed, we truly needed it," Doc said, "that we have entered an era not our own. Pole reversal is an old story in geological chronology. The earth's magnetic field wanders constantly, and sometimes shifts drastically. Add to that the concentration of Late Cretaceous land masses, before continental drift and plate tectonics began to spread the continents into their future positions and orientations, and compass needle deviation is not unexpected."

"There, that's better." Sandra donned her new blouse and, after the front was closed with the original thongs, she plucked the remaining hairpiece from her head. "Jane, thank you for the loan of your hair."

Jane smiled. "You are welcome. Cover breast?"

"Yes, and they're going to stay that way."

"You didn't always used to be this shy," said Scott.

Sandra scowled at him, then turned to Doc. "Pop, you'll have to pardon me for that outburst this morning. I guess it was a little impetuous. I'm sorry."

"My dear, we are all under a bit of a strain. Think nothing of it."

"Toad, I can't get over how—grown-up—you've become. I've never heard you apologize before. You've become quite mature. And you've—grown out, as well," Sam added with a smile.

"That's just because you haven't seen me for a year or so."

"Time flies, but it hasn't been nearly that long."

"More like sixty million," Scott said. "Or can you say time is passing when you're going through it backward? This is all so confusing that—" Scott jerked around suddenly. "There it is again. That honking sound. Only this time it's closer. I wonder what it is?"

The deep bass tone reverberated again.

"And it's coming this way," Rusty said.

Scott jumped to his feet. "You know, I really wasn't that curious."

"I believe there is more than one." Doc climbed up his cane and peered into the woods.

"More than one what?" Sandra said.

In quick succession two more toots rang out.

"More than one—source."

Scott said, "Jane, could that be some kind of dragon tone talk?"

As if she had done it all her life, Jane shook her head. "I not hear sound."

"What're you, deaf?" Sandra shouted.

"She means she's never heard it before. Jane, could it be some kind of dragon machine?"

She shook her head again.

The toots proliferated, louder than before, and were accompanied by grunts and the crashing of trees.

"Never mind," Sandra admonished. "We'll *see* it any moment."

Branches snapped off a nearby tree, and a blanket of vines fell to the ground. A green shape the size of a small tank pushed through the underbrush. The thing grunted.

Rusty crouched behind a moss-covered log. He held a palm frond in front of his face and peered through holes in the broad leaf. "It's an armored vehicle."

The tank that sauntered out of the shrubbery had four fat, stumpy legs, a thick caudal appendage that terminated in a swelling that made the tail look like a flexible club, and a body that was covered with pointed knobs and sharp spines. The snub-nosed beak rooted noisily through the grass. The cheeks puffed out as mouthfuls of foliage were crammed into the giant maw.

"What the hell is that?" breathed Sandra.

Rusty cast a glance at his mentor. "Doc?"

Doc seemed preoccupied, his eyes glued to the scene before him. "Oh, sorry. What was it you said?"

"What is that?"

Without interrupting his observations, he said, "Obviously an ankylosaur of some species or other, although not quite what I expected from studying their fossil remains. It appears to have a longer neck and a more upward stance than is usually pictured, and the tail is not as—"

"Pop! Just tell me whether it'll eat us."

"Do we run or hide or fight it off?" said Scott.

Doc shook his head. "I suppose we could shoo it away, or—"

The triangular-shaped head perked up. Beady little eyes peered out from under a ridge of bony plates. The beast looked straight at Rusty. The arm holding up the palm frond slowly lost its strength. The ankylosaur snorted. Then came a loud honking from behind it. The trees were thrust aside as a much larger but hunched-over dinosaur scuttled out of the herbage. Short forelegs exaggerated the size of its rear quarters.

"Now we run," Sandra said.

The ankylosaur spun around with agility that seemed out of place for one of its bulk and design. It wagged its tail like a happy puppy, but the swinging club was anything but a gesture of friendship. As it backed away from the intruder, its hindquarters came dangerously close to Rusty's place of concealment.

"Easy," Doc cautioned. "Easy. Do not alarm it."

"Who's alarmed?" Sandra fairly shouted.

The hunched dinosaur stood up on thick hind legs, to a height of some twenty feet. It balanced for a moment on its tail and looked down at the ankylosaur. The head was ornamented with a comb that protruded out the back like a trombone slide. The comparatively tiny mouth chewed a wad of conifer leaves. It swallowed. A moment later the air was rent with a loud, deep-pitched honk.

The ankylosaur turned tail and ran. Jane and Sandra screamed. Rusty fell to the side. Doc and Sam rolled out of the way as the armored dinosaur charged through their midsts. Scott was bowled over like a tenpin. The ankylosaur kept right on going.

Scott clambered to his knees, feeling his body. "I'm okay."

The tall dinosaur honked again. Off in the distance, another of its kind honked in return. Short arms stripped leaves off a nearby tree and stuffed them into its mouth. Wide-set eyes stared down at Rusty. Out of the corner of his eye he saw a bronze statue poised for action.

Death Wind stood in a clearing with a crudely fashioned spear aimed at the tall beast's throat.

"Do not attack," Doc called out in a scratchy voice. "It is only a hadrosaur."

"So what is that, an endangered species?" Sandra said angrily.

"They're all endangered here," Rusty said.

"So are we. But I'd feel better if they're more endangered than I am. Pop?"

"No need to worry, my dear. They are harmless herbivores."

Death Wind lowered his weapon. The hadrosaur paid him no mind, but went about its business of consuming leaves. It swung its mottled brown body broadside and ignored the band of people. It continued sounding its horn as it browsed.

"Nothing twenty feet tall or with a body full of pikes is harmless. What I want to know is where these things came from."

Scott dusted himself off. "Eggs."

"I know that. But I thought everything was supposed to have been wiped out. How come these guys survived?"

Doc sat up and composed himself. "Probably because they do come from eggs. Shell material is not gas permeable, so any eggs laid prior to the arrival of the death bomb could still hatch healthy chicks if properly incubated."

"That monstrosity was no chick," Sandra complained.

"Pardon my lack of precision, but I do not think the English language has evolved a word description for hatchling dinosaurs. I rather think the presence of livestock explains that wall." Doc indicated direction with a wave of his hand; nothing was visible but a grove of oaks and willows. "This is a game preserve for herds of domestic dinosaurs. That hadrosaur over there—more specifically, a parasaurolophus—is a farm animal."

The hadrosaur rose up on its hind legs, honked, and meandered out of sight.

"By the way, the hollow crest atop its skull is merely an elongated sinus passage from nostril to windpipe—a resonating chamber that functions as a recognition signal between individuals, or for warning of predators, perhaps even as a mating call."

Scott readjusted his G-string. "Doc, how come you know so much about dragons and dinosaurs?"

"I have studied them. It pays to know one's enemy." Doc's smile faded as he glanced at the surrounding forest. "Invaders are at a distinct disadvantage because they are unfamiliar with the territory and its inhabitants. That is why we survived against the dragons who invaded our time, and that is why we must move cautiously in the dragons' time."

"Right now I move that we get the hell out of this dude ranch," Sandra said. "I'll feel a whole lot better on the other side of that barricade."

"My sentiments exactly. Death Wind, what did you find?"

The Nomad stood tall with the butt end of the spear pressing into the soft soil. The honed tip rose two feet above his head. "One guard on each side of gate. Drawbridge controlled from either side. If we kill inner guard, outer guard is warned."

"Ah" was Doc's only comment.

"Hey, Jane's got the solution to that," Scott said. "She's been using her weaving skills again. Go ahead, show them."

Jane untied a coiled vine from where it hung down off her hip. "I make rope."

"You *made* a rope."

"I made a rope." She held it out to Doc. "It is a vine. I—plaited?"

"That's right." Scott kissed her on the forehead. "Not only does she absorb information like a sponge, she's highly creative—an inborn trait that's been stifled by a life of bondage."

Doc inspected Jane's handiwork. "She has both talent and natural aptitude." Doc patted her hand. "My dear, you are going to get us out of this mess. Shall we go?"

"We climb?"

"We climb."

The wall was thirty feet high and solid enough to keep in the largest of the multiton beasts of burden. The orange plastic had been poured into crude forms without regard for architectural elegance. Rough protrusions and extruded plastic produced a surface that Jane's long fingers and toes gripped with prehensile ease. She scaled the wall as if it were a ladder. After she reached the top, she tied the bitter end of the rope around a notched protuberance and dropped the other end to the grass-covered ground.

The rope uncoiled into Scott's waiting hands. "Who's first?"

"I'll give it a try." Sam was strong. He leaned back and had no difficulty walking up the wall like an experienced mountaineer.

Death Wind tossed his spear up like a rocket; Sam grabbed it. Then the Nomad scampered up with the agility of a red squirrel.

"Next?" When no one stepped forward, Scott offered the rope to Sandra.

Sandra looked down at the loose fold of material hanging from her G-string. "Thanks, but I'll go last."

Scott smiled. "Your pleasure."

"I guess I'll go." Rusty wrapped the rope around his wrists. He threw his feet against the wall and struggled for several seconds without getting anywhere. His lean arms could not lift his entire body weight. He clung to the wall like a limpet and sought the bulging knobs as purchase for his feet. He was thankful for the wraps of hide made from the skin of the morning's breakfast package; they protected his soles from serious scraping. The others cheered him on, but it was a long hard climb full of frequent rest stops. Most of the time he had his eyes closed. His strength was nearly gone when Death Wind grabbed his hand and vaulted him over the top. Rusty collapsed on the broad platform, sweating profusely inside his appropriated technician's vest. "Thanks."

"I do not think my performance will be much better. These old bones are not what they used to be."

"Come on Methuselah, I'll make it easy for you." Scott tied a loop around Doc's chest, and snugged it under his arms. The bunched material of the dragon vest offered padding. "Okay, take him away."

Death Wind and Sam hauled him up like a sack of potatoes. "How ignominious," Doc said.

When the rope was let down, Scott offered it again to Sandra. "How about for my pleasure?"

"Not on your life."

Scott winked at her, grasped the rope, and raced up the wall only slightly slower than Death Wind. "That leg is still a little sore." As he climbed over the top, he pulled up the rope just enough to keep it out of Sandra's reach.

"Hey, you, let down the rope."

"Did you want to come up?"

A hadrosaur honked in the distance. Sandra glanced frantically over her shoulder. "Scott, you drop that rope this instant," she screamed.

Scott smiled at the Nomad. "Death Wind, I sure hope you don't mind me teasing your wife."

Death Wind shrugged. "Someone has to."

CHAPTER 15

From the top of the wall the view was almost unlimited. The landscape ranged from gently rolling hills blanketed with luxuriant green foliage and dotted with sequestered stands of conifers, magnolias, and dogwoods, to lowland swamps steeped with palmettos, ferns, and placid ponds.

"It looks like we've got a long way to go," Sam said.

"So this is the land of the 'terrible lizard.'" Sandra coiled the rope and handed it to Jane. "I never thought it would be so beautiful."

"Looks can be deceiving. What is smooth from a distance is often rough upon close inspection. The terrain may be more difficult to traverse than it looks." Doc leaned against his cane. He untied the thongs and let his vest flap in the breeze. "Notice the predominance of angiosperms, and the lack of ferns—"

"What kind of sperms?"

Doc smiled. "Flowering plants that produce seeds that must be fertilized. They dominate the swampy forests of the Cretaceous, but soon will yield to plants like the fern, which reproduce by dispersing pollen to the wind. For some reason, the fertile ground of the Tertiary was kinder to the germination of airborne spores. It has been theorized that a worldwide forest fire may have decimated the angiosperms, and ferns, being smaller and growing more quickly, took over afterward. It is, of course, only one part of a biological cycle. Angiosperms eventually came back—but the dinosaurs that fed upon them never did."

"That's okay by me. I don't ever want to see another one of them oversized crop crunchers."

Doc rubbed his beard thoughtfully. "Even though the dragons undoubtedly nurtured the hatching of the domestic fauna we have just encountered, we may come across some survivors in the wild: stragglers, so to speak, who lived beyond the dominion of the world's overlords."

"Yeah, well, we'll burn that bridge when we come to it. I

109

say let's blow this burg and get some miles under our feet. I'm antsy."

Doc rolled his eyes. "Sam, why did you let this child watch so much video?"

Sam shrugged. "Growing up in a subway tunnel wasn't easy. At the time, video seemed like a good way to show the kids what the world used to be like."

"I do not think it was ever like the way it was portrayed on video." A shiver of revulsion coursed through Doc's thin frame. "Shall we be on our way?"

"I go first." Jane threw out the rope, stepped over the edge, and walked down the wall backward.

Doc went next, and one by one the others followed.

Sandra was last in line. It was not until she was halfway down that she saw Scott grinning up at her. "Scott!" she screamed. She lit beside him and threw a punch at his naked chest. "You beast. You're more prehistoric than that 'ankle sore' back there."

Scott partially deflected the blow. "I was just steadying the rope for you."

"Do me a favor, and don't do me any favors."

She stalked off across the field and did not speak for nearly an hour. The ground was soft and loamy. The short grass buzzed with attendant insects that all too easily transferred their attentions to her bare legs. She continually reached down to dislodge the little biters, none of which she recognized.

Doc plucked plants and bunches of fern, and inspected them minutely.

"Pop, we didn't come here to study the wildlife, you know."

Doc chewed thoughtfully on the leaf of a small shrub. "My curiosity is more than academic. The first priority of any invasionary force is to find food. We are at a distinct disadvantage because most of the indigenous flora is foreign to us, and we certainly do not want to consume vegetation that is inimical to our systems."

"What difference does it make, Pop? Meat is meat. Leave the herbage for the grazers. I'll stick to steak."

Sam rustled through a patch of thin, waist-high stalks resembling wheat. "Toad, ever since you were a baby your mother and I had trouble getting you to eat your vegetables. Now—"

"Now I'm a big girl, and I can eat what I want."

"How many times have I told you the human body can't sustain itself on a diet of meat."

"I know all about uremic poisoning, Daddy, but I'd rather take my chances with that than eat leaves." She pointed to Doc. "How do you know that stuff isn't full of deadly toxins?"

"Well, I—Henry, how do we know? Aren't you taking an awful big risk sampling unknown substances?"

Doc held out the macerated stem. "In the case of this particular leaf, I am not. I observed the ankylosaur eating it. I also recognized several varieties that the dragons transplanted to our time. I cultivated some of them myself."

Rusty said, "In Maccam City we lived almost entirely on vegetable protein extract."

"Listen, you guys wanna eat fodder, be my guest. Me, I'm going after the first game we see. Right, DW?"

The Nomad shrugged. "Food is food."

"I knew you'd agree."

Death Wind handed the spear to her.

"What's this for?"

He pointed to the edge of the clearing, where the long trailing limbs of a willow tree shimmered in the breeze. "Look close."

Sandra pinched her eyes. She saw movement, like leaves blowing across the ground. "What is it?"

"It's not an it. It's a them." Scott pulled out his needle and held it like a dagger.

Sandra saw a greenish, rabbit-sized creature scuttle through the underbrush. Then she saw another—and another—and— "They're all over the place." She crouched low and stalked silently through the grassy field. She placed a finger across her lips. "Shush."

The ground was alive with scurrying, lizardlike animals. As Sandra approached they spread out in the woods, some climbing trees and others scampering over moss-covered rocks. A few stopped and peered back with dark, curious, bulging eyes. Swinging the spear around her head, Sandra dashed into the middle of the flock. The little creatures suddenly stood up on two legs, tucked their forelegs along their sides, and bolted in all directions. Sandra lowered the spear so it grazed the ground at grass-top level. She caught one animal in the head and swept the legs out from under another. She stamped on the injured one and pinned it to the ground. The other had a crushed skull.

Scott chased futilely after the fleet runners; he never even got close. "These things are fast."

Sandra picked up her trophy by the scrawny neck and held it out triumphantly. "Now this is what I call dinner."

"But what are they? And what are they covered with?"

Doc took the still-living creature and examined it closely. "Feathers." He wrung its neck, then plucked a handful of dark plumage from its back. "Not true bird feathers. They look more like flaky, elongated scales that continually bifurcate until the tips resemble fanlike filaments. It must represent some dead-end evolutionary offshoot of avian ancestry."

"It's a blizard," Scott said triumphantly. "A cross between a bird and a lizard."

"Let's get a couple more." Sandra picked up a fist-sized rock and hefted it for weight. "Watch me pick off that turkey on the boulder. I'll cook his goose."

The round, grayish boulder was the size of a small bungalow. One bird-lizard perched on its hind legs and flapped its arms, while two others struggled up the craggy surface on all fours.

"That's strange," Doc ruminated. "Everything else is covered with moss or fern—"

The rock struck with a dull thud just below the clawed feet of the uppermost bird-lizard. The creature blinked and jerked his head, but made no other movement until the boulder on which it stood rippled. Then all three of them scampered into the underbrush and dashed off.

"What the heck—" started Rusty.

The boulder trembled like a giant blob of gelatin. The woods came alive with madly racing bird-lizards. Jane screamed as part of the flock swept past her in their curious upright, tucked-in posture. Sandra was too shocked to strike out at them. The boulder seemed to grow in height, as if it were being pushed up out of the dirt. Two massive, treelike columns lifted the gray mass like hydraulic pistons. A fat, ridged appendage unfurled, reminiscent of an elephant's trunk; it swayed from side to side.

"Uh-oh," said Sandra.

One hook-toed foot left the ground, tearing up logs and leaves and clinging vines. The beast pivoted. As the tail swung out of sight, the drooling, leering head came into view. Long, daggerlike teeth filled a mouth that was over five feet long. A protruding brow ridge topped dark eyes that burned with anger. The thick tongue darted out with a screech that sent chills down Sandra's spine. Her legs went limp when the animal rose to its full vertical height; it was as tall as a skyscraper.

"It's an allosaurus," shouted Rusty.

"No, allosaurs lived in the Jurassic. I rather believe it's a Tyrannosaurus rex. Notice the ridiculously tiny two-clawed forelimbs—"

"Forget the taxonomic classification," Scott shouted. "Let's get the hell out of here." He grabbed Doc by the vest, spun him around, and shoved him off. He gathered Jane in his other arm and pulled her along. "Come *on.*"

The tyrannosaur roared again, precipitating a complete rout.

Death Wind snatched the spear that was hanging limply from Sandra's hand. *"Run!"* She needed no other urging.

They raced across the open field skirting the antediluvian swamp forest. Shrubs with pointed stems stabbed Sandra's legs, but she hardly noticed. The weakness of fear left her body as the adrenaline took hold. Her heart fluttered wildly. She glanced over her shoulder and saw the portly behemoth stride out of the trees. Its stance was not upright but angled forward, the enormous head counterweighted by the bulky tail. White teeth glimmered in the sun. The beast swung its snout in ever-widening arcs, as if it were trying to locate its prey.

Its screech fulminated across the field, sending chills down Sandra's spine. The hideous head pointed directly at her. Its nostrils flared as if it could sniff her human odor. The head lowered and the tail raised, forming a body-line perpendicular to the ground. With another piercing screech the tyrannosaur charged. Taloned feet ripped up the earth at ten-foot intervals. This was no slow lizard: the carnivore advanced with the speed of a cheetah.

Sam veered for cover. "Head for the trees!"

The party in flight followed his example. A wall of shrubbery rose waist high in front of the palmettos, while five-foot-long segmented leaves cascaded down like a pall. Sam hit the leafy barrier first; he was stopped as surely as if he had hit a brick wall. He clawed and fought his way through the dense, closely packed bushes.

Death Wind leaped into the air, grabbed a low-lying limb,

and swung over the barrier. Scott dived headlong, hit the
ground on a roll, and came right up onto his feet. Rusty's long
legs easily vaulted over the shrubbery. Doc hit the ground and
crawled under the foliage. Jane executed a scissors movement
with her legs and ducked her head under the palmetto leaves.
Sandra fought her way through behind her father.

Scott grabbed Doc's hands, dragged him out from under the
bushes, and yanked him to his feet. "Come on!"

Jane hung back and parted branches for Sandra. "Hurry!"

Sandra raced past Death Wind, who stood grimly facing the
field with his spear raised over his shoulder, ready to launch.
From far ahead she heard Sam shouting "This way!" and
spotted Rusty crouched and waving her on. She stopped to wait
for her grandfather.

"Come on, Pop. Get the lead out."

Doc hustled by, half dragged by Scott and Jane. Sandra ran
just fast enough to keep in front of them without losing sight of
them in the brush.

"Over here," Sam called out. His naked chest was covered
with scratches. As the group closed on him, he turned and
made off through the trees. From behind came the feral
screeching of the enraged tyrannosaur.

Sandra hopped across a tiny brook. Tangled tree roots
eroding out of the shallow embankment snagged her foot. She
fell down in a heap, but was up and running in an instant.
"Watch it," she yelled back. She heard what sounded like a
giant threshing machine mowing down the woods. By the
clamor she judged the beast was less than a hundred feet away.

Splashing noises from ahead kept her attention on where she
was going. She broke out of the trees onto a grassy bank that
dipped gently to a slow-moving creek perhaps fifty feet wide.
Sam was already halfway across, in water up to his crotch.
Rusty plied through knee-deep water along the edge. Sandra
leaped into a pile of what appeared to be lily pads except that
the floating leaves were the size of pillows. The rubbery leaf
bent under her weight, but she did not tear through. Instead,
her momentum carried her forward. She felt like a frog as she
slipped off the green pad into the warm water and submerged
completely. She floundered about for a few desperate seconds
until she realized the depth was only three feet. She got her feet
under her, waded into the shallows, and continued her flight.

"Come on." Scott pushed Jane and pulled Doc into the

creek. They followed Rusty onto a sandbank in midstream, then across a reed-filled swamp. Jane tripped over a partially submerged log and went completely under. She came up sputtering. As Scott straddled the log it moved sinuously underneath him, tossing him five feet to the side. He landed sitting, in water up to his neck. "Watch it, Doc!"

The thirty-foot-long crocodilian writhed between them. Its body was covered with brownish leathery plates; its head looked like a frying pan with the long snout stretched out like the handle. Doc fell back, his jaw ajar and his eyes bulging. Scott whipped the plastic needle from its sheath. With a mighty swing he plunged the point into the depression between the two periscopic eyeballs. The needle promptly broke in two.

The crocodilian lurched forward with a powerful sidesweep of its broad tail. The wash knocked Scott down. Doc gulped. Scott slapped his hands against the surface of the water, regained his balance, and reached forward for Doc. "Come on."

The monster bent its body double, lunging back at the trio. Death Wind entered the arena with his spear, which he snapped down on top of the knobby head. The shaft broke off, but the mouth full of cruel teeth was driven beneath the shimmering surface. Death Wind leaped past the crocodilian before it came up for air. He grabbed Doc under the armpits and plucked him out of the water like a child would pick a flower.

"No waste time." Death Wing hauled Doc to the opposite bank.

The trees were sparse and offered no places of refuge. The terrain was mostly semi-open forest angling up onto dryer land. The ankle-high grass blanketed the earth as it would a pasture. Fields of yellow flowers contrasted brightly against the vivid emerald background.

"Hey, there's the road." Scott pointed to a horizontal elevation that carved an artificial orange path through the verdure.

"Let's start hitchhiking," said Sandra. She looked back at the creek just as the tyrannosaur crashed through the swamp forest on the other side. "And *now*!"

They took off running. The tyrannosaur teetered at the water's edge, tail swishing angrily.

"I hope that thing can't swim," Rusty said.

The tyrannosaur crouched like a hen about to squat on her

eggs. It screeched and bounded upward as if a colossal spring had released under its tail. The tremendous leap carried it halfway across the stream. Its huge feet swung forward with the claws outstretched. It landed with one foot on the crocodilian's head, pinning it to the sandy bottom. The tyrannosaur bent forward with its cavernous mouth agape, its lips pressed back exposing a horrible array of teeth. In one incredibly swift rending motion it clamped its jaws on the crocodilian's plated back and ripped out a chunk of flesh that weighed as much as a large man. It tossed its head back, devouring the bloody meat in one gulp. The crocodilian writhed in the tyrannosaur's unyielding grip; part of its backbone was gone, and what was left of its organs slopped out into the water. Then the tyrannosaur bit the crocodilian between the shoulders, tore out another huge chunk of flesh, and swallowed. The crocodilian lay still, surrounded by an immense pool of blood that stained the creek a frothy red.

Sandra wanted to throw up, but did not have time. She clambered up the rough, extruded embankment, and onto the flat orangetop. The poured plastic roadway extended as far as she could see in either direction, straight as an arrow but undulating with the terrain.

Doc bent forward at the waist, huffing and puffing. "Need a—moment to—"

"We're not out of the woods yet, Pops." Sandra watched the tyrannosaur finish its meal. It stood up on its haunches, licking its gruesome, drooling lips. "Come on, gang. Let's keep moving."

"I don't—think—"

"You can do it, Henry." Sam took Doc by the arm and urged him along. "You have to."

"That thing looks like it's still hungry," Scott warned. "And it's caught sight or scent of us."

Doc nodded weakly. His cane tapped on the road surface as he picked up the pace. "We can't outrun it."

"It's on the move and coming this way," Rusty said.

Scott took off at a trot. "I'll scout ahead for a place to hide."

"It's our only chance," Doc said, breathing easier, loping hard.

The tyrannosaur galloped across the open field with a speed that seemed impossible for a beast of five tons. Great clods of earth flew up from behind its taloned feet.

"There're no buildings, no—" Sandra looked around frantically for anything that might offer protection. "DW, come on."

Death Wind hung back with his truncated spear poised.

The tyrannosaur gobbled up distance like an express train. It stopped momentarily at the steep embankment and cocked its head from side to side, as if deciding how to negotiate the climb. It crouched and jumped, and in an instant stood atop the orange roadway. It screeched like a banshee.

"Hey! Down here!"

Sandra saw Scott sliding down the embankment to the grassy field. He plunged through some low scrub into a narrow brook.

"It's a culvert."

Rusty and Jane plowed through the brush after him. Doc slipped on the scree and tumbled down the slope into the soft earth.

Sam skidded down after his father-in-law. "Quick! In here."

Sandra's feet hardly touched the ground as she skipped down the angled roadbed. Death Wind leaped completely over her head and landed with a plop in the muddy water. With the tyrannosaur screeching wildly right above her, Sandra ducked under Death Wind's upraised spear, stumbled, and fell headlong into the circular opening. Death Wind ducked in behind her, spun, and jabbed the point of the spear into the tyrannosaur's gaping, cellarlike maw. The beast chomped down on the spear and snapped it as if it were a toothpick.

Foul, fetid, carnivorous breath gushed into the cylindrical drain pipe. The beast gnashed its teeth and howled in crazed frustration. The head forced its way into the culvert, but the twisted neck and bulbous body prevented farther advance. Sandra wrapped her arms around Death Wind's chest and looked past him into the glaring dinosaurian eyes only a few feet away.

The beast retreated. For several seconds the air was rent with its awful screeches. Great gray legs swept past the opening. The monstrous head reappeared and pecked at Death Wind. Sandra's scream reverberated throughout the short tunnel and knocked dirt off the ceiling, but the Nomad did not flinch.

The tyrannosaur pulled out its head. It continued to stalk the culvert entrance, occasionally stooping to screech in rage at the prey just barely out of reach. It was a long time before the beast finally wandered off, a longer time before its howls were no longer audible.

Inside the culvert, no one moved or spoke. They huddled together like a brood of baby rabbits. Sandra's heart pounded so hard she was sure Death Wind could feel it.

Eventually, the sun set and ended their first day in the Cretaceous.

CHAPTER 16

Sandra sniffed the meat suspiciously. "DW, where'd you get that?"

"You kill."

"Death Wind, I thought I taught you better than that." Scott gladly accepted the chunk of meat the Nomad handed to him. It was raw, but he was not about to quibble. He gave his portion to Jane.

"Yes. Sandra, you killed it. Before big lips." Death Wind cut another strip of flesh and held it out to Scott, who passed it farther down the line. "I picked it up, tucked it under belt."

"Wow, I was so startled by—big lips, as you call it—I forgot all about the little lizards."

Death Wind shrugged. "No sense to leave behind."

Scott cringed, but did not correct Death Wind's English this time. He knew how often he could point out the Nomad's curt speaking mode before he would clam up completely. "All I had on my mind was hightailing it out of there. You know, we only made it into this culvert by the skin of our teeth."

Rusty chewed on a tough meat strip. "More by the skin of its teeth. Did you see the size of its tonsils?"

"Are you kidding? I almost died of dinosaur halitosis." Scott scooted his backside higher up the mud bank. There was not enough room to get his feet out of the trickle of water that flowed through the sewer pipe. "Doc, how big do you think that thing was?"

"My powers of observation were unfortunately diminished by what I would like to call the exigencies of the situation, but which I cannot in all honesty refer to as other than pure fright. My altered sense of perception tells me it was the size of a small mountain. However, upon careful reflection, I would estimate that stretched out in running mode it spanned a full fifty feet from tip to tail, somewhat less than half that in erect posture. A postmortem would undoubtedly provide paleontol-

119

ogy with long-sought enlightenment on details not available in the fossil record."

Sam's deep voice echoed in the darkness. "My clinical interest ended when I saw that thing grin with a mouthful of croc."

Scott extracted another thorn from his macerated thigh. "Mine ended when it first stood up. Sandra, I think you should let sleeping tyrannosaurs lie."

"Shut up, you." Sandra's eyes were undoubtedly spitting fire, but in the total darkness of the culvert Scott could not see them.

He mocked her in a high-pitched voice. " 'So this is the land of the terrible lizard. I never thought it would be so beautiful.' "

"You're cruisin' for a bruisin', buster."

Scott patted her knee. "Nothing personal, my dear. I'm just experiencing a normal human reaction to traumatic events. It's called post fear syndrome. I've been scared silly, and I'm trying to laugh it off. Right, Doc?"

"I thought psychiatry was a defunct profession."

"Naw, we all studied it in Maccam City, didn't we, Rusty?"

"Yes. Part of our programming was the recognition and treatment of mental disorders arising from our highly confined and artificial living conditions."

"Rusty, get the computer lingo out of your head. Logic circuits are programmed, people are taught."

Rusty said, "Same thing."

"Yeah? Well, I'll tell you what my reaction is." Sandra stretched her legs across the narrow confines of the culvert, placing one foot between Scott's legs and one between Death Wind's. "I'm tired of being chased by nightmares that should have been dead for sixty million years."

"I'm just plain tired," Scott mumbled.

"I want guns. I wanna kill someone. I wanna blow something up."

"My dear, I have no doubt you will get your chance. Excuse me, son, but is there any more of that delicious meat?"

Death Wind served a second course.

Scott leaned forward and melded his chest to his knees, then arched his back as best he could in the round pipe. He was sore, tired, and dreadfully uncomfortable—but glad to be stuffed into a place where the rapacious tyrannosaur could not crawl. "It sure has been a long day. Somebody wake me up when—"

"Quiet!"

Scott instantly froze. He could not remember Death Wind ever raising his voice. No one moved, or breathed. Scott listened intently, but heard nothing other than the hollow echoing of air—like the sound of a seashell held up to the ear. He knew that the Nomad's senses were finely tuned, his perceptions acutely sensitive: the result of a lifetime of training that Scott, in his underground upbringing, had not developed.

Soon he detected a faraway wail, like the pleading call of a night creature. At first the sound was steady, without modulation, but soon it rose in pitch and loudness. A faint glow suffused from both ends of the culvert, detectable only because of the otherwise stygian blackness.

The sound became a whine. Looking out the tunnel Scott discerned shrubs and trees in the growing light. The shadows rotated with ever quickening speed. The whine dopplered to a roar. With a loud whoosh something passed overhead. The light reached full brightness and began to fade as the sound receded and dropped in pitch.

Death Wind tumbled out of the culvert.

"DW!"

Scott climbed over Sandra's legs and splashed out into the open. He scrambled up the slope, his eyes glued to the ball of light that shot down the road like a flaming meteor. "It's a car! It's some kind of dragon vehicle."

Sam crawled out the other side of the tube and climbed up onto the orangetop. "Battery driven, I'll bet. Everything else they operate is run on storage batteries."

The rest of the group came out of hiding. They looked like strange caricatures in the ghostly white fog that enshrouded the nighttime landscape. A few stars poked through the mist-filled sky. The slight drop in temperature with the setting of the sun was more than offset by the high humidity.

"I daresay you are correct." Doc rolled his shoulders and flexed his arms. "I detect no carbon monoxide or other exhaust fumes usually associated with the internal combustion engine."

Scott stared at him dumbfounded.

"There were still a few around when I was a lad. Well, as long as we're up and about, I suggest that we follow that cab."

"Aw, come on, Doc. I'm beat. We've been up for two days

straight, and constantly on the go—to say nothing of what we've been through, including the time barrier. How can you even think of staying up another night?"

"It is not a matter of choice, my boy, but of necessity. Our position is precarious. Apparently, even though the death bomb decimated the indigenous population, enough predators survived, or were hatched afterward, to harass the unarmed and unwary traveler. The gauntness of that tyrannosaur is an indication of how scarce a commodity the local prey must be."

"Doc, the thing was as fat as a tub."

"I think not. The dispatch with which it assailed us so soon after gorging itself on that crocodilian demonstrates its near starvation. I think we would be safer prowling at night and resting during the day."

Scott sighed deeply. He could not refute Doc's logic. Where did the man get his energy? "Okay, Doc. You win. Let's start walking. If I stand here another minute I'll fall fast asleep."

Jane placed her arm around Scott's middle. "I help."

Scott managed a weak smile. "Thanks."

The motley squad ambled along the orange road in the direction the speeding car had taken. Scott's feet dragged listlessly along the plastic. Even the warmth and tenderness of Jane's touch did not arouse him from his lethargy. He barely paid attention to the conversation the others resorted to as a way of staying awake. He heard only snatches of overlapping dialogue.

"Dinosaurs had quite a cosmopolitan distribution, so it makes sense that a few sur—"

"Did you see those withered hands, with only two useless fingers—"

"—the contrary, the dinosaurs were amazingly successful. They dominated the earth for over a hundred and thirty million years. Man has existed in his present form for a mere hundred thousand—"

"—no problem. Lots of drinking water and plenty of culverts to—"

"—must have a high speed of growth, to go from egg to adult in a few mon—"

"—like deer dropping their kids, they have to get up and walk—"

"—much more cursorial than specula—"

"Hey, you got any skin scrapings on that pelt? I could eat a dinosaur."

"—without pharyngeal speech the dragons have done quite well for themselves in the art of communication—"

"—than being eaten—"

"—what is sluggish to us. The dragons survived despite the speed of contemporary predators the same as man survived against the fleet-footed lion: by stealth and—"

"—all we need is a nocturnal—"

"—a genius at dactylology: deaf-mute fingers-and-hands speech. I saw her signing with a tech—"

"—intelligence, not wisdom—"

"—can find tubers—"

"—dragons are descended from lizards that were cold-blooded, or ectothermic. The body temperature is environmentally dependent: they bask in the sun to gain heat, hide in the shade to shed heat. At night they become inactive, although the friction of muscle movement can generate—"

"—gimme a bazooka and I'll show 'em who's—"

"I wonder if they hibernate in the winter?"

"Mammalia and dinosauria coexisted for millions of years, but mammalian evolution was stunted by the dominance of dinosaurs. After the Great Dying there was nothing to prevent mammalian growth—"

"—diversification of species—"

"Are you kidding? She's as smart as a whip. You're just jealous—"

"—high basal metabolism of warm-blooded animals, whether dinosaurian or mammalian—"

"Mesozoic and Cenozoic are eras; Cretaceous and Tertiary are periods."

"—never had to kill anyone. But she has other—"

"—thermoregulatory—"

"No, I think the oceans absorbed the contaminant and killed off everything from ichthyosaurs to plankton."

"—called minimum population density. Sure, a lot of individual animals survived the holocaust, but you need a large gene pool for the species to propagate. Extinction is a function—"

"—think there's a lot more going on between you two than a simple father-daughter relationship. I've seen the way she hugs—"

"—purpose of sexual dimorphism. By having both male and female gametes there is a greater chance of—"

"A scute is like a scale, isn't it? Like the plate on a turtle shell?"

"—glue them together to make a 'scale' model—"

"Because I've seen you two kissing, that's why. You never kissed me—"

"—not quite true. The hind brain of the stegosaurus, for example, was twenty times the size of the brain in the head."

"—two heads are better than one—as long as you only put your heads together—"

"Cockroaches have been around for three hundred million years—from the time of the Coal Age. I am sure they will outlive all of us."

"Just the same, I don't like her pawing you."

"—speaking, they are not dinosaurs. The plesiosaurs—"

"Yipes! Look at that!"

Sandra's scream shattered Scott's reverie. His eyes popped open. He saw a huge, bright orange ball rising up from the road ahead. The fog had cleared, and the stars shone down brilliantly except in a large arc above the fantastic orange globe.

"Wha—quick, get off the road!" He dragged Jane to the shoulder. "Come on!" The rest of the squad just stood there. Scott implored them with one arm outstretched. "Hurry!"

Rusty grinned and slapped his knee. "Scott, you look so funny."

Scott glanced at the mysterious ball. It was larger than any object he had ever seen in the sky except the sun and—"It's a flyer!"

Sandra put her hands on her hips. "Don't be silly. It's just the moon."

Scott look again. "But it's so big."

"Due to refraction through the earth's atmosphere, the apparent diameter is always larger when the moon is low on the horizon," Doc explained. "But it is closer now than it will be in our time. The tides must be higher as well. Beach front property must be rather ephemeral."

The adrenaline was still flowing through Scott's veins. He held Jane tight as he watched the near-perfect sphere break contact with the ground. He breathed a sigh of relief. He did not even mind when everyone laughed at him.

CHAPTER 17

"Scott. Wake up."

The voice that reached Scott's ears was dim and faraway. It was part of a dream.

"Come on. It's time to go."

Every muscle in his body ached. He moved sluggishly, and squinted through narrowly parted eyelids. A shaft of light stabbed into one corner of the room, glinting off dust motes that jiggled in the sunbeam with the random pattern of Brownian motion. For a moment Scott had no idea of where he was—or when he was. He dug his fists into his eyes and rubbed out the matter that had collected there like clots of earth. Rusty's image slowly took shape in the mists of his mind.

"What's the rush? I won't be born for another sixty million years."

"If you don't jump to it, you may become the first person to leave this earth before he entered it."

"Maybe my future body is a reincarnation of this previous life."

"We can discuss semantics later. Right now we've got a coach to catch. It leaves in ten minutes."

"Save me a front row seat." Scott gathered his legs under him and pushed himself upright. He stretched languorously. His body was covered with sweat; there was no circulation of air in the cubicle, and the heat of the day was stifling. "Where is everybody?"

"Working."

"Yeah? On what?"

Rusty slipped past the barrier intended to keep large marauding dinosaurs and their smaller cousins out of the now-empty storage shed. Immediately beyond the doorway stood a wall that crossed the opening like a tee. The narrow corridor extended twenty feet in either direction, under a thick plastic ceiling, and was barricaded by a swinging mesh of woven acetate fibers that was fitted with a simple latch.

"Jane's been translating instruction plaques, so we've been able to gain access to the main yard and operate some of their mechanisms."

"No kidding?" Scott followed Rusty into the sun-filled lot. The highway ran through a shaded concourse that was straddled by a complex of fenced-in buildings and enclosures. "Why didn't you wake me earlier?"

"I tried. So did everyone else."

"What can I say? I need my beauty rest."

"It didn't help." Rusty ran a hand through his curly red locks. "You look like you combed your hair with an eggbeater. Anyway, it's apparent that besides being a substation—you heard the transformers humming—this place is also a maintenance facility and stopover point. It was crawling with dragons an hour ago, and—"

"With dragons?"

Rusty blinked at him. "Yes, you know—the guys with the long necks? The eight-foot-tall lizards that walk on two legs?"

Scott rubbed his scalp vigorously and brushed the tassels of blond hair back over his head. The cooler air of evening was a welcome relief. "They were *here*?"

"Scott, the road goes right through this place." Rusty spread his arms, indicating the small outbuildings, the canopied areas, the electrical compound, and the sprawling structure on the other side of the road. "It's like a pony express stop—traveling dragons can eat, sleep, and change vehicles. The corral's this way."

"Whoa. Wait a minute. What are you talking about?" Scott looked both ways before crossing the highway. He saw no traffic in either direction. The sun was about to drop below the horizon. "You mean, there were dragons and vehicles running around and I didn't hear them? Where are they now?"

"Gone. I'd guess in its heyday a labor contingent stayed here full-time, to patronize truckers servicing the time transporter. Now, with the population deficit, there aren't enough left to dragon the place. The convoy carried trained workers with them."

"Hey, the gates are wide open."

"I told you we got in." Rusty's long legs ate up the plastictop. "The dragons don't lock things for privacy, only against danger. Because of their biological predilection and their highly structured class system, they probably don't have theft or other crimes of possession. That's what Doc says, anyway, after listening to Jane's descriptions."

Scott shrugged. "Makes sense to me. I always thought doors were sound barriers. I never saw a lock until we had to leave—" He flashed back to those final hectic moments when he and Rusty were forced out of Maccam City as acidic gas crept up the ventilator shafts corroding everything it touched. While Scott was usually able to ignore his feelings about the catastrophe, he knew how sensitive Rusty was about the loss of home, family, and friends. He rushed on, "Did the dragons leave the gates—"

"Wake up, Scott. I told you, Jane's been reading all the operation signs. The motor contactor is actuated by an external switch. We just had to flip up a protective cap, press the button, recite 'open sesame,' and entry was ours. Actually, we watched the dragons do the same thing. Still, Jane was a big help once we got inside."

They walked into a huge parking lot filled with vehicles of all descriptions, from single passenger models to tractor-trailer rigs. Each sat on a thick plastic chassis whose wheels were protected by armored fenders. All storage compartments were enclosed in bubbles of clear acrylic. The smaller cars were equipped with single rotating turrets, while the trucks and multipassenger coaches sported any number up to four; a laser nozzle poked out of the top of each turret.

Scott ran his hand lovingly over the squared-off, purely functional body of the nearest vehicle. "Look at these machines!"

"I knew you'd be excited. Anything with moving parts fascinates you."

"Hey! Over here." Scott turned at Sandra's shout. She leaned against the forward turret of a jitney and stroked the barrel of the laser gun. She thrust out her fist with the thumb up. "Now let one of those bastards get in my sights."

Scott whispered out of the corner of his mouth. "Sandra's got her security blanket." He smiled at her as he approached. "You know, you look your best when you're wearing a gun."

"Hey, man, I'm dressed to kill."

Sam climbed out of the front door. "Toad, remember that we're to use the gun for defense only."

"I hear you."

To Scott, Sam said, "Some people are trigger-happy, but she's trigger ecstatic."

Scott put his hands on his hips and surveyed the situation. "Rusty, when you said the bus was pulling out, you weren't kidding. How's it work?"

"Like everything else, it runs on universal, chargeable, interchangeable battery packs. Retractable cables pull out of that wall and plug into the charging port. The dragons either stop long enough to recharge their batteries, or a maintenance crew changes battery packs, or they turn in their vehicle for one fully charged. And look at this." Rusty held up the single-shot stun gun. "There's an adaptor for fitting this into the receptacle. It's rearmed and ready to fire."

"And where are the transformers fed from?"

"Underground. The main power cables run under the highway. I can only see where they come out of the packing glands in the service tunnel, but I suspect the plastic road surface is poured over the top of the wires as added insulation and protection from damage."

Scott nodded. "Telephone poles wouldn't last long in this country. The tyrannosaurs would use them as scratching posts. I would have thought—"

"Well, well, my boy. I see you're up at last." Doc carried a large plastic carton under one arm. Jane was one step behind him. "Did you get your nap out?"

Scott smiled sheepishly. "Sure, Doc. I was really exhausted. Jane, what's in the boxes?"

Jane held out the plastic container so he could see inside. "Rations."

Doc tossed his own package into the bus. "It is not exactly what I would call living off the land, but the food is quite good once one gets used to the added preservatives. The cafeteria has not been restocked for quite some time, but we managed to scrounge up some victuals. Are you hungry?"

"When isn't he?" Sandra called down from her perch in the turret. "Hey, here comes DW. Let's get this caravan on the trail."

Death Wind carried a double armful of slender branches. "Bow and arrows."

"Rearmed, recharged, and rarin' to go," Sandra sang out. They all climbed aboard.

"This is all going a bit fast for me." Scott sat down in the oddly shaped window seat behind the driver's compartment, noticing the cutout in the backrest where a dragon's tail was intended to slide. "Now I know how an infant feels in an adult chair." Furniture made to fit squatting dragons was not molded for the human form.

Sam took his place in the driver's seat. "All aboard?"

"Are you sure you can drive this thing?" Scott said.

"No. But what better time to learn."

Jane thrust an open plastic box into Scott's lap. "Eat?"

Scott sniffed the concoction in the container. It smelled awful and looked worse: bloody red chunks of meat the size of his fist. The grumbling in his stomach forced him to taste the unappetizing rations. He screwed up his face as he gulped it down. "If this is dragon cuisine, I'd rather have grubs."

Sandra laughed raucously. "Scott, that's the first time I ever saw you make a face at food."

Sam fiddled with the controls. The dashboard annunciators came alive. "Jane, which button was the searchlight?"

Jane pointed to a tag covered with scratches.

"Thanks." He applied power to the electric motor by pushing a rheostat lever. The coach rolled smoothly ahead. "The joystick makes the bus go forward and backward, applies braking action by reversing current flow, and alters the direction by forcing one set of wheels ahead of the other in a scissors movement: every pair of wheels is on a split axle." He demonstrated how the coach drove at an angle to its facing axis. "It's extremely responsive, and if you pull the tiller all the way to one side it'll go around in circles. So far, I've only pulled it out of its parking spot." Sam demonstrated the turning radius in the lot. "If you want to stop you can either slow it down gradually by cutting the power, or throw it into emergency braking by applying reverse power. Hang on."

He yanked back on the lever. The polymerized wheels screeched on the orangetop. Scott was thrown forward by his own momentum as the coach skidded, halted, and started off in reverse.

Sam brought the vehicle under control. "It's fast and has tremendous torque. And with every wheel independently powered, it can probably travel off-road just as well as on. It's quite a machine." Sam veered in a large curve and steered the coach out the gates. "Death Wind."

The Nomad leaped past Scott and out of the coach. He

touched an inset switch on the garage wall. The massive gates swung closed. When Death Wind was back in his seat, Sam closed and sealed the armored hatch. Ventilators opened and airflow fans went on automatically.

"Next stop, dragon land city," Sam announced to his passengers. "Sandra, keep a sharp eye open." The coach rolled smoothly out onto the highway, but went into wild gyrations when Sam pulled the lever to the side to execute a turn. The vehicle zigzagged like a drunken sailor until he got it facing the right direction and resumed a straight course. "The steering's going to take a little getting used to."

The sun had dipped below the trees, and the first stars of twilight were upon them. The highway maintained its arrow-like course through the swamp forest. The coach accelerated with a quiet whine up the gentle hills and coasted noiselessly downhill. A ground mist hung low above the bogs, creeping eerily across the road. Trees on high ground had been cut back to offer an unobstructed view in case of stalking predators. The night orchestration of prehistoric insects was damped by the acoustical properties of the acrylic housing.

Scott tossed down another chunk of preserved meat. "This is too good to be true: the dragons providing us transportation not only into the past, but to their city. And I thought we were going to spend weeks trudging through the swamp and fighting off dinosaurs. Unbelievable."

Jane winked at him.

Sam adjusted the temperature controls for maximum comfort. "We can only travel at night, though, when the dragons can't see who's driving this bus."

"Wait a minute." Scott squirmed in his seat. "You mean, we're not going to run off the road at the first sign of another vehicle?"

Doc chuckled. "There is no reason to, my boy. They will not expect to find us driving so boldly along a main thoroughfare."

"But what about when the future dragons relay information about our escape into the past? Won't they be on the lookout for us?"

"I have no doubt they will, but not in a stolen vehicle. No, I think we should maintain a course of intrepidity. The way to win a war is through active aggression. We should never allow—"

Rusty placed a hand on Doc's forearm. "Please, Doc, no more dictums."

Doc stopped with his mouth open. He slowly turned his gape into a smile. "Quite right, my boy. Quite right."

"Besides, we can always blast our way out of trouble." Sandra climbed down from the turret. "DW, gimme another one of them tubers."

Death Wind handed her what looked like a maroon banana. "Already cleaned."

"Hey, what's that?" Scott said.

Rusty took another out of a plastic sack. "It's actually a bulb." He gave it to Scott. "And quite tasty."

Sandra took a bite off the end. "Not bad for a vegetable."

"Honey, would you mind closing the hatch?" Sam said.

"Sure, Daddy." Sandra climbed back up into the turret and sealed the upper hatch. She sat on the gunner's chair and hunched forward over the firing mechanism, but her feet came nowhere near the rotation control pedals.

"Sam, watch out!" Scott practically choked on his food.

The coach swerved sharply as Sam yanked the joystick back and to the left, forcing the vehicle to slew sideways with the wheels racing in reverse. The coach bumped off a grayish shape, lurched to a halt, then backed up until Sam let go of the lever and stopped the engine altogether.

Scott twisted around and saw the dinosaur standing in the middle of the road. It was quadrupedal and sported a splayed neck shield with scalloped edges. Tiny horns, little more than enlarged thorns, topped each beady eye, while one long fat horn jutted off the snout. It twisted its neck and looked at him with obvious lack of concern, chewing a mouthful of vegetation. Scott swallowed the unchewed bulb at a gulp.

"It's a triceratops, and you broke off its horns."

Sandra slid off her seat and jammed the foot controls. The turret spun until the gun pointed in the dinosaur's direction. Then she jumped back into the seat and lowered the elevation of the barrel.

"Don't shoot! Don't shoot!" Sam shouted.

"I ain't gonna, unless I hafta."

Jane squeezed into the seat next to Scott. She snaked one arm around his middle. "Okay?"

"You, me, or it?" Scott kept his eyes on the creature as Sam switched on the searchlight and stabbed the beam in its face. It had a beak like a parrot, a body like a cow, and a thick tail that rested on the ground. "I don't see any blood."

The dinosaur let out a loud bleat that rose Scott's hackles. It lifted its multiton mass halfway up on thick hind legs, pivoted, and charged off like a scared rhinoceros at a speed inconceivable for a beast of its bulk. It tramped down brush and small trees as if they were grass. Sam kept the bright beam on the creature until it disappeared among the trees.

Scott felt Doc's hand on his shoulder. "I doubt if it was hurt."

"But the horns—"

"It is a member of the short-frilled ceratopsians: a monoclonius. It is supposed to have only one large horn. Sam, if we have not sustained any damage, I suggest we proceed with caution."

Sandra scowled. "You'd think they'd have a dinosaur crossing sign."

"We're out of here." Sam applied power, and the coach eased ahead at a snail's pace. "I can see that one of the first rules of driving is to keep your eyes on the road. I'd better concentrate on what I'm doing."

Uneventful hours later they came to a crossroad.

"So now what do we do?" Sam brought the coach to a halt. "Wait for a dragon vehicle to lead the way?"

"Jane, my dear, are there any hidden symbols to guide us?" Doc said.

"I still think we oughta go back to the time transporter now that we're armed, go back to our time and blow the structure to kingdom come." Sandra drummed her fingers on the laser gun's power amplifier. "We got the might, we got the right."

"My dear, we have already settled that issue," Doc said.

Scott was in a quandry. "We have?"

"While you were asleep," Doc explained. "Our principal aim is not to destroy, but to learn. We do not know what secrets we may uncover unless we seek with an open mind. Wonders of the universe may unfold—"

"Doc!" Rusty screamed.

"Sorry, my boy. But it is in our best long-term interest to storm the walls of dragon land before we retreat, to ensure that when we close the portal to the Cretaceous it is forever."

"Seems like I missed a lot by oversleeping," Scott said.

Rusty whispered, "An argument with Sandra is something you can afford to miss."

"I heard that, you worm!"

Rusty cringed and rolled his eyes.

Jane peered out the windshield as Sam played the searchlight beam across the road surface. They were surrounded by open fields of tall grass. No buildings marked a way station, and no poles indicated direction of travel.

"There." Jane pointed down at the middle of the intersection. "Dragon scratch." Her thin brows beetled as her eyes raced across instructions etched in the plastic surface of the road. She held out her right arm. "There."

Sam executed a right turn. He left the searchlight pointed straight ahead, illuminating the road in front of the coach. Thirty minutes later they passed a lone building sequestered in a desolate tract of forest. It was dark and seemingly abandoned. A few minutes after that they came upon a cluster of sheds constructed of universal poured plastic. Just beyond was a rural complex consisting of single unit structures of different sizes and shapes.

"Nobody's home," Scott said.

"We must be on the outskirts of a city," Doc said. "We may soon encounter occupied dwellings."

"Hey, what was that?" Sandra dropped out of the turret and hit the floor with a thud. "Over there, to the left."

Sam brought the coach to a halt and swung the searchlight to where his daughter was pointing. A huge mound of freshly dug earth towered next to a deep hole. A truck-sized vehicle with a blunt grill was parked next to a pile of dead dragons stacked like cordwood. Sam took the coach closer to the grisly scene. The pit was crammed with the bodies of naked dragons. Long necks intertwined with protruding legs and paws and snakelike tails. Leering faces glared up at the stars. White teeth gleamed sardonically.

"There must be thousands of them," Rusty breathed. "Millions."

A flock of pteranodons fluttered over the decaying remains with rapid motions of their twenty-five-foot wingspans. The ungainly monstrosities pecked with long beaks at sightless eyeballs and lolling tongues. With the rear cranial ornament protruding as far to the rear as the toothless beak stuck out in front, the pteranodons presented an otherworldly profile as they hastened to consume the proffered morsels.

"The dragon metropolis must be a charnel house that is yet being cleansed." Doc leaned back in his seat and closed his eyes. "I fear, my friends, that we are about to enter the city of the dead. Let us do so with as much trepidation as daring. The future of the world is in our hands."

CHAPTER 18

A long dragon convoy trundled by in the opposite direction. The leading vehicle was a flagcar filled with caped dignitaries, the rest were heavily armed freight cars. Sam kept up his speed to allay suspicion. He slunk down in his seat, and hid his face with a curtain of dinohide. The others lay flat on the floor.

"All clear," Sam sang out.

Scott stared out the rear window at the retreating searchlights. "You're right, Doc. They must assume we have a right to be on the road."

"Dragon psychology—the best weapon in our arsenal."

"I'd still rather beam off their family jewels," Sandra glowered.

"My dear, besides the trivial biologic fact that lizards do not display external genitalia, we have a better chance of preventing dragon reproduction by continuing our clandestine crusade. Silence is our watchword, stealth is our method, and bold—" Doc peered at Rusty. "Anyway, you get my point."

"There are more lights up ahead." Sam did not slacken speed. "But they appear to be stationary."

The moon had long since risen. Scott was getting used to its increased apparent diameter. A steady stream of pure white light shone down on the landscape, highlighting a jagged escarpment that rose thousands of feet above the surrounding prairie. Castellated ramparts were plainly visible.

"It's a fortress," Rusty shouted.

"The size of a city," Scott added. The battlements extended as far as he could see to either side. "A *big* city."

"That long talus slope must be the entrance ramp. Sam, slow down so we can see what we are getting into." Doc said to Jane, "My dear, let us know of any scratched warning we should heed."

"Yes, Doc." Jane positioned herself by the windshield. "I read."

"Sandra, I am not expecting trouble, but you be ready to man the gun—er, woman the gun—should the need arise."

"When it comes to blasting dragons, I'm always ready."

"Scott, please stand by the rear turret."

"Gotcha."

"Death Wind, how are your weapons systems coming along?"

The Nomad carved the finishing touches on a wooden shaft and held it out for inspection. "Wood is strong, it make good arrow. Feathers okay." Fitted into the sliced grooves were the coarse scale-feathers from the carcass of the turkey-sized creature Sandra had clubbed to death. He twanged the taut bowstring. "Plastic line not so good—too much stiff."

"In your hands, I am sure it will be exceptional armament."

Death Wind hefted his new spear. "This is very good." The shaft was shorter than that of the other spear, before it had been reduced to a ruler splintered at both ends, but it was tipped with a formidable, finely honed white point.

"Where'd you get that?" Scott said.

"From tyrannosaur. It broke off when I stabbed."

"Death Wind the dentist. Extractions free of charge." Scott admired the six-inch tooth lashed to the end of the spear. "I have to hand it to you, you are some scavenger. You don't miss a trick."

The highway headed straight for the cliff face. Other pikes merged from both sides. Abandoned vehicles lay scattered across the shoulders where they had apparently been towed. Many were smashed beyond repair. The lights ahead did not seem to be getting any closer: in the open, desertlike expanse leading to the dragon aerie, perspective was distorted by distance.

Many minutes passed before the coach came within clear view of the huge concourse that siphoned all the highways into a seemingly single broad orangetop entrance hundreds of feet wide. Two searchlights were mounted atop tall gun emplacements on either side.

"That must be how they keep marauding tyrannosaurs out of the city," Doc commented dryly.

"But how do the dragons keep the traffic in order?" Rusty wondered. "In all the video movies I've ever seen, cars had lanes—"

"That must be what these ridges are for," Sam said loudly.

"I've been driving right over them. Jane, what do these scratches in the road mean?"

"In. Enter. Come."

"Close enough. Well, Henry, we didn't get shot to pieces by the first defense, so I guess this is going to go as well as you thought. What do we do next."

Sandra said, "I still say let's just find a cache of explosives and leave a delayed charge in the time transporter, and blow the thing after we go through."

"My dear, we will do that eventually, but we have priorities of more importance. We must explore this magnificent city, not just out of idle curiosity, but to gather knowledge about the dragons as yet unknown to us, and which may be of monumental importance to future events. They have at their digittips a power of awesome strength and a technology of incredible complexity. We cannot simply destroy their time transporter, we must ensure that they do not build another and escape once again from their proper place in the history of the world."

Sandra grimaced and pounded the back of the seat with both fists. "I hate it when you're right. Okay, Pop, we do it your way." A broad smile split her face. "You just let me know when I can do some damage."

Doc nodded gratefully. "My dear, your cooperation is deeply appreciated, and serves as a fine illustration of deferring tactics to strategy. You are to be commended—"

"Sam. There." Jane pointed to the left. "Follow symbol with two line."

"Lines, Jane." Scott stood behind her and rubbed her shoulders. "Two implies the plural."

Jane smiled. "Okay."

"Looks like we're coming to a tunnel." Sam hunched low and peered upward. "No wonder. There's a sheer cliff above us."

The coach entered a conduit wide enough for a dozen vehicles. Ripples in the dull orange plastic lining gave the appearance of a lava tube. It was dimly lighted by solitary fluorescent fixtures spaced at hundred-foot intervals.

"Looks like they're conserving electricity," Rusty observed.

The grade was no more than fifteen degrees; it may have slowed down a heavily laden freight car, but the coach hummed along at its normal gait.

"Stay in line," Jane read.

"I'm sorry." Scott laughed. He jerked his hands off her shoulders. "I wasn't trying anything funny."

Jane's thin eyebrows pinched together. "I not under—stand."

"Jane, your linguistics is improving at a fantastic rate, but you're not yet ready to embrace the pun." Scott winked at her. "But I'll teach you."

"Don't do her any favors." Sandra leaned against the turret ladder. "Maybe she didn't learn much from Daddy, but you can ruin her."

Sam huffed. "I think she did very well in the two months we had together. She at least caught the rudiments of the language so Scott—"

"Why do you keep saying two months? What were you doing the rest of the time?"

"The rest of what time? I was only there for two months."

"Where?"

"In the dragon city. Where Jane lived."

"So where were you before?"

Sam winced. "I was home, of course. With you."

"What the hell are you talking about?" Sandra came erect, and her voice became a squeal. "That was a year and a half ago."

"No, dear, get your times straight. The hunting party was out only a week when we got—" Sam's eyes clouded over.

In front of them the lights grew brighter. The tunnel flared out as the ripples in the road surface curved away from the middle. The ceiling yielded to the open canopy of the sky; faraway stars twinkled through atmospheric heat inversions. Shapes hovered in the ground shadows below the searchlight stations.

"What's happening up ahead?" said Rusty.

Sandra ignored him. "And that was a year and a half ago."

Scott's mind filled with comments about all the incidences taking place in the future, not the past, but his attention was split between Sam's evident consternation and disorientation, and the spectral display they were fast bearing down upon.

"I—I—can't remember—it seems as if—"

"Hey, those are armed soldiers!" Rusty screamed.

Sam shook his head. He stared out the windshield, but his mind obviously was not taking in the scene before them. He was frozen.

As the coach leveled out where the ramp split into half a dozen thoroughfares, a bank of searchlights burst into full brilliance. The inside of the coach was illuminated as if by the noonday sun. An entire panzer division lined the walls of the tunnel outflow. Ground troops filled the spaces between the armored tanks.

Sam shrank back in his seat, oblivious to his surroundings. When his hand left the lever, it automatically resumed the middle position. The coach slowed down. Doc leaped forward and jammed the joystick as far forward as it would go. At the same time, a barrage of laser blasts crisscrossed in front of them. Two energy beams penetrated the windshield and left smoldering holes in the acrylic.

"It's an ambush!" Doc shouted.

The sudden acceleration threw everyone on the floor. A second volley arced through the side windows, blasting holes through the seats or going out the other side of the coach.

Doc kept his hand on the joystick. "Sandra, I believe that your wish for action has been granted."

Sandra sat up, her face showing signs of shock. "What?"

Scott braced himself against a backrest, wrapped his hands around Sandra's waist, yanked her off the floor, and thrust her against the turret ladder. "Shoot 'em." He climbed over Death Wind and scrambled up into the rear turret. His legs were not long enough to reach the foot pedals from the seat; he stood awkwardly with his spine bent backward in order to rotate the turret while he adjusted elevation manually.

His first shot went wild, gouging a hole in the orange road surface. His second shot barely missed a dragon soldier taking aim with his pack-mounted laser gun. Doc turned the coach away from a vehicle blockade, throwing Scott to the side; his hand clutched the trigger as he grabbed the discharge mechanism for balance, and he succeeded in blasting a hole in a second-story balcony.

The coach turned in a wide circle just inside the lethal perimeter. Scott spun his gun to starboard, shooting bolts of electronic lightning as quickly as the capacitors recycled. He and Sandra pasted a deadly broadside into the dragon ranks, felling soldiers and drilling chassis. One lucky shot hit a vehicle's recharging unit; the battery exploded in a shower of sparks and flying debris.

"Way to go, Toad!" Scott shouted enthusiastically. His

fighting blood was flowing. He braced himself against the clear plastic walls of the turret, aimed down the barrel, and cut down the dragon hordes with reckless abandon. The slow-moving soldiers, made more sluggish by the nighttime chill, responded lethargically to the passing high-speed coach.

"It's a turkey shoot," Sandra yelled over the sounds of battle and exploding fusillades. "Give 'em hell, Scott."

The heavy-duty laser cannon reeked with raw power. Scott worked the trigger like a lab animal jolting itself with bursts of gratification through brain-stimulating electrodes. Every deadly discharge released pent-up emotions. He was more alive than he had ever felt before. For a fleeting moment during the heat of battle he understood that Sandra's aggressive nature was not prompted by feelings of hostility or inadequacy, but by a sense of almighty dominance over a situation of previous impotence. He was the weak devouring the strong, the innocent conquering the culpable. He was getting even.

An enemy laser beam bored through the turret; Scott winced as hot fire touched his abdomen. His moment of reverie was gone. He was scared again.

Sam suddenly came alive in the driver's seat. The windshield was riddled with holes, and smoke poured out of the dashboard. Jane huddled in a heap where she had been thrown against the hatch. Doc lay in a prone position; he kept his hand on the throttle and directional control. "Henry, I've got it." He thrust the lever from side to side, causing the coach to dodge erratically. Bolts of pure energy stabbed at the vehicle; the fenders may have been proof against tyrannosaurs, but the laser beams penetrated the plastic guards like hot foils through butter.

"There're too many of 'em," Sandra shouted. "Get us outa here."

Sam steered for an opening in the barricade of vehicles. Soldiers from the after ranks moved forward to take the place of their fallen comrades. They wore cloaks to protect their bodies from the cool air. Hand-held weapons leveled at the coach.

Sandra blasted away from the front turret. "I'll make Swiss cheese outa them."

Scott, frustrated at not being able to direct his fire forward, picked off troops along the sidelines. His turret was punctured by three laser beams almost simultaneously. The breech of his gun was blown in half. Scott fell back, ricocheted off the seat, and dropped like a stone into the cab.

Death Wind softened his crash to the floor. "You okay?"

With a shake of his head, Scott said, "I think so."

A rending crash sent them both forward. All the windows on the port side blew in as the coach scraped alongside a building. The coach leaped into the air as the wheels rolled over a dragon soldier. The coach reeled at so sharp an angle that Scott thought it was going over. It righted itself with a crash. The follow-up gyrations were not caused by Sam's lack of control; the coach had suffered serious structural and mechanical damage. A fire raged in the rear compartment.

Sandra plopped down on the floor. "I think it's time to abandon ship. My gun's on strike."

An awful screech emanated from under the floorboards; the misaligned axles were grinding to pieces. The coach looked like a sieve. Seats and bulkhead insulation were smoldering. What was left of the windshield was splattered with the blood of the run-down soldier. The ambushing vehicles had broken formation, and a full battalion of dragons was creeping along the street.

Doc squirmed out of the miscellaneous wreckage on the floor. "I think a propitious retreat is appropriate."

"I've lost the hydraulics." Sam punched buttons on the darkened instrument panel. "The door won't open."

Death Wind slung his bow and dinohide quiver over his broad shoulders. He climbed through the cluster of bodies, grabbed hold of an overhead rail, and swung his feet through the remaining glass. He kicked out the windshield, then hopped through. "My spear."

Scott picked up the weapon as the others climbed through the opening. He waited until the rest were off the coach before passing the dangerously tipped spear to the Nomad. Splinters of glass pricked his feet, but the dinohide moccasins were tough enough to prevent the shards from breaking through. "Now what?"

"We should take a lesson from the lowly flatworm and move away from the disturbing stimulus," said Doc.

"Go where the dragons aren't," added Rusty.

Jane screamed at the same time Rusty discharged his one-shot stun gun at a leering lizard face. The soldier dropped as if pole-axed. Jane shook her head. "No good door."

Death Wind buried the tyrannosaur tooth into the heart of the soldier that took its place. "Run." He led the way along the sidewalk.

The human squad scuttled after the Nomad. Searchlights roved along the roadway and illuminated building walls. The abandoned coach blew up with a tremendous roar of fire and flame; a chunk of quarter panel knocked over a passing single-turret vehicle, and burning fragments scythed through nearby soldiers with the devastation of a grenade. The flaming roof turned end over end until it smashed into a third-story balcony. The chassis separated into its component parts; wheels ricocheted from walls like billiard balls off a cushion.

As they ducked into a narrow alley, Doc looked back at the scene of destruction. "So much for secrecy."

CHAPTER 19

Doc reconnoitered from the top of the watchtower. The dragon metropolis sprawled in front of him as far as he could see. It had not been built from scratch like the concentrically designed outpost in Holocene South America; it was a hodgepodge of slave pounds and domiciles, barns and sties, industrial plants, warehouses, and lofty spires that punctuated the urban scenery with add-on irregularity. The city was bigger by many times than any that modern man had ever constructed.

"Here you go, Doc." Scott pounced into the room with a handful of supplies. "We raided another storage locker and found all kinds of good things to eat."

"Yeah, and he's already sampled most of 'em. You'd better chow down before he consumes the whole lot." Sandra unloaded her booty by the door. "With the elevators out of order, this is quite a hike."

Doc said, "That is the idea—to deter dragon scouts from locating our base camp."

"No chance of that. They're spread as thin as dielectric on a resistor." Scott handed a faded brown, fist-sized cube to Doc. "Processed meal, probably made for the slaves."

"Thank you." Doc gratefully accepted the dried, compacted food bar. "Did you check the basements?"

"Yeah, there's not a soul anywhere," Sandra said. "Not any that haven't already gone to heaven. Man, there are bodies everywhere. Millions of 'em. It'd take a month of Sundays to clean 'em all out."

Scott chewed on a mouthful of meal. "And the cellars go on forever. There's an underground maze all interconnected with the topside structures. I'll bet you can go anywhere in the city without getting a suntan. And, Doc, we've got the key to the city. There are abandoned cars all over the place, charged up and rarin' to go. I even tried my hand at the stick."

"Yeah, and he almost creamed Jane when he lost control."

"It's not as easy as it looks."

143

Doc sighed. "Perhaps I'd better come down from my aerie and perform some useful work. All I've done all day is stare out the window. Oh, yes, I scared some pterodactyls out of the attic—or was it the other way around?"

"But, Doc, that's what you were *supposed* to do."

"What? Scare pterodactyls?"

"No. Watch the city for movement, for military maneuvers, for dragon activity."

Sandra harrumphed. "While those lizards are busy hatching eggs, you better be hatching one hell of a plan."

"Yes, well, that is what bothers me. For once in my life I have no plan. My grandiose scheme to delve into the world of dragons past has so far gained us no advantage. Nor can I excogitate a discernible future plan. I keep waiting for an inspiration—for some direction. But three days cooped up in this lavish apartment"—he swept his hand to indicate the plush furnishings, the alien architecture, the convenience appliances silenced by the loss of electric power—"and I haven't got a clue as to how to proceed. I underestimated the dragons once and it nearly ended our campaign. I do not intend to do it again. I need more input from you young scouts."

"I wanna stop skulking around like a pack rat," Sandra said, "and eliminate some lizards—if I can find out where they're hiding."

"Not an easy task in a city designed to house tens of millions, and occupied by a mere pawful. They must have a stronghold that I fear must now be heavily defended. The dragons do not seem to have made the mistake of underestimating human ingenuity."

"Yeah, they sure knew when we were coming, and how."

"That is precisely why we must tread with caution. I realize now that they have been studying our psychology as much as we have been studying theirs."

"There isn't much they could learn about this outfit by watching those dunderheads back in the present—or the future—or whatever you call it." Sandra strode to the window and glanced outside. The sky was a clear deep blue with practically unlimited visibility. Clouds like cotton puffs floated serenely overhead. "So how could they do that?"

Doc was caught off guard, lost in thought. "Do what?"

"Study human psychology. Did they read Freud's *Beyond*

the Pleasure Principle, or did they experiment with two-legged guinea pigs?"

Doc jerked back so hard he almost tripped over a tail rest. His jaw hung slack, and he was momentarily speechless. When he regained his composure, he said haltingly, "My dear, whatever possessed you to peruse such an erudite volume?"

"Hey, I didn't spend all my time as a kid watching movie vids—just most of it."

"I don't know," Scott said with a smile. "It sounds like a title that would attract her attention."

Sandra pinched her brows and poked out her finger as if she were going to yell. Instead, she threw back her shoulders and said calmly, "Scott, I may have some personality faults, but at least I'm working on them."

Scott rolled his eyes. "I guess I asked for that. I apologize."

"Accepted. So what—"

Rusty and Death Wind joined the powwow. "We've had an interesting morning," Rusty said.

"DW!" Sandra threw her arms around her husband and gave him a resounding smack on the lips. They had not seen each other in several hours. "Where's Daddy—and Jane?"

"They stay behind."

"Together?"

"Alone is not safe."

Sandra pouted, "I don't like it when those two—"

"Hey, don't you want to hear what we found?" Rusty interrupted. "A library."

"You mean, with books?" Scott said enthusiastically.

"Made of the sheerest synthetic vellum. I'm telling you, there's nothing the dragons can't do with organic polymers. They read it, wear it, build with it, drive on it—I wouldn't be surprised if they eat it, too."

"Yes, well, judging by the taste of this stamped-out cubic nutriment, they do." Doc placed the food bar on a countertop, and wiped his mouth with the back of his hand. "As food for thought, I hope what you have to say about this prehistoric atheneum is more digestible."

"Unless you're a termite or a silverfish, you'll love this." Rusty paced the room with the practiced gait of a thespian. "There are more books on these shelves than the legendary Library of Congress—or was that real?" He shook his head. "It doesn't matter. The important thing is that Jane can read everything but the technical journals. Did you know that when she was a little girl she stole grammar books from the schoolhouse? She was studying dragon scratch when she was supposed to be sweeping the floors." Rusty flung his hand past his ear. "Anyway, the information retrieval system is serviced by computer and, knowing the dragon's penchant for uniformity, I'll bet it operates in identical fashion with the one I played with in the North American dragon outpost."

Scott jumped for joy. "You mean, you can enter through a keyboard terminal and access their data files?"

"No."

The expression of glee on Scott's face took a long time to fade into a frown of misunderstanding.

"They've turned off the electricity to the entire complex." Rusty faced Scott and placed his hands on his friend's shoulders. "But our mechanical and electrical wizard can trace the wiring circuits back through the distribution panels and plug us back into the main power supply. Then we'll show these lizards mammals in action."

CHAPTER 20

"Uh, Henry, can I talk to you for a minute?"

"Of course, Sam. What seems to be troubling you?"

Sam looked both ways, saw that they were alone in the dark, underground corridor, and said in a hushed voice, "It's about—my amnesia."

Doc pinched his eyebrows. "Is some of your memory returning?"

"No not exactly." Sam pursed his lips and again checked the empty hallway. The only light emanated from the battery-operated lantern at his feet. "That is—I've been thinking about it a lot and, well, I've been waking up at night with the shivers. My chest feels like a block of ice."

Doc wiped perspiration off his brow. "Not the reaction one would expect in this heat."

"It's the dreams, Henry. It's coming back to me: a sensation of—utter cold. I can remember when I woke up—after being shot. I was freezing. My teeth were chattering, I was shaking like a leaf, my skin was frosted—"

"Not an uncommon response to the temperature suppressive affects of anesthesia on the hypothalamus. Vasodilation coupled with long-term immobility—"

"No, Henry, this was different. It was intense cold, like—I don't know—like I'd been buried in an iceberg."

"When I was practicing medicine in my younger days, back east, I often saw similar responses in patients after long surgical procedures. People sometimes suffer memory loss after a traumatic accident."

"Did they lose a year out of their lives?" Sam said desperately.

Doc tilted his head. "No, of course not. But then—"

"This was *different*. I wasn't shot with a stun gun. I *remember* looking down the nozzle, I *saw* the burst of light, I felt the laser beam drill through my chest like a red-hot branding iron. And, Henry, I don't even have a scar."

"The mind often plays tricks on the brain; it can go awry like the printed circuits of a computer. Oxygen starvation to the cells will cause synaptic breakdown—"

"I know my physiology, Henry. I studied under the best doctor in the profession—you. I'm also a wise enough physician to know that a doctor is his own worst patient. That's why I'm telling you . . . my impressions. Please don't explain them away so hastily. Just—think about what I've told you. And remember what I'm going through. I'm trying to account for a big gap in my memory. I'm trying to reconstruct—"

Death Wind padded along the corridor like a breath of wind. Only the intentional thumping of his spear warned of his approach. "Scott says throw the switch."

Sam nodded and glanced away. He ducked into the electrical closet, held the lantern up high, and wrapped his hand around the engaging device of the liquid circuit breaker.

"Sam, do not look at the contact blade in case it arcs."

"Right." He closed his eyes as he rotated the mercury-filled vial that made the electrical contact. "Hey, no sparks." The vial stayed in the horizontal position, instead of spinning to the vertical and breaking the flow of electrons. "Let's go upstairs and see if we're in business."

By the time they threaded their way along the convoluted corridors and up the stair towers into the library, Scott had his instruments clamped to the exposed wiring in the central distribution panel. He touched the probes to various terminals. The window on the plastic meter box flashed runic symbols.

"How's it look?" Sam said.

"So far, so good."

Sam looked over Scott's shoulder at the readout. "How do you know what all that stuff means?"

"I don't," Scott said matter-of-factly. "I never have. At least, not most of it. And Jane's dragon vocabulary doesn't extend into technical jargon. But I used the same kind of instrument to check wiring circuits on the dragon computer in our time. I know I'm checking voltage because the lead goes from a hot wire to ground; amperage is gauged by putting the meter in series with the circuit. These scratches are integers to base eight—dragons apparently developed their numerical system by counting their toes. I figured this out through interpolation. How many volts or amps, or what amount of resistance we've got, I just don't know. But it doesn't matter, as long as I remember that the numbers are consistent with the readings I made before. So, let's give it a shot."

Scott rotated the mercury tube until it rested against the detents. As slow as the dawn, the light in the room waxed from nothing but lantern glow to the equivalent of bright moonlight to the luminous intensity of the noonday sun.

"Dragons have an interruptor rheostat that prevents power surge from blowing the fuses again. It's quite clever. Well, let's go see if there's enough light to read dragon tales by."

"I do not believe I fancy getting close enough to a dragon to read its tail."

"Doc," Scott said with surprise. "Aren't you getting our roles reversed? You're the serious one; I make the jokes."

"Solemnity is a condition of inflexibility to which I refuse to adhere. Do not let this cane confuse you: my bones may be aged, but my wit is sprightly."

They passed under an arch that could have been the center span of the Brooklyn Bridge. The grand exhibition chamber that housed the principle book collection was a ten-story-tall geodesic dome whose walls were crisscrossed with ramps that began at four points on the floor and which took off in alternating directions: a quadruple helix that wound upward to the transparent ceiling with inward protruding study platforms at the intersections.

Rusty sat at the computer console in the middle of the vast room. He was surrounded by a vast complex of keyboard terminals and tiered monitors. Sandra lounged against a printer station. Jane ran her finger along a row of labeled switches and read out their meanings.

"Is it hot?" said Scott.

"The place ain't exactly air-conditioned," Sandra retorted.

Scott ignored her. "Rusty, do you have power?"

The redhead did not look up. He wore a newly made pair of gloves with claw extensions sewn into the fingertips. He tapped away at the keyboard. The control panel lit up like a Christmas tree. Rusty grinned like a Cheshire cat. He flexed his hands. "All the power I need."

Using pointed thumb and forefinger like ice tongs, he plucked a program capsule from a storage bin and inserted it into a square depression in the control panel. The weight activated a servomotor that siphoned the matrix cube out of the capsule and introduced it into the scanning recess. A bank of monitors sprang into life; their display screens filled with line language.

"This model is highly sophisticated. It can boot all six superficies at once."

"Huhn?" Sandra said, frowning.

Rusty waved a hand over the hundreds of other capsules. "Each one of these crystals contains an operating format and memory unit coded at the molecular level, and containing as much information as every volume in this library."

"Get outa town," Sandra said.

"No, I'm serious. Microminiaturization is the key to dragon dominance of the world. It enabled them to produce a computer that worked better than their own brains."

"So what? We had computers that could outthink people."

"No, we didn't. We had computers that could calculate faster and store more information and retrieve data quicker than their programmers, but they could not think. They were simply programmed logic circuits that operated at the rate of electron flow—essentially the speed of light. By comparison, although the human brain carries thoughts at a snaillike pace, it has the ability to create ideas."

"That didn't help me any on my math homework."

Rusty went on without interruption. "Early computers using vacuum tube technology took up a five-story building just to add simple figures. Second generation computers used diodes and transistors, analogues for neurons in the human brain, and became much more efficient. But *this*"—he stabbed a clawed finger at the control panel—"using a multilevel scanning system, reads data stored in a finely grown crystal lattice in terms of the positions the atoms occupy within the lattice. Perpendicular laminations provide internal access—"

"Whoa, whoa, whoa." Sandra waved her hands in front of her face as if she were warding off a horde of hornets. "Just give me the short version. My brain can't even keep up with an abacus."

Rusty sighed.

"He hates being cut short when he's on a roll," said Scott.

"If I may interpolate," Doc said, "it may help to understand that the human brain is biologically superior to—that is, its construction is more complicated than—the lizard brain. At least, in the accumulation and processing of data. Which is not to say that we are necessarily smarter, only that we reach conclusions more quickly—and sometimes jump to them."

Rusty said, "The dragons have designed a computer better than their own brain, possibly even better than ours. The internal search and seizure interval is almost instantaneous, giving it the semblance of true thought. Of course, it can't make decisions that it hasn't been programmed to give. That's the difference between memory capacity and intelligence."

"From my experience with dragon soldiers," Doc added, "they function either by instinctive reaction or conditioned response. That is why they will fight to the death. Technicians have the ability to learn. Administrators can actually think for themselves, although almost always within predictable parameters. On the other hand, the mammalian orders are somewhat adaptable to situations of stress. In man, this flexible response to circumstances has reached the highest degree of versatility. The irrational approach to uncomfortable predicament is called emotion, my dear, and it is one of your greatest attributes."

Sandra stared slack-jawed at her grandfather. Before she could cry a rejoinder, Doc, smiling quixotically, rushed on, "And I intend that as a compliment. You see, one of the most effective ways for a numerically inferior force to overcome a stronger adversary is to catch him off guard, to attack from an uncertain direction, to do the unexpected. Your compulsive conduct under pressure often leads to unpremeditated victory. That is why, although I chastise you for your hasty actions, I always forgive you. You exercise a genetic quality that has a positive long-term effect."

Slowly Sandra regained muscular control of her mandibles. "I'll remind you of that the next time we get in a tough spot."

"I am sure you will."

Sandra picked up a cube and held it so that it glinted in the light. She pushed open the slider; the crystal dropped out of the clear plastic housing and into her hand. "Oh! I'm sorry. Do I have to be careful of breaking it, or scratching it?"

"You can't hurt it. I've already dropped a few without ill effect. The data is locked permanently into the crystal lattice; the bonded carbon atoms can't be dislodged by shock, magnetism, or electricity. And since it's diamond, you can't scratch it either."

"Diamond!" Sandra held the gem by the corners and admired it with newfound awe. Like a prism, the crystalline structure split white light into its component parts. The rainbow spectrum that played across her palm disguised in colorful ostentation the true value of the jewel. "How many carats?"

Rusty shrugged. "I don't know. But its storage capacity is in the hundreds of gigabytes. Each one of these cubes holds uncountable reams of dragon knowledge."

"All of which we can use to our advantage," said Doc.

"Capturing the enemy battle plan is the ultimate victory in a spy operation." Scott pounded a fist into his palm. "With all that information at our control we can wage a guerrilla war that'll blow the dragons to kingdom come. We'll be a worse plague against what's left of the lizards than the Great Death was against mankind. I think it's time to get to work. What do you think?"

Rusty flexed his fingers, tapping his clawed gloves against the keyboard in front of him. "I think we're about to make history."

CHAPTER 21

"I have a plan."

"I knew you would come up with something eventually, Pop."

Doc pulled the shish kebab off the fire, inspected the chunks of canned meat, then put it back over the flame. "I am sure it is one that will meet with your approval, my dear, since it involves dragon bloodshed."

"Now we're talking turkey."

With his teeth Scott pulled a bite of meat off another steel spit. "Tastes more like stegoceras to me. I wish they had pictures on the boxes, so I could be sure."

"May we dispense with the repartee and get down to business?" Doc waited for a moment of silence. Scott and Sandra exchanged raised eyebrows, the others nodded silently. "Thank you. Now, we all understand how important it is for Rusty to familiarize himself with dragon science and technology via the library computer terminal. Whatever we learn about our enemy may play a significant part in our triumph over the survivors who would bring dragon rule back into the world. But the library computer is not a control computer; it can only read and access data. It is not tied in to the defense network, or other actionary devices. I think it is equally important, therefore, to explore more than the dragon state of knowledge. We need practical intelligence as well. And we need to disrupt and demoralize their ranks. I propose we do this by coordinated sniping."

"Tell me more." Sandra grinned.

"We split into three teams. Rusty will stay at the computer console, with Jane to help with translation. Death Wind and Sandra will work as a combat unit, Sam and Scott as an exploration party. We go out only at night, and we forage as far and wide as vehicular operation will allow during the hours of darkness. I want everyone to report back at daybreak."

"Pop, I love it."

"Sounds great to me, Doc." said Scott.

Sam tossed more trash onto the fire. The courtyard in which the rebels dined was surrounded on all sides by five-story living accommodations. "Do you have specific objectives?"

"Only those we've already discussed. The main emphasis should be placed on crippling their utilities. Since virtually everything in the city operates on electricity, shutting down or disabling the generating plants is the number one priority. Scott, you must study the distribution system in order to ensure that we do not cut power to the computer."

"Hey, what about the time transporter?" Sandra wanted to know. "This is a nice place to visit, but I don't wanna live here."

Doc raised bushy white eyebrows at Scott.

"Sure, Doc. No problem. That substation where we stole the bus is an electric facility as well. I'm sure there's enough battery power there to make several time transfers."

"Good. I always feel comfortable having a backup. Sam, keep an eye open for dragon operations. If we can determine a specific survival plan we may be able to circumvent it."

"Right, Henry."

Doc held up his walking stick. "Death Wind, Sandra, your main objective is to act as a diversionary force by raising Cain. Kill, loot, plunder, burn, do anything you want—but always on the opposite side of the city from where Sam and Scott are conducting their activities. We will operate in random fashion so the dragons never know where we will strike next. Do not conduct major assaults, just hit-and-run warfare. That is the strength of the guerrilla tactic." Doc paused and glanced around at his meager but multitalented squad. "Are there any questions? I am always open for input."

Doc took the skewer out of the fire, tasted the meat, and found it favorable. He slid the other pieces off the spit and onto a plate, then passed the feast to Jane. She smiled. The first chunk of charred flesh she offered to a shrewlike creature she cuddled in her lap.

"Does she always have to keep vermin?" Sandra said through clenched teeth.

"My dear, it is only a pet, and keeping pets is part of human nature: one of the distinguishing characteristics that separates man from the lower animals." Doc held out a tiny morsel, smiling as the cute critter wrinkled the nose on its long snout and nibbled at the proffered food. "Who knows. Perhaps someday the descendants of the little fur ball will evolve into the larger mammals of the Tertiary—perhaps even into the Primates. We certainly wouldn't want to take the chance of killing it, would we?"

Eyeballs roved, but no one spoke. The plate circulated around the group of warriors, returned to Doc with several bites left. Sam poked the fire with an iron rod. Death Wind rotated another skewer in the yellow flame.

"I suggest that we finish eating and get a good day's sleep. We have a world to change, and, despite the availability of temporal displacement service, very little time in which to do it."

Death Wind stole along the open street toward the lighted building, *whoosh*ing before the hot wind like a leaf in an autumn gale. His tooth-tipped spear led the way.

He stopped just outside the cone of light and melted into the shadows. He stood as still as a bronze statue. He detected no movement inside the doorway, he heard no sound; but he smelled the ripe odor of lizard flesh. Dragons were nearby.

All his Nomad instincts welled within him. With his back pressed tightly against the plastic wall, Death Wind peeked around the jamb. A sleepy guard perched on a stool; its tail flicked to the slow rhythm of a lizard heartbeat. The long neck looped like a horseshoe, letting the guard's lower jaw rest on its scaled breast. It wore a cloak of thick dinohide. On the floor, leaning against its hindquarters, stood a battery pack and laser pistol.

Death Wind rushed into the room, a wraith with a will. He buried the tyrannosaur tooth into the dragon's chest and punctured the three-chambered heart in between beats. The guard did not have time to breath its last.

The tripod formation of tail and legs kept the motionless lizard on its stool. The only sign that it was dead instead of asleep was the viscous flow of blood that dripped over its fat belly and pooled on the floor. Death Wind slung the backpack over his shoulder and readjusted the long straps to their shortest extension. The battery pack rode uncomfortably on his lower back beneath the bow and quiver, but could not be raised higher. He doffed the backpack and left it with his spear by the door. Bow in hand and arrow notched, he strode farther into the building.

A palatial spiral ramp coiled clockwise from the floor of the antechamber. Only night lights were lit. Death Wind crept up to the second floor. A long corridor stretched out before him. A guardroom stood to one side, occupied by two lounging lizards. The Nomad slipped past them quietly. He stopped at the next room, lifted the latch, and eased open the heavy door. He ducked into the darkness.

When his eyes adjusted to the gloom, he saw that the apartment was tenanted by a lone dragon lying naked in the sunken pit that served as a berth. A gold cape hung on a wall rack. Death Wind slowly released the tension on the bowstring. He put the arrow back in the quiver. He drew his knife.

Crouching low, he flowed across the room at a glacial pace. Every sense was alive, every muscle attuned. Unfamiliar insects buzzed in the air like dive bombers. A winged monstrosity landed on Death Wind's bare shoulder; he ignored it. The knife rose in the air. Death Wind balanced on the balls of his feet as he lowered himself to within striking range. His nostrils flared and his chest expanded as he forced air into his lungs.

Scaled lids fluttered, the squat body stirred.

Moonlight glinted briefly off the steel blade as it plunged downward with all the force Death Wind's corded muscles could bring to bear. The dragon lurched in slowly dawning awareness. The knife sheared off the breast bone at the same time that the long tail whipped around and caught the Nomad in the head. He was flung backward by the force of the blow. He crashed noisily over a stool and into the hard wall, absorbing most of the concussion with his brawny back.

The wounded dragon hissed as its head rose up like a rattlesnake's, tongue darting. Blood spurted from its chest. Death Wind regained his feet and charged. He leaped into the air, came down at the base of the dragon's neck and somersaulted over the clutching claws. Death Wind executed a perfect roll. When he came up, the dragon's head lay flat against the mattress. It gurgled once, then went limp.

Death Wind yanked out the bloody knife. He wasted no time in flinging open the door and whisking down the corridor. One guard was already half out of the watch room. It was in the act of bringing its stun gun to bear when the Nomad bolted by with his knife upraised. The razor-sharp blade rasped across the tough underside of the leathery throat. The guard recoiled, but by that time the Nomad was halfway down the ramp.

He stopped at the junction of the hallway and let out a series of war whoops. The uninjured guard waddled to the railing. In one smooth motion Death Wind pulled an arrow out of the quiver, notched it, and let it fly with deadly accuracy. The honed plastic tip buried itself in the soft, fat underbelly. The guard hissed as it clutched the half-buried shaft with one paw and grabbed onto the balustrade with the other. It steadied itself. Still hissing, it turned and waddled off.

Death Wind stood there for several minutes, waiting for something to happen. Escape at this point was too easy. When a squad of soldiers finally appeared on the landing, he whooped once, turned, and ran before their stun guns could be brought to bear.

He snatched up the spear and backpack on the way out, then hung around the doorway and waited for the dragons to catch up. When he was sure they had spotted him, he jogged in full view down the middle of the street. He stayed just beyond stun-gun range. Dragons did not move fast, but their long legs carried them far with each step. Several of them fired their guns.

Death Wind let out a whoop as he approached a darkened alley. He stepped over a thick rope stretched across the street. When the dragons reached the same spot, Sandra pulled the rope taut and snugged it around a hydrant. The first two soldiers were caught in midstride and went down headlong. The next three reacted too slowly to stop their forward momentum; one of them tripped, the others leaned beyond their balance points, but flung their tails out backward and remained upright. The two in the rear crashed into the melee, knocking them all down.

"Gimme that laser gun!" Sandra shouted. She burst from the alley like a jet from an aircraft carrier boosting track. She jerked it out of Death Wind's hand, flipped off the safety, and fired. The power pack recycled again, and again, and again. The street filled with smoke, and with the stench of burned flesh.

When Death Wind finally convinced her to stop shooting, there was nothing left of the dragon soldiers but fried meat.

Sandra wiped tears from her cheeks. "Take that, you bastards."

Sam swung the dragon lantern nonchalantly. "If anyone is in here we'll see their light a long way off."

The corridor was as black as a coal bin, and every bit as dusty. Scott held up his lantern and cranked up the rheostat. The light gradually grew brighter until he could see the pipe racks along the ceiling. "Still the same coding." Scott referred to the plastic tablet. "According to Jane, a loose translation would be something like 'main power circuit district eight.'"

"Did you bring the dictionary?"

"Yes, but I'm not that proficient in using it. I'm not as quick a learner as Jane."

Sam nodded. "A bright gal."

"A veritable Rosetta Stone as far as I'm concerned." Scott held the lantern next to the pipes on his side of the corridor. The markings had not changed. "Jane is . . . Sam, I—I—can I ask you a personal question?"

"Of course."

Scott dimmed his lantern until it threw out barely enough light to show the way: more as a mask to prevent their discovery. "Sam, is—is there anything—between you and Jane?"

Sam answered calmly and forthrightly. "Yes."

Scott gulped. He stared straight ahead. "Oh."

"But not the way you think."

Scott stole a glance at his companion. "How do you mean?"

"You've been taking too much stock in Sandra's innuendoes. Sandra sometimes sees what she wants to see, the result of insecurity mixed with childhood fantasy. She means well, but she's confused about her feelings, and by her feelings."

"I thought she was the most secure person in the world—next to Death Wind."

"Considering there are only seven of us in the world—this world—that's not saying much. Actually, her outspoken audacity is merely a cover-up for the fragile person inside. It's not her fault, really. We did a lot of traveling when she was a baby—either chasing after dragons or running from them. Until we stumbled on the subway people we lived in caves, in tents, in demolished buildings: always hiding, always on the lookout for the enemy. Then, after we moved into the subway, we were apart a lot. I was foraging, or hunting, and she was stuck in the tubes watching videos with her mother. She's never forgiven me for abandoning her."

"But, Sam, it wasn't your fault that you had to go out for food."

"Oh, I know that. And she knows it, too. But the child inside her doesn't know it. She needs love and acceptance, but doesn't like to have to need it. That's the conflict she faces. And until she comes to terms with it, until she finds a situation in life that she can live with, she will be an unfulfilled woman. As her father, all I can do is understand her—and love her. I love Jane the way—as my daughter. The great, fulfilling love of my life has been lost, and once lost can never be regained. You'll understand that someday."

"Well, I . . ."

"Scott, it's blatantly obvious you're smitten with Jane. The eye embraces, the touching, the long walks together, they all give it away. Don't try to resist the temptation of longing; go along with it. I would—if I were in your moccasins."

"But you—"

"Forget about me. I'm not a competitor. Whatever relationship Jane and I have is not affected by your relationship with her, nor vice versa. If anything, they complement each other. Now, what do you suppose that glow means up ahead?"

Startled, Scott looked up. He had been staring at the floor for so long he had forgotten their mission. "This must be it. We must be close to the generating station." The corridor broadened, and the pipe racks spread outward in various directions. "This is how it looked in the nuclear power plant in the outpost in our time. This is a much larger scale, of course. We should see a—" Scott drifted toward a plastic retaining wall on which were mounted lighting distribution panels, insulated pipe lines, and equipment shelves and cabinets. "Here it is: a radiation counter."

He pulled the device out of its compartment, flipped a switch, and watched with satisfaction as the clear plastic faceplate lit up. "This is unbelievable!"

"What? High levels of radiation?"

Scott shook his head. "No. There's nothing but normal background emission. But now that I know something of the dragon language, I can understand the readings. It never made sense to me before. Come on." Holding the radiation counter in front of him, Scott led the way through the maze of duct work. "The reactor should be nearby."

"I can't believe there aren't any barriers," Sam said.

"According to Doc, it all has to do with dragon hierarchy. They have a class system of such enforcement that no dragon would ever think of entering an area for which it wasn't authorized." Scott shrugged. "It doesn't seem strange to me. Where I come from the ideal of community welfare was taken for granted. And even though we've been raising hell in the city for the past two weeks, they don't have enough soldiers to guard against intrusion."

"Let's not get overconfident." Sam warily scanned the sidelines. "It's getting brighter up ahead."

Scott found himself whispering. "Better switch off the lanterns."

They entered a mechanical space full of humming motors and clacking contactors. Emergency lights suspended below the overhead pipe racks shed an eerie yellow glow. The room was as big as a house. A pump came on, and the discharge of water was clearly audible in the distance, reverberating in the tomblike structure.

"Shouldn't a nuclear power plant be humming with technicians?"

"Naw, they're fully automated," Scott explained. "Back home, in Maccam City, the only time we had more than two people watching the monitors was during a core change. But there may be a maintenance crew wandering around—if they have the personnel to spare on anything but emergencies. As long as we stay clear of the control shack we should be okay."

The floor inclined upward; dragon architecture did not include stairs. Since the pipes ran horizontal they gradually dipped beneath the plastic surface. Soon the auxiliary generator room was behind, and Scott and Sam found themselves in an enclosure the size of a large stadium. The monstrous structure that occupied the center stage was a sleek-skinned, five-hundred-foot long lozenge whose lower portions were cribbed with external crossmembers that doubled as an interlocking series of catwalks. Stars shone through the transparent dome.

Scott stopped in his tracks, ogling the ultramodern structure. "This is the strangest nuclear containment system I've ever seen. I don't see any access panels for the exchange of fissionable materials."

Huge magnetic coils protruded from either end of the five-story lozenge. Peripheral machinery whined steadily. The smell of ozone was thick in the air. The floor thrummed with power, sending a tingling sensation through Scott's feet.

"Oh, no."

"What is it?" Sam jerked his head from side to side. He drew the laser pistol from its holster and thumbed the safety. "What's wrong?"

"I can't believe it."

"Talk to me, dammit!"

Scott walked forward slowly. His arms hung limply at his sides. He paused at an engineering station long enough to stare at the cluster of gages and the dazzling array of annunciator lights. He passed under the catwalk ramp. He did not stop until he was within arm's reach of the dull orange surface of the generating lozenge. When he held out his hand, every hair on it stood on end as a result of the static charge.

"Scott, what is it?"

Scott's mouth was full of cotton. He licked his lips and swallowed hard. "It's a plasma shield, Sam. This a fusion reactor."

CHAPTER 22

"Rusty, my boy, wake up. Wake up, lad."

Rusty sat on the tripod stool with one arm dangling down and the rest of his body sprawled across the keyboard and function switches. His curly red hair was matted where his head had lain against his hand. He groaned, but did not move.

Doc clutched a sheath of foolscap against his chest. Half a dozen printers clattered behind him while reams of newsprint collected on the floor and threatened to inundate the library. "You may as well lie down if you are going to sleep."

Rusty's head lolled. The circles under his eyes were dark. "No time to sleep," he mumbled. His voice was craggy and barely audible. "Work to do."

"Yes, I understand." Doc deposited his fanfold on a workbench. When he lifted Rusty off the stool the youth's legs buckled under him. Doc let him down as easily as he could.

Rusty curled into a ball. "Incubator." He breathed deeply and evenly.

"He is okay?" Jane said in an unfaltering tone. She stopped scribbling English transliterations long enough to stoop and place her hand on his forehead. "He is hot head?"

Doc smiled. "It is the other way around, but never mind. He has a mild fever. Nothing to worry about. Just overwork. He has been glued to that console for more than thirty-six hours straight. His longest stretch yet."

Jane pinched her eyebrows and looked up at Doc. "What is incubator?"

Doc rubbed his beard thoughtfully. "It could be the beginning of future adversaries."

A dragon soldier waddled out of the building with its gun drawn. Behind it marched a vested technician. The armored car squatted only yards away, engine idling; the gunners sat in their turrets.

162

Death Wind loosed an arrow from a second-story window across the street. It was a long shot that glanced off the soldier's scaled flank. The twin turrets slowly rotated, the gun barrels elevated. By the time the laser beams stabbed through the opening, blasting away the framework, the Nomad was long gone.

Sandra fired her pack-mounted laser from half a block away. She did no more damage than to crease the pavement between the technician and the car. She was forced to duck the blast from a second soldier leaving the building. As soon as her gun was recharged, she poked the nozzle around the corner of the alley and let go a wild shot. The concentrated fire from ground troops and gun turrets bit into the walls and street surface around her, blowing out droplets of molten plastic.

She ducked back and threw her arms across her face as protection against the incandescent blobs. She scrabbled to safety on all fours. With her aim to draw fire accomplished, she got up and ran. Ten minutes later, and half a mile and three subbasements away, she met her husband in an abandoned storeroom.

"It ain't easy as it used to be," she said, breathing hard.

Death Wind nodded. "They are on guard. We must keep them that way."

Scott huddled in a corner of the library, using crumpled papers for a makeshift mattress. He heard a rustling behind him. When he rolled over, he saw Jane holding out a steaming mug of tinted water. Scott smiled at her. "No matter how far people go, in space or time, they take their customs with them."

Jane grinned. "You like tea?"

"Very much." Scott pushed himself to an upright position, leaning against a shelf of books. He took a sip of the brew. "Hmmn, very good. What's it made from?"

Jane shrugged. "That means I do not know."

"I know what it means." Scott gave her a peck on the cheek.

"Do I say good morning, or good evening? You wake up, so it should be morning. But it is dark outside."

Scott humphed. "I don't know. Leading a nocturnal existence for a couple months throws one out of perspective. I think it's a matter of choice."

"Do always have choice?"

"Yes. Always. Or at least, you should. I know that's hard for you to understand, being brought up as a human slave." Scott took another sip and raised his eyebrows in consternation. "That's why we're fighting this war. So we can have a choice in what we do with our lives."

"I understand. It is difficult to make up mind after years of—dragon telling. I think—I like it. I not like dragon control. I not know this before." Jane placed her hand on her breast bone. "I have turnings in here."

"Feelings, Jane. Those are feelings."

Jane sidled closer on her knees until their skin was touching. "I have other—" She chewed her lower lip. She clenched her hand into a fist and lightly tapped her chest. "Pain in here—but not hurt."

"Huhn?"

"Not the words." She took Scott's hand and pressed it against her bare breast. "What is—love?"

Scott was caught between a gulp and a tingling in his groin. "Where—where did you hear that?"

"Sandra say it with Death Wind. Say 'I love you.' What is love?"

"Well, it's, uh, it's a word that—has to do with feelings, and with the heart. Not the physical heart. That's just a poetic description, I guess, because when your feelings are hurt you feel pangs in your chest. Actually, the seat of emotion is in the brain. It's part of your personality, part of your being, part of—your soul."

Jane looked at him blankly.

"All right, I guess I'm not explaining this too well. Love is—the way you feel about people. Not that you love everyone. At least, not in the same way. It's a feeling of—warmth, I guess, of wanting to be near—of wanting to touch."

Jane brightened with glee. She rummaged through the accumulation of scrap paper until she found a plastic box whose sidewalls were fully of tiny cutouts. She unsnapped the lid, reached inside, and pulled out a furry rodent with a long snout and twitching whiskers. "I touch. I feel warmth."

Scott rolled his eyes. "That's not exactly what I meant." He went on quickly when Jane started to pout. "I mean, you can love your fur balls, but that's only one kind of love. There are other kinds of love. Like—do you remember your mother?"

Jane nodded expressionlessly.

"Well, you had feelings of love for her. And it hurt very much when—she was taken away. That's the bad side of love. Some people aren't even aware of love until they lose it. But love is a very great thing. It describes the depth of your closeness to someone, it's a bond between two people, it's a one-word summation of a million mixed-up emotions that are too complicated to explain. And you can love people in different ways, and on different levels. You have one kind of feeling for your fur balls, another for your mother, and yet another for Sam, and Doc, and the others."

Jane stroked her pet as she pondered Scott's description. "What kind of feeling I have for Scott?"

Scott inhaled deeply. "That's something that only you can know."

Doc rolled the six-foot diameter hemisphere across the floor of the library. He shuffled through papers that were strewn everywhere—tens of thousands of pages filled with laser-burned dragon scratch. The sheets of vellum were also piled high in every available nook and cranny of the main level. When he reached the space for the half globe he let it fall; it rolled around in circles for nearly a minute, winding down like a child's top, before it came to rest.

"There it is: the great continental mass of Cretaceous dragon land." Doc dusted off his hands. "Although it is not exactly the way geologists reckoned it would look."

"A hundred-foot change in water level could make a big difference in coastal contours," Sam offered. "Polar ice pack could account for it."

Everyone gathered around, sitting on stools or lounging on deck pads that had been brought in for bedding.

"It was believed that the supercontinent of Pangaea split up long before the Cretaceous." Doc ran a gnarled finger along a separation zone on the raised surface. "I can see here what may represent fault lines, the rifts of modern day plate tectonics, but I believe we will have to rethink our theories on the time scale of prehistoric geological processes. Empirical evidence takes precedence over—"

"Pop, this is all very interesting, but what does it have to do with your plan of attack?" Sandra sat cross-legged, one arm crooked around Death Wind's elbow. "Wouldn't we be better off using the city map?"

"Quite right, my dear. I was simply trying to set the stage for Rusty's discourse: to give an overview of this microcosm in which we find ourselves. We do not want to rush into anything we do not fully understand. Rusty?"

Rusty bounced to his feet with a sprightliness he had not shown in weeks. He passed a wand over various dark splotches of the curved map. "These are dragon municipalities, fortifications actually, in various portions of the world. According to the videos—"

"Videos!" Sandra shouted. "You mean while we've been out there tailing dragons you've been watching *videos*?"

Rusty's face was a blank. "Part of the time yes. Uh, may I continue?"

Sandra maintained her frown.

"Thank you. Now, according to the videos the dragons maintain a feudal state in which remote rulers occupy tracts of land surrounded by fenced-in forts, or plastic castles, whose sole purpose was to provide a place of refuge from marauding carnosaurs. There were no battles between warring vassals: they all paid homage to the central government. Toward the end of the dragon regime they managed to wipe out most of the wild predators while corraling many of the herbivorous dinosaurs. The newsreels end with the coming of the death bomb, but it's fair to assume that all the border legions died in the great genocide. However, some of the slave population here in the city managed to survive because they live cooped up in underground units. The bigwigs lived in the multistory apartments and were all killed. I believe that most of the administrators and technicians returned here from our time."

Like a schoolchild Sam raised his hand. "Doesn't this social and technology disparity seem strange? On one hand we have a highly advanced science that has harnessed the energy of nuclear fusion, while on the other hand we have a civilization that relies on slave-drawn carts. And in between is a pervasive and unemotional desire to kill off an intelligent race predisposed as inferior. There's no evenness in their culture."

Doc grimaced as he tugged his beard. "I daresay we can find appropriate parallels in mankind's recent history: one country living in riches and comfort while another lives in squalor, the hunting of animal species to extinction, even pogroms against adjacent nations. Dragons may not be fundamentally different from mankind, only more ruthless. And where man chose spaceflight as a way to leave his planet and expand the race, the dragons opted for time flight. Just because we do not understand the physics of time transport does not mean that it is an esoteric science."

Rusty plucked a diamond off the computer console. "I may not understand it, but this crystal lattice does. Each cube is a data storage packet programmed on a specific topic—with a great amount of cross indexing. I hold in my hand the secret of time travel."

"Let me see that," Scott said.

Rutsy tossed the carbon crystal to him. "One facet is also a history module. Initially, the dragons built a sending unit large enough to handle their death bombs. When the coast was clear they sent through the personnel and materials to build a reciprocal unit—the push-pull system is more efficient. The time transporter then becomes a harmonic device that can both send and receive in the same space at the same time, with interlocked safety features that prevent passage into a space already occupied. Once synchronized, the double transfer utilizes hardly any more power than a one-way dispatch—operating on the same principle as an elevator with a counterweight."

The wand touched a spot on the semiglobe. "Not knowing what they were getting into, the dragons built their time transport structures in the boondocks. Here is the one we came through. And here, given sixty million years of geologic displacement, is the North Atlantic TTS we blew up: an outpost intended as the first phase of their expansion program. Eventually, they would have built more transporters in the Cretaceous to correspond with the positions of the continents in the Tertiary. Because of the chaos created by the death bomb that massacred the home force, it took months for them to send the relief mission that captured us. I suspect they thought we were previously captured outlanders and not responsible for the 'accident.' "

"All that is in this little cube?" Scott held the diamond so the beam of light shining down through the transparent dome focused on the floor in prismatic design. "I can't see it. But seriously, Rusty, how about skipping the history lecture and getting on with the plan."

"Uh, sure." The wand danced across the land mass concentrated in such a way that a full globe was not necessary to depict it all. "The city is built on this escarpment that according to my geographic knowledge doesn't exist in modern times. Perhaps future tectonic movement—"

"Rusty!"

"Sorry, Scott." Rusty moved the pointer. "The distance between the TTS and the city is several hundred miles—"

"Several hundred miles!" Sandra called out. "We were only on the road a few hours."

"You probably didn't notice how fast we were going because of the dark. Sam kept the throttle pushed to full acceleration. Anyway, the lizards never got around to building the other transporters because their existence was terminated by a new order of intelligence—the mammals. Uh, Doc, how about bringing out the city map, please. I'll point out the objectives, then you can take over."

"Of course, my boy." Doc slid the hemisphere across the floor. He was still crouched over it when a beam of light flashed under his nose. A hole appeared in the middle of the supercontinent. The odor of burning hair wafted across his nostrils. "Wha—" As he stood upright he felt heat against his chin. His beard was smoking.

"Dragons!" Death Wind tackled Doc just as another laser blast arced across the room. The Nomad rolled in the air so that he hit the floor under Doc and padded the older man's fall.

There was a mad scramble for weapons. Lightning bolts ionized the atmosphere as soldiers poured into the room through the archway. Two dragons wearing strange harnesses stooped down on all fours; on their backs were heavy-duty gatling guns with barrels the size of saplings. Gunners straddled the bearers' tails and fired with abandon. In seconds the library was a psychedelic light show. Books were blasted off the shelves, shelves were blown off the walls. Fires started among the litter.

Rusty ducked under the console as pulses of pure energy lashed at the computer station. Monitors exploded from direct hits, showering glass and electronic components all over him. He scooped up a sheaf of papers and tucked them inside his vest.

"What the hell're you doing!" Scott crashed down beside his chum. He held the nozzle of his laser pistol over the countertop and fired blindly. "Start crawling toward the rampwell before they think to cut us off."

"I need these notes."

Scott grabbed Rusty by the collar and dragged him backward, keeping the computer terminal between them and the dragons. "You need your life, too."

The laser gatling guns chewed so many holes through the control panel that it looked like a colander. The room was a mass of flames fanned by the nonstop machine-gunning. A solid wall of soldiers advanced through the flickering orange fire, kicking the burning paper out of the way with clawed hind legs.

Rusty worked his legs ineffectually. Sandra plopped down next to him and took a fistful of material. She and Scott dragged Rusty so fast that he was strung out like a mannikin. He was choking on the hide bunched around his neck.

"Where's Jane?" Scott shouted above the tumult.

As the three of them rolled down the ramp, Jane yelled, "Here." She cowered by Sam's legs as the man provided cover with a laser gun.

Doc and Death Wind were behind Sam, halfway down the ramp. Scott disentangled himself from the twisted limbs of humanity. Sandra pulled Rusty to his feet. The squad beat a hasty retreat to the lower level. The precautionary barricades they had built across the underground passageways were being blasted in by flanking soldiers.

"Down the escape shaft!" shouted Sam.

They all piled into an electrical closet. Scott closed and barred the door behind them. One by one they climbed down the raceway opening where cables and conduits came up from the subbasement. The trays that fastened the components to the wall doubled as ladder rungs. When they finally came to a halt in the lowest level, they were all sweating from their exertion.

Sandra gasped, "Pop, I'm all for rushing this plan of yours—whatever it is."

Doc fingered his singed beard. "My dear, I hadn't intended to implement it with such expedition, but circumstances force me to agree with you."

"Wait a minute," Scott rejoined. "We can dodge these slowpokes from now till doomsday—there are millions of places to hide. I could spend years studying dragon machinery."

"And I love a computer with overbyte," Rusty added. "There's so much data to assimilate."

"Love?" Jane said questioningly.

"I'll explain later," Scott told her. "Doc, the dragons have built a truly magnificent metropolis. We've got all the time in the world, why rush it? There are other computer centers where we can set up a base. Let's not run like scared rabbits the first time they swipe at us."

"Speed of flight does not necessarily connote abdication, nor withdrawal surrender. Any goal must be set with limitations, and I feel that we have reached a point where further ambitions can only be approached asymptotically. As Sandra would undoubtedly state it colloquially, it is time to cut bait and be satisfied with what we have already caught."

Sandra nodded fervently. "Right on. Besides, it's becoming almost impossible to find dragons anymore. They're really on their claws. And when we do stumble over a work party, they're so heavily guarded we can't get close enough to count coup. We can't get a shot in edgewise. They've been withdrawing to a tightly knit perimeter around their precious reactor."

"You see, Scott, I am afraid that if we do not act soon, we may not be able to act at all." Doc hunched into a corner. He picked up his bad leg and massaged it with his fingers. "We can study dragon culture ad infinitum and never understand it completely. Man never reached an understanding of his own culture, and he evolved with it. With soldiers nipping at our heels, I believe the time has come to execute our grand design. We must stop living in the past and look toward the future. That is where our destiny lies."

CHAPTER 23

"As far as I have been able to ascertain there is no genetic distinction or specialization. They all come from the same eggs."

Sam scratched his black beard. "So they're not like ants, creating drones and soldiers and workers and queens by chemical injections or forced feeding?"

"Not at all, no." Doc watched Rusty splice the remote computer terminal to a multistranded cable. Scott and Death Wind were stringing wires inside the access trunk. Sandra stood guard at the end of the corridor. Jane ran her finger along the wiring diagram as Rusty referred to his notes. "Dragon class structure is a social convention. Impulsive promiscuity between administrators, or kings, and female slaves, or drones, confers universal gene pooling. Hierarchical division results from aptitude: the smarter ones become kings, the stronger ones become soldiers, the active ones become workers, the listless ones become drones. Some dietary management during rearing increases physical bulk, but that is not analogous to the gross anatomical distortion achieved by ants. After all, dragons are lizards, not insects."

"A dragon in any other vest would look the same," Sam misquoted.

"Precisely."

Death Wind peered down through the open ceiling panel. "Steady ladder."

"Got it." Sam braced the giant A-frame against his shoulder as the Nomad clambered down the makeshift rungs.

Scott climbed down next, carrying a satchel full of dragon tools and instruments. "The place is a maze of ventilator shafts, conduits, junction boxes, and terminal boards. We were only inches away from a maintenance worker. He never knew we were *inside* the incubator computer console. It was unbelievable."

"What about the heat exchanger," Rusty wanted to know.

"This is one mammal that's going to destroy a whole nest full of lizard eggs. I jumped the temperature control circuit so they'll never know when things start to heat up. By the time they figure it out and shut down the power, it'll be too late. Every egg in there will be soft-boiled—a generation gap the dragons'll never overcome." To Rusty, "Now that the heat's off us, are we ready to sabotage the reactor?"

"Almost. Thanks to Jane I'm fairly fluent in dragon scratch, which is what shows up on the computer screen, but they use a line language for programming that's something like Morse code. We've got to make three-way translations without making any mistakes. You just get me to the reactor control room, and I'll patch in the interruptor circuit. The time delay will give us twenty-four hours to get to the TTS before shutdown occurs."

"I know you can do it."

Rusty shrugged. "I'll finish the programming in the car."

Doc clapped his hands. "I am already forgetting the past and planning for the future. Sam, how is traffic this time of night?"

"No wonder we haven't found any stray dragons in the past couple weeks," Sandra said. "They've all been at the same party."

In the buildings surrounding the fusion reactor containment structure temporary accommodations had been established. Dragon kings and workers slept while drones milled in the courtyards. In the gloom of night it was impossible to see all the fortifications, but by the static glow emitted through the reactor dome Doc could discern that the entire area was cordoned off by a girdle of armored vehicles like a wagon train in circle defense against a tribe of attacking Indians.

"Even the guards have guards."

"It all makes sense," said Doc. "Your ambushes were so successful that it forced their paws. They retreated to the most vulnerable part of the city while they sent out shock troops to track us down."

Rusty leaned over the parapet. "I'll bet they got onto us by tracing power consumption. They must have switch gear to detect load peaks. Even though we kept the lights off, their technicians could trace where the electricity was going. And a computer that size draws quite a few amps."

Jane still wore nothing but a G-string and the coiled rope

clipped to her waist, but she now carried her large dinohide bag by a strap over her shoulder—like a twentieth-century designer outfit. She took out a sheaf of computer printouts and Doc's carefully drawn map of the city with a detail of the power plant. She pointed to a thirty-foot-high featureless rampart. "We get in there."

Sandra scowled. "What're we gonna do, melt our way through with these." She pulled the laser pistol out of its holster and ran her finger along the notches she had carved into the handle. "I wanna get them dragons as much as you do, but this time I wanna get 'em all. No more pickin' 'em off one at a time. Right, Pop?"

"My dear, you are becoming a master strategist. I compliment you." Doc stroked his beard; another group of whiskers blackened by the laser blast broke off in his hand. "It is indeed frustrating to have such well-laid plans come apart at the seams."

"Don't break your arm patting yourself on the back."

"I take no credit for the original ideas. I merely took the observations of others and put them together into a cohesive whole."

Scott, Sam, and Death Wind joined the others in the tower. Sam said, "It's no good, Henry. They've corked all the basement corridors with blobs of plastic. You'd need a division of tank-mounted laser guns to burn through that kind of barrier. And they've probably got guards on the other side."

"Dragons move," Jane said calmly.

Everyone rushed to the balcony. Two blocks away and several stories below, milling lizards did not appear to exhibit any untoward movement.

"Finger speak say leave."

"That means our electric frying pan's in action," Scott said gleefully. "If we're going to strike, one way or another we'd better do it now."

Sandra said, "Yeah, let's act emotionally and throw 'em off balance. We'll go in with guns blazing. You know, Pop, the old mammal trick their lizard brains can't grasp."

"Odd that you should remember that so well. Jane, what is this idea of yours for gaining access?"

"I climb wall." She patted the coiled rope attached to her G-string. "I drop rope for Sam. We open door."

"Henry, it sounds simple enough to work."

Doc rubbed his beard. "Yes. It is so direct and against such odds that it is not an option I would normally consider. Therefore, we will do it. But—" He pointed an errant finger at Sandra. "No blazing guns."

Sandra crossed her heart by drawing diagonal lines between her breasts. "I promise."

Doc gazed at the lightening sky. "The sun is almost upon us. Let us make this our last day in dragon land. And let us make it the last day for dragons."

CHAPTER 24

"Excuse me, Sam, but could I, uh, talk with Jane before you go? Alone?"

Sam pinched his eyebrows, then nodded slowly. "Of course." He scuttled back into the shadows of the alley, toward the tall rampart that surrounded the fusion reactor building.

Scott fidgeted for a moment; if his G-string had had pockets, he would have shoved his hands into them. Instead, he kept his eyes plastered to the ground while he nervously untied a leather cord from the connecting thread of his brief apparel. When he brought up his hands he held a crystal that sparkled in the bright light of the setting moon. He held the jewel between his face and Jane's.

"I hung onto it when Rusty tossed it to me because I—well—because I wanted to present it to you, uh, as a token of my, uh, my feelings. For you. I couldn't find a setting for it. Besides, it's too big for a ring. But I bent this platinum wire around it and made a loop for a thong. It'll have to be a pendant. It's the best—I could do."

Jane stared at him expressionlessly.

Scott stumbled on. "Uh, you're supposed to wear it. Around your neck. It's a custom that signifies—friendship. When you look at it, you're supposed to remember the one who gave it to you." He spread the leather necklace with his fingers and worked it over her head. After it fell around her neck he spent several awkward seconds pulling her waist-length hair through the loop. The diamond lay snugly against her throat.

Jane took Scott's open palm and cupped her left breast with it. "I remember you always—here." She looked deeply into his eyes. "I love you, Scott."

"I—I love you, too, Jane." He gulped loudly. "I have—for a long time."

"Sixty million years?" she said innocently.

Scott broke into a broad grin. "At least. And I will love you forever. Now, uh, you'd better get going before the sun comes up—and something else as well." He gave her a peck on the cheek.

Jane clutched him when he pulled back and drew him close. She pressed her lips against his. Scott ran his hands down the smooth skin of her back and pulled her hips tight against his. She kissed him long and hard. "We make love later?"

Scott felt the blood rush to his face. "Yes. But we've got work to do now." He spun her around, patted her on the seat, and gave her a little shove. "Now move it," he said, smiling, with more cheer than he felt. The wrenching inside him was not all longing, for it was tempered with thoughts of what they yet had to face. "I'll be waiting."

He promptly turned and rushed back to join the others. They took up their vigil by the roadway that led to the reactor stadium's loading platform. And there they waited—and waited—and waited.

First light glimmered, casting long shadows across the courtyards. Dragon slaves stirred in preparation for dawn. The temperature skyrocketed as the sun made its debut. Neither Sam nor Jane put in an appearance.

Doc sat down next to Scott. "Are you worried about her, my boy?"

Scott jerked to attention. He had not realized he had been so deeply lost in thought. "Uh, not really. She can take care of herself. Besides, if anything went wrong I'm sure it wouldn't have gone wrong quietly."

"Quite right, my boy. Quite right." Doc leaned back against the wall. He unbuttoned his vest. "I always experience the jitters before I go into battle. I almost wish for the kind of fight that comes unexpectedly. Fear itself is short-lived, but the continued anticipation of fear can rack one's nerves. So much of my life has been subjected to the anxiety of imminent death that I sometimes take survival for granted."

Scott humphed. "You do come off pretty blasé."

"Do not interpret a calm exterior as a defiance of my own mortality. I am too well aware of such inevitability. Life is a commodity to be savored, for who knows when that vital spark shall be forever quenched. And even though I believe to a certain extent that what will be, will be, yet I strive to alter the world in which we live along precepts that I find personally acceptable. We have but one life, therefore we must life it to the fullest."

"I've certainly learned a lot about life since getting my head out of the ground," Scott said. "Although I can't say that I accept it with your equanimity. To be honest with you, Doc, I've been bored to tears the past couple months. Don't get me wrong: taking apart dragon machines and vehicles to see what makes them tick has given me a great deal of satisfaction. That's a side of me I've always had. But ever since I entered the real world, ever since I joined the war against the dragons, I've been developing a need for—excitement. For danger. I actually revel in it. And it bothers me because it's something I never felt before; or, at least, was never aware of before."

"The maturation process induces changes in the hormonal balance of the prepubescent body. Growth induces modifi—"

"No, Doc, this is more than a chemical stimulation. It's a psychological dependency: an adrenaline rush that I can't get enough of. It's become an addiction."

"Adrenaline is a chemical—"

"That is emotionally induced. Its physiological effects can't be denied, but control of its release is a matter of inner security. And I'm finding out that I don't have the security I thought I had. That's what hurts. I want to be like Death Wind: strong, austere, confident, a man of the forest. Instead, I end up acting like Sandra: wild and irrational."

"Perhaps you should concentrate instead on being more like Scott. We are all born with our own strengths and weaknesses. One should cultivate one's strengths and protect one's weaknesses. Who you are, and who you can be, is greater than your desires otherwise."

Scott tilted his head resignedly. "Sure, Doc, I understand all that. My problem is a condition of too *much* self-awareness. I *know* from within that I'm looking forward to what we're about to do. I'm enjoying the destruction of this world, and that feeling is destructive to my inner being. I should want to build up, not tear down."

"When a house falls into disrepair it is necessary to remove dilapidated walls before constructing new ones."

"There you go, talking in parables again." Scott shifted the backpack and pulled the laser pistol out of its holster. He slapped it in his palm. His hands tingled with the knowledge of the power he held. "Maybe you're right. I guess a planet can't be restructured without a little damage first. And dragon land isn't long for this world." Shaking his head, he stared at the plastic surface between his feet. "You know, I have the feeling I've done this before: cracking their eggs while we sneak in the back way. We did that a few months ago along our time stream, but sixty million years in the geological future. It's so confusing—like a case of pre-déjà vu. Let's call it préjà vu. And they still don't know what's coming. It almost seems unfair to play the same trick twice. It's so unoriginal, even though in universal time sequence it's never been done before."

"Semantics aside, would you rather give them a warning?"

"Doc, I'm not that confused. Besides, we've come such a long way to get where we are. Every time Sam and I sabotaged one of their fission reactors, I knew it was leading up to this moment."

"You did an excellent job of concealment, I might add. It was a master stroke disassembling the control panels and performing electronic lobotomies where the dragons could never see them, then putting the external circuitry back together so it appeared that the reactors were simply shut down, and not permanently impaired."

Scott shrugged. "They can be repaired, but it'd take years and a whole lot more personnel than they have available to do the job. I didn't want them to have alternate resources in case this job doesn't go as smoothly as planned. Once they're out of power, their civilization comes to an end. And the sooner we can get on with our own lives."

"What does that mean for you—now?"

Scott thought for a moment. "I know I could never go back to my old lifestyle. I love the outdoors, and the freedom of movement. Maccam City doesn't seem real anymore. It's a dream I just woke up from." He looked into Doc's eyes. "I want a world of my own choosing. I guess—I guess I want Jane to share it with. There's probably a lot more I want. I just haven't had time to think of it yet."

Doc raised bushy white eyebrows. "It is want that provides motivation in life. It is that quantity that keeps us moving forward, that prevents stagnation. Of course, we do not always get what we want. We sometimes have to roll with the punches."

Scott made a fist. "I'm going to throw a few punches first. Then I'll—"

Sam and Jane ran briskly into the alley. Death Wind maintained his vigil at the terminus as the duo stopped to catch their wind. Scott jumped up, leaving Doc to climb slowly up his cane.

"It's all set," Sam gasped. "The door's open." He took a few more deep breaths before going on. "We got up the wall with no problem, but we had to stay out of sight till the techs abandoned their stations. Once the eggbeater started going full speed they left like rats deserting a sinking ship."

Jane pouted and hugged her gadget bag closer to her chest. She pulled out her pudgy rodent pet and stroked its sleek fur.

"Sorry. No aspersions intended against present company. Anyway, they left a few guards behind, but we can take care of them, no problem."

Scott threw his arms around Jane's slender shoulders and kissed her on the forehead. "That's my girl."

Jane fingered the diamond brooch. "I not forget you."

Laughing, Scott said, "I should hope not. It's only been an hour."

"Hey, if you two can stop smooching, we've got a job to do." Sandra drew her gun and stroked the barrel with the same tender motions that Jane had used on her protomammal. "Let's get in there and pull the plug on them lizards. I got a date for tomorrow I don't want to be late for."

Rusty said, "Your date's not for sixty million years. But if we hurry we can make it before we die of old age."

"Lead on, wise man."

The guerrilla squad double-timed into the outer compound. After months of roaming deserted streets, the lack of dragon personnel did not seem out of the norm. None of the inner doors possessed locks. In a trice they found themselves skulking along silent corridors.

"There's likely to be a couple of meter readers on watch," Scott cautioned. "Be careful not to zap any gauges or electrical cabinets."

"You afraid of damaging what you're going to put out of commission?" Sandra said haughtily.

"I want to shut this reactor down right. Jane, do you have the computer printouts?"

Jane pulled a sheaf of fanfold out of her handbag.

"Good." To Sandra, he explained, "Remember that I've never worked on a fusion reactor before, so I'm a little out of my depth. From what I can make out of that dragon scratch, the control circuits are pretty much the same at the monitoring end. The main difference is what effects they cause. I'll follow the same procedures I would follow for a fission reactor shut-down—except that we'll use Rusty's delayed action device to give us getaway time. Once I've got—"

Death Wind held his hand up high, signaling for silence. Everyone froze. The Nomad crouched and advanced cautiously on the balls of his feet. He was a mountain lion stalking its prey. He bent back his wrist and grasped the spear halfway along its length. He hefted it once or twice for balance. Very slowly, he bent until his knees touched the floor. He laid down the spear.

He peered around a door jamb. When he stepped back it was to notch his bow. Quickly he stepped into the rectangle of light. His shadow spread behind him like a huge black giant. Three arrows thwacked into the room, a low murmur of a hiss escaped. When he bent to retrieve his spear, he nodded once.

The three dragon technicians lay sprawled on the floor, each with its throat transfixed by one of Death Wind's plastic-tipped arrows. The Nomad quietly went about recovering his ammunition.

Scott slapped the Nomad on the back. "Death Wind, you make it all seem so easy."

"Death is always easy."

"Yes. I guess it is. The shame is that it's necessary. Oh, well." Scott unlimbered his tools while Jane spread the blueprints across the desk. "Rusty, have you got that timer programmed."

"For about an epoch and a half."

"The Mesozoic doesn't have epochs, only periods."

"Lucky Mesozoic," Sandra chafed. "Scott, can you get on with it? I'd like to leave the Cretaceous before I become a grandmother."

"I didn't know you were trying."

"Shut up, you."

Scott held up his hands in defense. "Sorry. Just remember that you can't hurt me until I make these connections. Sam, take down that panel with the flow gauges. Death Wind, you make the solder connections. Rusty, get into the CPU and follow what I'm doing on the simulator."

Jane took the soldering iron out of her gadget bag and gave it to the Nomad.

"Is there anything I can do?" Doc asked

"Help Sandra watch for dragons. This is going to take some time."

Sandra marched out of the control room with her gun drawn. "The Cenozoic's right around the corner."

Three hours later, except for the dead technicians, no one would have known that the reactor station had been compromised. The timing device was concealed behind a panel, the reactor was generating its full load of electricity, and none of the gauges indicated pending trouble. Sam and Death Wind dragged out the bodies and hid them in a pump room.

"Just like clockwork, Doc. I feel like an old hand at this."

"The booby trap is set?"

"Yes. If some smart cookie does figure out what's wrong, it'll blow as soon as he tries to disconnect the timer. Otherwise, we've got twenty-four hours to reach the transporter before the bomb goes off and demolishes the main control circuits. Then the reactor quietly shuts itself down and the power begins to fade. Even if the focusing nodes are discharged when we get to the TTS, as long as the transmission lines are intact the reactor will recharge the capacitors to full power in a couple hours."

"And they can't restart the fusion reaction?"

Scott shook his head. "It takes an immense external power source to supply heat and compression. Once fusion is started the reactor is self-generating, but with all the fission reactors down they won't be able to initiate the system. Batteries just can't generate the amps."

Rusty said, "I'd still feel better if we could have cracked the plasma containment hull, or fractured the magnetic generator housing."

"Both made out of pure iridium, one of the heaviest metals in nature. We'd need explosives a lot stronger than a shorted battery pack to split foot-thick walls."

"Then the countdown has begun and there is no turning back." Doc nodded slowly as he rubbed his beard. "So this is the way the world ends; not with a bang, but a whimper."

CHAPTER 25

"Doc! Doc! We got dragons breathing fire down our necks!" Sandra skidded into the control room with her laser gun drawn. "It's a whole horde of techs and a coupla battalions of soldiers. They're onto our ruse. The jig is up."

Scott hastily threw the battery pack over his shoulders. "Come on, Doc. It's propitious retreat time."

Jane grabbed her handbag and took out the single-shot stun gun. "This time I fight."

Scott spun her around and shoved her out the door. "Let's hope we don't get that close to them. Rusty, get the lead out."

They raced along the corridor and into the reactor room. Sam and Death Wind met them with weapons in hand.

"There's a squad of soldiers coming in the back way," Sam shouted. "But they didn't see us."

"They will now." Sandra jerked a thumb over her shoulder. "There's half an army right behind us, and they ain't just whistling Dixie."

Doc pointed his cane in the direction from which Sam and Death Wind had just come. "I believe the path of least resistance is that way."

The words were barely out of his mouth when the vanguard emerged from the control room corridor. The wall of lizard flesh waddled into the open. The lead soldier hissed loudly as Death Wind's arrow buried itself into the flesh above its forelimb. It dropped its gun, but kept coming. There were two more behind it, ready to fire.

"I believe you," shouted Sam as he turned to run.

It was strangely quiet in the reactor room despite the sudden call to arms. The only sound dragons were capable of making was a sibilant hiss. The roar of atomic fusion was damped by the thick iridium walls of the plasma bottle. The clacking noise of auxiliary motors and pumps was absorbed by the acoustic properties of the plastic structure. The action progressed like a reel from a silent movie.

As the rebel squad approached the emergency exit, the rear guard shuffled into view. Scott saw the trained gun nozzle. He stopped so fast that his moccasins slipped out from under him. In an uncontrolled skid he crashed into a dynamo casing. The ring of fire from the upheld weapon burst into the air like a great green amorphous bubble. The coruscation dissipated harmlessly over Scott's head.

"Hey, they're using pain guns instead of lasers," Sandra shouted. She crouched by Scott and sighted along the barrel. "That means we can outrange 'em."

"They don't want to damage the equipment," Scott observed. "And neither do we."

The others took up defensive postures in the cluster of machinery adjacent to the plasma containment lozenge.

"It doesn't make any difference at this point. They know we're here."

Doc spoke with a deep, calm timbre, "We would like to keep the electricity flowing until we effect our passage through time. Unless you would like to become a permanent teratology major."

Sandra pulled back her wrist and aimed the nozzle at the faraway ceiling. "Oh, yeah."

Death Wind let loose another arrow that caught the dragon blocking their path of retreat squarely in the breastplate. The long tongue shot out its mouth, but no hiss emerged. It kept walking forward even as blood spurted between jagged teeth and curled lips. It finally fell forward like a wooden cigar store mannequin.

As dragons converged from both sides, Sam peeped over a cooling coil. "We've got to shoot our way out, Henry. There's no other choice."

Another arrow twanged through the air.

"I must concede to logic," Doc said. "Here, let me hold that spear for you, Death Wind." Doc glanced quickly at the attacking minions. "Commence firing at will."

"But be careful!" Scott called out. He took careful aim and drilled a back door dragon in the gut. It clutched at the hole in its abdomen as it reeled to the side like a drunken sailor.

Sandra blasted one in the face as it emerged from the control room corridor; its head exploded as the laser beam tore out the back of its skull. Sam caught another at the base of the sinusoidal neck. Because of the distance between gun and target, the energy field was spread out at the point of contact: it gouged out a large gaping wound rather than burning a needlelike hole. The end result was the same either way: death by invasive maneuver.

"Hey, there're techs slipping along the walls!"

Scott looked where Rusty was pointing his stun gun. "If they're trying to outflank us, why aren't they doing it with armed soldiers?"

"Beats the pants off me," said Sandra. She zapped one before it waddled out of sight behind a computer console. "But as long as they're afraid to shoot back with real beams, I love it."

Rusty shook his head. "They've got to have something up their sleeves: gas bombs, or knock-out beams, or something."

"You must be right, my boy," said Doc. "They can't take a chance on wrecking their only source of electricity. If I were—"

"Up!" shouted Jane. "Up!"

All heads turned toward the catwalk overlooking the plasma injector at the far end of the fusion reactor. A lone dragon stood on an observation sponson; a long, golden cape flowed around taloned hoofs. Half-lidded eyes watched the fight stories below, while claws plucked at the strings of a harp.

"That's the one! That's the bastard that got me." Sandra drew a bead on the bulbous body. "Buddy, you just crossed your last time zone."

"Don't!" shouted Scott.

Sandra checked her fire, frowning. "What's wrong?"

"It's standing in front of essential control circuits. If you miss, you may fry the output electrodes."

"Damn." Sandra pounded her knee with her fist. She glared at the caped dragon with staunch resolution. "Oh, well, it's so far away, I probably can't do anything more than give it a good hotfoot. All right, I say it's time to bust out of here."

"A sensible suggestion, my dear." Doc stood up, held the spear in front of him like a lance, and hobbled toward the soldiers blocking the emergency exit. "Char-rr-rr-rge!"

Caught unawares, the rest of the team were still clambering to their feet as the white bearded scout halved the distance to the back way. Sam and Scott spread out behind him and fired crossing beams past his head. Two dragons fell smoking. Sandra stabbed out with her laser over Doc's snowy mane and grazed another soldier in the chin. A red tongue darted out with a hiss as the beast veered into a wall.

Another soldier lurched into its place. Doc buried the tip of the spear—the tyrannosaur tooth—into the creature's heart. The jaw dropped and the dark eyes widened in pain. Still, the sagging soldier brought its gun to bear on its attacker. Doc grabbed the scaled forelimb and shoved it aside just as the soldier squeezed the trigger of the stun gun. The blob of light that burst from the nozzle narrowly missed the old man. Coruscations of energy wrapped around a capacitor bank that protruded out of the floor. Sparks flew into the air. A miniature lightning storm raged over the device, crackling explosively and erupting blobs of molten plastic like a toy volcano.

"Uh-oh."

Scott, Sam, and Sandra poured a deadly volley of laser beams into the escape corridor. Soldiers armed only with stun guns were unable to retaliate effectively. So many energy fields were discharged in such a short amount of time that the air simmered; the static charge built up enough to make Scott's hair stand on end.

Death Wind leaped past Doc and buried his knife into the throat of the soldier Sandra had wounded. It died squirming. He then braced his foot against the other beast's breast and yanked out his spear.

"What have I done?" Doc shuffled backward across the floor away from the pyrotechnics. The floor bulged in front of him, accompanied by a deep-throated whump. "What's happening?"

Scott grabbed Doc by the armpits and pulled him to his feet. "I think the capacitors overloaded and burned out the magnetic flux accelerator coils."

"Nice going, Pop."

"I do not feel the need to apologize for my audacity, although the result was unanticipated. The final action was strictly in self-defense."

"It's too late to worry about it now, Doc." Scott fired into the distant mass of reptilian flesh. The distance was too great to kill, but the beam of energy checked the speed of the advancing soldiers. "It just shortened our getaway time a bit. There's still enough reserve power to last for days."

"Then I may as well cook my goose." Sandra took careful aim and fired a bolt of electricity at the gold-caped dragon some five hundred feet away. The energy field reached it in such a weakened condition that it merely singed its scales, but the harp strings melted in its paws. Having talked its last tone, it turned and ducked into a control cubicle. The blackened cape fell away in ashes; its back smoldered like a dying ember. "Bastard."

"Scott! Take at look at this." Rusty stood in front of a panel of gauges, the labels of which Jane hastily translated. "We're in trouble."

Scott recognized most of the symbols from his study periods with Jane, when he was learning how to sabotage the reactor control boards. "Uh-oh."

"I believe I already said that," Doc said. "How serious is it?"

Internal detonations continued to emit bass sounds dampened by the plastic flooring. Needle gauges and numerical readouts were on the rise, although the fusion reactor demonstrated no distress.

Sam fired his laser gun down the escape passage, keeping the way clear. "Come on. Let's get going before they send reinforcements."

Sandra kept the advancing hordes at bay. "I could use a little help. This ain't supposed to be a one-woman stand."

"Real serious." Scott ignored the importunities. "The power surge shorted the high voltage transformer coils and fused the flux reinforcing bus bars."

"I fail to comprehend the significance of that." Doc rubbed his beard more quickly than usual. "Does that mean the loss of electrical power sooner than expected?"

"Worse than that. It means we can't shut down the reactor at all. The feeding circuits have been isolated into a self-generating loop. Without a load it'll pour all that power back into the magnetic deflectors buried in the floor."

Sandra joined the caucus. "Ain't there some kind of interruptor circuit? We can always blast our way back into the control room—or come back another day."

"No good, Sandra." Scott's spine crept with chills as he

watched the mounting figures on the dials. "Our bobby trap is irrevocable."

"What about triple redundancy—"

"I wrecked all the backups. And there isn't going to be another day." Scott did a quick mental calculation. "Doc, you'd better start whimpering, because this thing's going off with a bang. In about ten hours this city will be a hole the size of the Mediterranean Sea."

CHAPTER 26

Not only was their escape vehicle in ruins, but the cleverly disguised ambush nearly caught them unawares. Only Jane's timely warning kept the fleeing squad from the clutches of dragons.

"Danger! Do not touch!"

Sandra jerked her hand back from the trip wire across the open seal. "Now what? Ain't it bad enough they smashed in the windows—"

Jane pulled Sandra a safe distance from the nondescript black box. She indicated the squiggles on the plastic sidewall. "It say danger."

Sam placed his hands on his daughter's shoulders. "It's a good thing Jane can read that dragon scratch. They've got the whole coach rigged with explosives. One touch—"

Death Wind loosed an arrow that caught a skulking technician in the midriff. The tip penetrated the hide at an angle and lodged against the hip joint. The dragon hissed as it limped behind a road barrier. The Nomad stared up at the tall buildings surrounding the parking lot. "More with no guns."

"Get away! Quick!" Doc dashed for the protection of a sidewalk partition. "It's a command detonator."

The others followed his example without further explanation. No sooner had they leaped for cover than the coach blew up with a deafening roar and a tremendous sheet of flame. Burning debris and molten plastic rained down for nearly half a minute. Scott was caught in the open and slammed into a storefront by expanding gases. His face was numb from the blast. When he convinced his battered muscles to move, he found that his body was relatively unscathed; but his vision was blurry. Something hung down over his left eye. When he brushed away the obstruction, he saw clearly for only a moment before a shadow again fell across his eye.

"Hold still, my boy." Doc knelt by Scott's side and cradled the blond head in his calloused hands. Sandra screamed, and

Jane thrust her fist into her mouth. "I'll have this fixed up in a jiffy."

"What is it, Doc? What's wrong?"

"Jane, give me some of that vellum, please."

Jane fumbled with her handbag and handed Doc a sheaf of computer printout. She stifled back a tear.

"Doc, what happened? What's wrong with my eye? It's blurry."

Doc quickly but professionally wound the continuous roll around the top of Scott's head, across the side of his face, and under his chin. After several wraps he tucked the loose end under the bottom fold. "There. That ought to hold." He peered into Scott's eyes one at a time. "Your eye appears to be all right. But a flap of skin was burned off your scalp and fell across your brow. It may sting some when the shock wears off."

"It stings already." Scott fingered the makeshift bandage. "I think it's bound too tight."

"No, that's the epidermis drying and stiffening. You'll have to suffer with it, my boy."

Scott felt a laser blast near his head and heard Sam's capacitor recycling. With his good eye he saw soldiers emerging from an alley. Sandra fired with telling effect.

Scott stumbled to his feet. "Why do I feel like a planarian?" He staggered a few steps in the direction away from that of the oncoming soldiers, until Rusty wrapped his lanky arms around him and yanked him to a halt.

"That's it. That's exactly what they want us to do. React in a prescribed manner to a specified stimulus."

Scott's jaw did not move well because of the shriveled skin and the paper wrappings. It was an effort to talk. "Let's go, Rusty! This isn't the time for philosophical dissertations."

Rusty gripped Scott with uncommon strength belied by the emaciated look of his arms. "That's exactly what they want us to do: move away, and probably into another ambush. What we should do is the exact opposite."

"Sounds like a good emotional response to me," Sandra said. "Let's rush 'em."

Doc raised bushy eyebrows. "I do not think it is truly emotional once one takes the time to reason it out. But the effect should be the same."

The rebel squad launched a frontal attack against the

remaining soldiers in the alley. Scott lumbered along uselessly, his gun undrawn. He was barely conscious enough to observe the proceedings. The next thing he knew Jane was dragging him past dragon bodies and into a waiting troop transport.

"Rusty, you're all right in my book," Sandra shouted with glee. "Daddy, can you run this thing?"

"Can a pterodactyl fly?" Sam switched on the power train and engaged the drive controls. The annunciator lights flashed on silently. "All systems are go." When he advanced the throttle the motor hummed softly and the vehicle moved forward with a barely perceptible lurch. "Hang on, people. We're homeward bound."

Scott fell into a seat like a lump. The side of his face felt as if it were pressed against a hot iron; his left eye was full of gravel. Jane sat next to him and cradled his head against her breast. Her nipples were erect and hard against his cheek, but he was in too much pain to take pleasure in the fact. She worked her fingers around his temples in a circular motion. The warmth and the love of her touch was a greater comfort than Scott had imagined possible.

"I don't want to beat a dead dinosaur, but are you sure there's no way we can stop the fusion process." Sandra climbed into the forward turret and fondled the laser gatling gun lovingly. "Can't we blow something up that'll do the trick?"

"Not unless you've got an atomic bomb in your back pocket," Rusty replied.

"Wouldn't that set it off?" Sam asked.

Rusty shook his head vigorously. "No. There is no 'setting off' a fusion reactor. But a big enough bomb would crack the casing. The magnetic field would instantly collapse, and the plasma would leak out. You'd still get a hell of a blast, but that would mostly be from the nuclear explosion. With the reactor isolated from the control circuits, there's no other way."

"Meaning, of course, that the dragons are as powerless as we are." Doc rolled his baby blue eyes. "Once they figure that out . . ."

"Yeah, well, it looks like they already have." Sandra rotated the turret as the truck sped through an intersection. Cutting in from the right was a two-dragon convertible. Long lizard necks peered through the tall windshield while blue capes were buffeted in the slipstream. "Hey, Pop, can I send these guys to their maker?"

"Please do."

With a rapid-fire staccato Sandra riddled the smaller vehicle with laser beams. Holes appeared in the bonnet and fenders. Sandra found the range on the occupants as the car veered off. She injected the bulbous bodies with bolts of energy until the vehicle went out of control and crashed into a building. The car scraped acrylic across plastic until the front wheel carriage hit an entrance ramp; then it careened on its side and skidded into a projecting rampart.

"Damn. I missed the batteries, and it didn't even burn."

"Good shooting, my dear, especially considering a five-foot-two tyke is firing a gun designed for a seven-foot-eight lizard."

"I'm still frustrated. I want to blow something up, and while I'm picking off dragons with a pea shooter, you set the whole damn world on fire."

"An honor of which I am not particularly proud, although in retrospect I can see now that it was inevitable. It is curious how we are bound by the dictates of the past, as if we were predestined to be here at this time in order to perform the changes necessary to ensure our own future. The mind boggles."

"Yeah, well, while you're boggling, how about consulting your crystal ball and tell me what it says about us getting the hell out of here before dragon land becomes an inland sea."

"I would not care to speculate, my dear. No course of action is a surety. I suppose the future holds secrets aplenty to keep us guessing for a long time—perhaps forever, if we can imagine such an infinite quantity. The past holds the key to the future only in a statistical sense which we as minor inhabitants of the microcosm—"

"Sam, do you know where you're going?" Rusty said.

"To Hell in a hand basket. Of course I know where I'm going. While you had your head buried in a computer console, Scott and I were taking a grand tour of the city. Maybe I don't know every corner and back alley in the red-light district, but the streets move in a pattern of right angles that're pretty easy to follow even without a road map."

Sam did not spare the amps. The army truck rolled through the deserted city like a sports car on a freeway, dodging vehicles parked in random fashion where they happened to be when the death bomb struck. Many still held the remains of drivers, their bodies dessicated after many months of microbial action.

It seemed to Scott like quite a while before he recognized the approaches to the tunnel complex that led down the escarpment to the plains below. This time no blockade awaited their passage. The sun was suddenly blotted out as the troop carrier entered the underground tube.

Doc hopped to the back of the truck and dabbed at a trickle of blood seeping through the vellum on Scott's face. "My boy, how certain are you about that time limit?"

Scott snorted. "It could be plus or minus fifty percent. I just made an assessment on the short-term accretion ratio and measured it against the danger markings on the dials. But if the rate of increase is exponential—"

"Hmmn. This is not as bad as it looks, although I daresay you will have a bit of a scar once it heals. There's some inflammation in the eye, but it is more like a flash burn than an injury. Assuming we survive the next ten hours you should return to good health in a few weeks."

"That's a pretty big 'if'."

"A positive outlook is the key to success in any campaign. Will can win where might may fall. One cannot achieve greatness without striving to be great. Triumph comes to he who tries. Good fortune smiles—"

"Doc!" Rusty screamed. "Can we skip a couple chapters?"

Lines creased Doc's forehead. He cleared his throat. "Forgive me, lad. I disguise my fear with rhetoric."

Jane continued to rub Scott's temples. "What will be, will be."

"That is a truism." Doc resumed his seat, then turned and raised his eyebrows at the girl. "My dear, I do not remember you being present at the conversation where that utterance was extemporized. Unless you were around the corner the whole—"

The troop carrier burst into the sunlight at the end of the tunnel at the same time that a tremendous explosion ripped through the aft end of the vehicle. One third of the gear train was gone, along with a significant portion of the passenger compartment and the rear turret.

"We've hit a land mine," Sam shouted.

Wind whipped into the open rear. Sandra dropped out of the

turret and hit the deck between the seats. "DW, are you okay?"

The Nomad stood up plucking shards of plastic from his back and sides. The seat fell away from under him, crashed onto the orangetop, and bounced end over end until friction brought it to a halt. Sandra dabbed at Death Wind's blood-smeared body with a cloth she pulled from one of the vest's many pockets.

Rusty shouted above the roar of air, "That means they were waiting for us. Watch out for—"

Two laser blasts from the main gun emplacements tore up the road in front of the vehicle. "Evasive action." Sam jockeyed the throttle to and fro and from left to right. "Sandy, keep 'em busy while we run the gauntlet."

Sandra careened back and forth as she dashed up the aisle to the turret trap. The troop carrier gyrated in a random escape pattern. Scott did not have the energy to man the gun in the middle turret; he gripped Jane to keep from being hurled out of his seat.

"I can't keep up the speed with two of our axles missing," Sam complained. "Good thing each wheel runs on independent motors."

A gigantic bolt of energy from one of the enemy laser cannons chewed up a chunk of road surface next to the truck, spattering the side wall with blobs of molten plastic. The arcylic windows melted in splotches. The wind whistled in chorus through holes of various sizes.

Sandra's shots ran wild. "Daddy, I can't hit a thing jolting around like this."

Sam maneuvered recklessly. "I ain't gonna stop just so you can get your jollies. They'll get our range."

Because of their size the laser cannons recharged slowly. A beam from the right hit aft of the racing vehicle and danger-ously close; another from the left creased the roof with its heat, causing the supports to sag and the center to belly inward.

"That was a close one." The carrier swerved crazily as Sam rotated the throttle in a way it was never intended to go. The undercarriage was a bed of indecision as the wheels swiveled in a circular motion that stressed the chassis in all its dimen-sions. Sam sang out, "Catch me if you can."

Jane dragged Scott off the seat and onto the floor next to Doc and Rusty. She clasped Scott to her breast like a mother would cuddle her child, rocking gently. With one eye closed Scott peered out the window. Death Wind crouched in the aisle on one knee, holding onto the seats for stability. Then they were past the center line between the two embattlements.

"Not as easy getting out as it was getting in."

Sam swung the control lever sharply in order to avoid a blast hole in front of the truck. The left wheels trundled over plastic moguls and caught the liquified edges of the furrow. The vehicle launched itself into the air, throwing the occupants against the inner wall. It banged down hard and continued on its way with solidified masses of synthetic plastic bonded to the wheel treads. The multiple motors hummed along to the tune of the bumps hitting the orangetop with jackhammer regularity.

"Hit something, Toad. Will you?"

"I'm trying." Sandra's body was stretched out between pedals and gunsight. She could aim only by eyeing the bottom of the barrel with her target while rotating the turret in the approximate direction. "I'm just not built for this."

Sam thrust the joystick all the way forward for maximum speed, while alternating its sideway motion haphazardly. The truck yawed with sickening caprice. Another laser blast gouged a huge crater right in its path. The wheels left the ground as the truck soared across the open space where the road used to be. The front axle hit the opposite side of the trough with such a bang that the whole vehicle shuddered with the shock. It squished through the plastic lava without slowing down. The front axle was smashed out of alignment, adding further torment to the truck's aberrant course. The wheels were recapped with a new coating of plastic.

Gradually they outdistanced the effectiveness and accurate range of the laser cannons. A few parting shots seared the road surface in their vicinity, but the energy field was so diffuse as to cause little damage.

Sandra dropped down into the cab. She pulled Death Wind's face against her side and kissed the mop of long hair that was blown in wild disarray. "Scott, are you okay?"

"No, but I'll live."

"Hey, I never thought I'd say this, but during the fight I missed your repertoire of wisecracks."

"I'll mention that the next time you disparage my drollery."

"Hey!" Sam called out. "We're not out of the woods yet. There's a roadblock up ahead."

Sandra leaped to her gun station. "Clear for action. I wanna blow the gizzards outa them lizards."

The two tanks parked broadside across the highway were not big enough to prevent passage of what was left of the troop carrier. But the guns they mounted were portable models of the stationary laser cannon.

Sam tacked furiously from side to side in order to forestall attack. "Sandy, I'm gonna keep dodging until they both fire. Then, while they're recycling, I'll straighten out to give you a chance to aim. But be quick about it."

"Gotcha."

Watching through the windshield, Scott saw the burst of light from the mouth of one of the laser cannons. The beam of energy seemed to be coming straight at him. The laser cut through a corner of the glass and went right out the open back of the truck. The air inside rippled with intense heat. Scott broke out into a sweat that was not all temperature dependent. The second beam contacted a guardrail to the left of the truck; shrapnel soared into the sky, but fell harmlessly behind.

"Now!" Sam steadied the vehicle on a diagonal track.

Sandra pulled the trigger and kept it depressed. Her gun was not as powerful as the laser cannons, but it recycled faster. She got off three shots before the enemy returned fire. Neither damaged the other.

"All right, I've got their charging time figured." Sam threw the truck into a long curve that evaded the follow-up shot from the other cannon. "Eight seconds, Toad."

As the truck straightened out, Sandra picked her target and opened fire. Her first shot clipped an armored fender, the second slammed into the main body, the third missed high, and the fourth grazed the base of the turret. Sam swung the truck just as the other tank let loose its bolt. A dazzling beam of amplified light dug a long trough in the highway shoulder and splattered hot plastic along the truck's left side.

"The turret's jammed on the one," Sam yelled. "I'm gonna head straight for the other."

Sandra locked the turret in the zero position and concentrated on the elevation. The first shot was short, but three in a row pronounced devastating damage on the hull. Sandra kept shooting. Beam after beam arced into the tank. No fire was returned.

Sam did not veer off course until the last moment. He narrowly avoided a collision. Both tanks were silent. "All in a day's work."

"Damn." Sandra shook her fist as the tanks were left behind. "Neither one of them exploded."

CHAPTER 27

"Daddy, can we make a pit stop."

Sam jerked his head around so fast his neck cracked. "What're you, crazy? The continent's on the verge of being blasted off the face of the earth, and you wanna take a break? Go off the back of the bus like everyone else."

Sandra's face was pale. She clutched her stomach tightly as she made her way to where the truck terminated in jagged pieces. She knelt on the floor, gripped the last seat for support, and vomited into the void.

"Motion sickness," Doc said, low enough so she would not hear. The troop carrier skewered along the road on a wobbly front axle and plastic-blobbed wheels. "How is your injury, my boy?"

"It hurts, but it's not too bad." Scott snugged the vellum against his nose. "My eye's still blurry. I can see better with the good eye when the bad one's covered."

Death Wind pulled up a floor panel and handed it to Rusty. "Smoke comes from battery. I can disconnect."

"That means we lose more power," Rusty said.

With four wheels blown off the rear, and the resistance from the drag on the front axle slowing them down, half the drive train was already out of action. The six working wheels were soon overloaded.

The Nomad severed the cables one at a time and covered the exposed wires with slashed seat-covering material. "Cannot help. This will catch fire soon." Slowly the flow through ventilation cleared the smoke out of the cabin.

"They sure don't build 'em like they used to." Sandra reclaimed her seat at the base of the forward turret. "Whatta we got—half speed?"

"Less," said Sam. The grinding axle parts screeched through the dashboard. "We gotta ditch this thing at the first pony express stop. It's got more rattles than a hill full of snakes."

The truck thumped and wheezed along the highway. They were out of the city environs and passing through lush swamp forest that buzzed with insectivorous life, most of which found its way into the troop compartment through the massive hull breaches. The sun was high, the heat and humidity unbearable. The force of time passed poignantly.

"Oh, no. What the hell is that?" Sam pulled back on the joystick and let the vehicle coast. "Looks like we got a brontosaurus sleeping on the road."

Doc crouched next to the driver's seat. "The brontosaurs lived during the Jurassic and have been long extinct. This is more likely a smaller descendant, the titanosaurus. It looks full grown. Dinosaurs must have a phenomenal growth rate in order to reach maturity in such a short—"

"Henry, we don't have all day to listen to your scientific speculations. And I don't care what you call it. It's got the road blocked. We're all likely to be extinct if we don't get around it."

The truck screeched as Sam pulled back the throttle and threw the strained motors into reverse. The titanosaur's body lay stretched out from shoulder to shoulder, while the thick neck and tail draped across the culverts. As soon as the forward motion stopped, he punched the door release. Nothing happened.

"The hydraulic system must be out." Sam climbed out of his seat and kicked the door until it sprang open enough to squeeze through. The rest followed him out.

Scott felt more energetic than he had in hours. "What a mountain of flesh." The body was so thick that he could not see over it.

Sandra placed her ear next to the abdomen. "I can hear all kinds of gurgling inside. The damn thing is taking a nap."

"I think not," Doc commented dryly. "I am not surprised that in a creature of this size organic processes continue after death. After all, twitching nerves cause muscle movement in animals long dead. A body of such mammoth proportions must die in stages."

Sandra stepped back shaking her head. "I don't get it. Why did the dinosaur cross the road?"

Scott groaned, but felt more like his old self. "Since this is the Cretaceous, that must be the oldest joke in the world."

"A joke on us if we don't get around—"

"Here!" Death Wind pointed his spear toward the grass divider between the road surface and the tree line. A man-sized monster lay on the ground, with smoke pouring out of a gaping hole in its chest. "Laser did that."

"So our dragon counterparts have been here recently," Doc mused. "Judging by that wickedly enlarged hind claw, I'd say we're looking at a deinonychus: a vicious carnosaur that—"

"Look! Over there. Tracks." Rusty indicated an area where two parallel paths flattened the grass. "If they went around, so can we. Let's go!" He dragged Doc by the arm. They all piled into the truck.

Sam jumped into the driver's seat and flicked the controls. "I don't know if this baby can hold together off road." He backed up until he reached the spot where the dragon vehicle had left the orangetop. "But it doesn't seem as if we have much of a choice."

"Notice the bloody longitudinal gashes on the titanosaur's throat. It is astounding that a six-foot-tall predator can dispatch a brute weighing tens of tons. Of course, it was common for a pack of hyenas to bring down wildebeest in the African savannah—"

"Doc!" Rusty placed his hands on Doc's cheeks and turned the older man's head toward him. "Cut it *out*. We've only got a couple hours—"

"Hang on back there." Sam yanked the throttle to the side and eased it forward. The split differentials spun in their joints, turning the wheels to the left while applying power. The troop carrier veered off the prepared surface and down the sloping embankment on a steep angle. The front wheels groaned as they impacted with the mushy grassland. "That wasn't so bad."

He throttled down as the truck bounced across the uneven ground. Clods of dirt spun out of the drive wheels like an arched rooster tail. The truck skidded and swayed as the tread dug up the grassy covering and churned the damp earth underneath into a muddy mess. He stayed in the grooves made by the earlier passage. As the path curved back toward the road he gunned the motors to full power. The truck ran up the slope on an angle, sideslipping as the gritty shoulder offered little traction. The wheels spun futilely, without the torque necessary to mount the final hump. Instead, wheels spinning madly and motors whining, the truck moved horizontally just below the crest of the shoulder.

"We ain't gonna make it."

Scott gripped his seat and willed the truck upward. His stomach muscles tightened. He let out a gasp when he felt the truck slip back. "Come on, baby. Come on. You can do it."

Smoke poured out of the armatures. The pungent odor was distinctive to Scott; he was used to working with motors and burnt-out windings. The treads issued a musty stink from the pulverized plastic. Still describing a diagonal heading, the weary and battered truck seemed about to rattle apart when the left wheel trains caught a slick of extruded plastic that bestowed solid traction.

The truck scratched upward, pounced over the shoulder and onto the orangetop facing sideways. Sam pulled back the joystick as the truck raced across the road and nearly went off the other side. The tortured wheels spun backward and brought the truck to a halt just before it careened down the opposite embankment. Scott felt like a billiard ball caroming off case-hardened cushions. Sam pulled the lever to the side, rotated the vehicle like a top, then thrust the lever all the way forward as soon as the broken bow was aligned with the lane marker.

Sam wiped sweat off his brow. "Whew."

"Way to go, Daddy."

"Expert handling, Sam." Doc breathed a sigh of relief.

"Anyone got any water?" Rusty said. "I could use a drink."

"We have no supplies, and I do not think we have time to stop by a convenient puddle. Other obstacles may await us."

"Hey, who are those guys up ahead?" Sandra's hand quaked as she pointed to a bunch of stick figures standing in the road.

"I don't know, but they're coming this way," Sam said.

Scott at first thought it was a human road crew, until one turned aside and he saw the long tail stretched out behind it. "They look like that carnosaur back there in the grass, except these are alive."

"Deinonychus," Doc pronounced slowly.

"You didn't say they traveled in herds," Sandra fairly screamed.

"The fossil record is devoid of behavioral characteristics. Bones tell us about an individual, not—"

"Forget it, Doc," Rusty said. "Sam, don't pick up any hitchhikers."

"We're going full speed, and if they don't get out of the way they'll be wearing plastic."

The carnosaurs stood upright on hind legs, balanced by whiplike tails. Clawed fingers graced humanlike hands held at half mast. Their heads were shaped like fat beaks. Fernlike ruffage covered their bodies in the way feathers covered birds. They were two-hundred-pound packages of meanness looking for a scrap.

Sam steered the truck for the middle of the flock. Tails rose and heads lowered as the carnosaurs went into a running mode, seemingly undaunted by the approaching vehicle. As the distance closed, the beasts split to the side—except for one deinonychus that leaped straight at the windshield with both hind feet stretched forward like an osprey clutching for fish in the water. It hit the clear acrylic talons first. The windshield splintered as the clawed feet came through, narrowly missing Sam's head. The edge of the roof caught the beast at the base of the short throat. The plastic snapped off in chunks, but retained enough structural integrity to fling the brazen carnosaur in front of the charging vehicle. The truck vaulted over the squirming body and hit the road with a crash.

"I guess that'll show 'em."

If the carnosaurs had the faculty of cerebration, they expressed other ideas. With catlike agility they reversed their direction of flight and fairly flew after the onrushing truck. They had no trouble keeping up the pace.

"Look at 'em go," said Sandra with consternation.

"They're catching up!" Rusty shouted.

Sandra dashed for the middle turret, which now stood at the end of the truncated troop carrier. "I'll slow 'em down with a light show." She climbed up the trunk and took a position behind the breech of the laser gun. One deinonychus ran so fast along the shoulder that it caught-up with the straining vehicle.

"It's coming in the door," Rusty shouted.

Death Wind's spear was too long to maneuver in the confines of the troop carrier. He knelt on the landing next to Sam, bow in hand. Wind rushing in through the shattered windshield blew his long hair about his head. He notched an arrow and pulled it back until the bow nearly curved back on itself. The deinonychus's throat was only a yard away. With a loud twang the arrow leaped instantaneously into the gaping, tooth-filled mouth and emerged from the back of the neck. The carnosaur's head swiveled around as if it had been jerked by a lariat; it fell dead in the road.

"Watch out the back!" Sandra screamed.

Scott was so intent on the Nomad's action that he forgot about the other carnosaurs. When he twisted in his seat he saw with his right eye that another deinonychus was climbing in the rear opening. Sandra screamed as the monstrous head darted up the turret tube. Scott rudely thrust Jane aside, grabbed Death Wind's spear, and, unable to turn it around in the narrow compartment, butted the carnosaur in the chest as hard as he could. The creature fell backward, but clawed fingers grabbed the backrests of the last two seats. Scott butted again, in the throat. The deinonychus screeched as it clutched for the object of pain, lost its balance, and fell out the back of the truck. It flayed in the air for a moment, but landed on its feet with uncanny litheness. The forward momentum carried it onto its face. A pack member leaped over its back. A moment later, the downed creature regained its feet and continued the chase.

"They're too close." Sandra dropped out of the tube and landed on her buttocks with a slap. If she was hurt, she paid it no mind. "I can't depress the muzzle enough."

Scott searched frantically among the seats. "Where're the guns?"

"Gone with the rear of the truck," Rusty said.

Sandra climbed into the forward turret. "Hold 'em off a minute."

"With what? My good looks." Scott held his stance with the spear as two carnosaurs fought to climb in the jagged opening while the truck rolled along at highway speed.

Rusty pulled out the stun gun he had been carrying all these months. He climbed over the starboard seats and jabbed it into the face of the closest deinonychus. The single shot paralyzed it; it fell limp onto the road. Scott thumped the other one in the abdomen, but it had too good a grip on the backrests. The hind leg came up so high that the extended talon brushed the ceiling. Scott fell away as the carnosaur gashed downward. The hoof hit the floor, and the other one came up to repeat the procedure. Death Wind stepped over Scott and picked up the fallen spear at the same time a laser blast burst through the roof and drilled the creature neatly through the head; the beam continued lengthwise through its body, frying its insides. It fell dead on the floor.

Sandra did not stop there. She raised the barrel and fired at the bloodthirsty entourage. She blew out most of the roof doing it, since the rear turret was in her line of sight. She knocked down one deinonychus, but since she could not see well through the roofing material, most of her shots went wild.

"There's a rest stop up ahead," Sam called out.

"And a stagecoach pulling out with a fresh charge," Doc added. A double-turreted vehicle turned out of the driveway and headed toward the time transporter. "Now I understand. The deinonychus herd killed the titanosaurus, then was interrupted by the dragons. They did not like having their repast disturbed, and chased after them. Since the dragon vehicle was undamaged, our lizard refugees soon outdistanced—"

"Who gives a hoot?" Rusty screamed. "We've got monsters behind and monsters ahead. What'll we do?"

"We gotta changes horses." Sam eked as much power as possible out of the dying troop carrier. "This one's on its last amps."

Scott let Death Wind pull him to his knees. "Don't those things ever give up?"

Half a dozen carnosaurs galloped behind the truck, heedless of the bolts of death punching the orangetop around them. Sam did not slow down as he turned onto the staging platform, but the beasts cut across the hypotenuse and raked their claws along what was left of the glass and sidewalls.

"Hang on, guys." Sam steered the truck toward the stockade, yanked the joystick over hard, and threw the vehicle into a sharp turn. The side with the clinging carnosaurs bounced along the wall, scraping off two of the monsters and crushing a third under the wheels.

The stockade doors swung open. The motors screamed in protest as Sam spun the joystick in a circle. The truck veered away from the heavy gates, but spun out and stalled. The cab was full of smoke.

Coughing, Scott swatted the air in front of his face. "What the hell's a tech—"

An enraged deinonychus reached the vested dragon in a flash, raised its hind leg high in the air, and with one swift downward slash ripped open the slow-moving lizard from neck to groin. Razor-sharp teeth clamped onto the snakelike neck as the dragon's organs spilled out over the roadway.

A passenger coach full of technicians trundled out of the stockade and was immediately set upon by the remaining pair of carnosaurs. No soldiers were ready at the guns. The two rampaging beasts clambered through the open front door and wreaked bloody carnage on the dragons hissing within.

Sandra fired a well-aimed blast at the deinonychus that was hurriedly swallowing the entrails of the dragon it had disemboweled. She waited until all sounds of lizard hissing ceased before emptying her magazine on the coach. When the power finally died, the coach was a mass of flames. "Damn! It didn't blow."

Sam kicked open the door and helped the others out of the wreckage of the troop carrier. "End of the line for this bus, folks."

"I have never seen such a feral, ferocious, single-minded animal—"

Rusty grabbed Doc's elbow and hauled him into the stockade. "Later, Doc."

Scott let Jane lead him into the newly selected vehicle: a low-slung, double-turreted sedan with barely enough room for them to fit. Rusty pulled the charging plug before squeezing inside. Sandra climbed into the forward turret, Sam took the joystick, the rest crammed into the two passenger seats and cargo space.

Sam wasted no time switching on the motors. "Hey, the power grid says we're only half charged."

"The electricity was off in the complex, too. None of the indicator lights was lit." Rusty turned to his companion, his face locked in a grimace of horror. "Scott, do you know what that means?"

"Yes." Despite the blurry eye, Scott could see all too clearly. "It means that no more power is being transmitted along these lines: either in or out. If the time transporter is operating off its own reserve power, it'll send through only one more shipment. We've got to get to the TTS before those dragons in the bus ahead, because the only one who gets away—is the one who gets there first."

CHAPTER 28

"No sign of 'em. They must really be hauling." Sam held the joystick all the way forward; he moved it slightly from side to side in order to correct his course. "I wonder if they know about the reactor."

"With the power out, the commlinks are down," Rusty said. "Since we didn't pass them on the road, they must have left the city before we did. Ergo, they are probably on a routine assignment."

"Yeah, they shuffle techs back and forth like they were telegrams." Sitting in the turret seat, Sandra spoke down the entrance tube. "You just get close enough, Daddy, and I'll send 'em on their last mission."

Sam shook his head. "Scott, I sure hope you know what you're doing. I still think we should have taken a couple of single-turret speedsters instead of this lumbering coach. The batteries are so weak I'm losing speed."

"I took enough rigs apart to repair them blindfolded. Open the door. I want to get rid of another seat."

Sam hit the hydraulic switch that operated the portal piston. Gale force winds whipped into the cubicle as Scott and Death Wind held the bench seat in the air and manhandled it over the other seats and thrust it out the door. It tumbled off the shoulder in one piece and plowed a furrow in the grass.

"Good. Now, get that other access panel off."

While Death Wind removed the floorboards, Scott worked with unwieldy dragon instruments on the cable connections. Jane held the tool box in her lap and with uncanny prescience handed him the strange devices as he needed them.

"Are you sure the overload will not damaged the motors?" Doc said.

"Sure. It'll destroy them. But by the time it does we'll either be sixty million years away, or it won't matter."

"Don't you dare disconnect my turret," Sandra called down. "We may need this gatling gun before the day's over."

205

"Oh, you just want to blow something up."

Sandra fumed. "That's beside the point."

Scott wrapped a wrench around a copper bolt and loosened it enough to slip out the terminal prong. "Besides, I'm shunting the laser power in such a way that either gun will work, but not both together. You're a fast gal, but you can't be in two places at the same time." To Doc, "By putting the other power module and storage battery in series with the power train I can increase the voltage to the drive motors. They'll run faster than they're supposed to, and the extra heat will eventually burn on the windings. But dragons built things to last, and I'm betting the motors will hold up beyond their design specs at least long enough to get us to where we're going."

"It is a calculated risk we are forced to take—considering the alternative. Today is judgment day for us as well as for the dragons."

Sandra said, "Yeah, well, as long as the better man wins, the lizards don't have a chance."

"Is that proverb or prophecy?"

"It's propaganda. To keep up my spirits more than anyone else's."

Scott tightened the final connection. "Sam, you want to take off the load while I make the crossover?"

Sam idled the motors by pulling the joystick into the middle position; he could still steer the coach by shifting the lever from side to side, but the power linkage remained in neutral. "All clear." The coach decelerated slowly on nearly perfect ball bearings.

"Okay, Death Wind, you can close the knife switch."

There was a momentary spark as the Nomad closed the contacts. Scott kept his good eye on the built-in meters. "Looks good. Ease it into gear, Sam."

As he slowly thrust the joystick forward, the motors hummed until they sang at a higher pitch then they ever had before. The coach topped its previous top speed by twenty-five percent. After the initial load there was no more arcing.

"Dragons are good engineers." Scott smiled. "They have their faults, but none of them are electrical."

"Soon their only faults'll be geological," Sandra commented wryly. "An observation we should leave to them. Come on, Daddy, move this thing like there's no tomorrow."

"An unfortunate choice of words," Doc muttered, "phrased

such that they are likely to prognosticate before they become clichéd."

"Whatever that means." Sandra stood on the seat and arched her toes so her head touched the turret canopy. "Hey, I can see the bastards up ahead. Battle stations, folks. Get ready for a shootout."

Scott readjusted his bandages. "There's nothing we can do, Sandra. You've got the gun, so it's all up to you."

"Has it occurred to anyone that without power the draw-bridge may be inoperable?"

"Pop! Why the sudden pessimism? What're you trying to do, destroy morale?"

"I was merely pointing out the obvious so that we can prepare for every eventuality."

"Well, if worse comes to worse, we climb the wall again. Jane must still have her rope. She has everything else in that bag."

Jane smiled innocently as she pulled out the coiled vine. "I have."

Doc smirked. "My dear, it certainly did not take you long to join the ranks of civilized women."

"The next thing you know she'll be wearing a blouse," Sandra scoffed.

"Okay, I can see 'em now," Sam said. "Whoops, they just went over that next rise. Sandy, I'm gonna come straight up on 'em so you can lock the swivel on zero degrees."

"Gotcha."

As the coach topped the hill Scott saw an orange barrier several miles ahead. The time transport structure was not in line of sight with the road, and, even though it sat high on a hill, it was hidden by the nearby trees. "It's going to be close."

"You know, if there isn't any power, it may not make any difference," Rusty said. "No one is going anywhere if the transporter isn't fully charged."

"Hey, cut the gloomsday predictions," Sandra yelled. "Let's cross each bridge as we come to it."

"I was just pondering the possibilities."

"Yeah, well, what're you guys gonna dream up next?"

"Flyer in sky," said Death Wind without intonation.

"Just what we need," Sandra said sarcastically. "DW, don't you start going funny on me, too. I've got enough worries—

Hey, what's that mountain moving across the road? Daddy, do you see that?"

"Yeah, but I can't make it out. It's as big as a house. It must be some kind of moving van."

"That is certainly going to complicate—"

Doc was cut off by Rusty's poignant shout. "It's not a vehicle. It's a dinosaur."

"And it's not just a dinosaur," Scott gasped. "It's a Tyrannosaurus rex. Maybe the same one we woke up before."

"This time I'm ready for 'im," Sandra said through gritted teeth. "I'm gonna put 'im back to sleep—permanently."

Sam pulled back on the throttle. "We sure as hell don't wanna run into it."

The road in front of the coach erupted in a violent orange display of molten plastic. Exploding globules splattered against the windshield and bubbled the acrylic.

"What the hell—"

The coach drove straight through the tempest of flying debris; it emerged intact, but with the front window opaque.

"I can't see—"

The coach still streaked along the road faster than full speed.

"Watch your heads!" Death Wind bellowed.

Everyone ducked as he swung the access panel like a discus. It sliced a neat horizontal slit in the acrylic windshield. Sam squinted as hot air hit him in the face. Straddling the highway like the Colossus of Rhodes, the tyrannosaur screeched angrily at the oncoming vehicle. Two-fingered paws clutched futilely as a cavern full of teeth gnashed the air in strident expectation.

"Holy—" Sam jerked the joystick. The independent axles swiveled so sharply that the coach skidded fifty feet before beginning to describe a vector. The heavy storage cells in the chassis gave the vehicle such a low center of gravity that there was no chance of it overturning. As the coach's forward motion curved to the left, Sam slammed the throttle forward and to the right. He narrowly missed driving off the edge of the steep embankment. When the coach swerved right it grazed the columnar hind leg of the tyrannosaur and ran over the beast's tail. The crash with the caudal appendage tossed the vehicle sideways. It skimmed along the opposite embankment and came to a halt teetering over the edge.

"I got no power," Sam shrieked. "Musta blown a fuse."

"DW was right. It *is* a flyer. And my gun is jammed."

Sandra tumbled out of the forward turret and scrambled down the narrow aisle and up into the after turret. "Damn. This one's dead, too."

Scott saw the tyrannosaur spin around and stare directly at him through the rear window. Close-set eyes gave the beast binocular vision and depth perception that Scott was temporarily lacking.

Sandra punched the trigger uselessly. "Scott, I thought you said—"

"They just went through the gate, and they're closing the drawbridge behind them," Rusty shouted.

"Ten o'clock high, and it's taking aim."

The tyrannosaur hunkered down low and charged.

Doc inhaled sharply in the sudden shocked silence. "Sometimes I wish I hadn't been born. And in a time such as this, I realize thankfully that I haven't."

CHAPTER 29

The explosion next to the coach jolted Scott to action. He leaped off his seat and in one smooth motion ripped off the dashboard access panel and reset the electrical breaker.

Sandra must have had her finger clamped to the trigger mechanism because as soon as power was restored Scott heard the staccato drumming of the laser gun. Through the clear thermoplastic turret he saw the flyer veer off as bolts of energy bit off its power nodes in bursts of bright sparks. Sandra rotated the turret and let loose a blast at the oncoming tyrannosaur.

Sam fanned the master control switch; all drive motors came on-line at once. The accumulated torque jarred the coach's delicate balance; it tilted forward off the edge of the steep shoulder. Sam engaged the wheels at the same time: most of them turned vainly because they no longer contacted the road surface. But the two axles that provided the pivot point offered enough reverse motive force to catch the coach before it plummeted off the road. It slammed down hard. As the rear wheels bit into plastic, the coach shot backward, knocking all but Sam and Sandra to the floor.

The joystick banged against the turning detent as Sam tried frantically to prevent the coach from darting across the road and off the other side. The odor of burning plastic wafted up through the disassembled floor as the wheels spun against the road surface. The coach gyrated sharply, aligned itself with the direction of the highway, then smashed its back end into the tyrannosaur's low-slung abdomen. The rear window splintered inward, showering the cab with slivers of plastic.

Sandra was knocked from her perch by the impact, pitched down the turret tube, and deposited with a thud in the aisle. The tyrannosaur leaned forward like a steam shovel and with one monstrous crunch bit off the after turret. The gun was ripped from its mount. As the power cables separated, a pyrotechnic display of thunderstorm proportions burst in the tyrant lizard's face.

210

Rubbing her posterior, Sandra scuttled away from the missing turret; chunks of metal and shards of acrylic fell away from the opening. "It didn't even faze—" She grabbed a backrest to keep from being hurled into the cascading debris as Sam jammed the joystick all the way forward and propelled the coach out of the tyrannosaur's kissing embrace. The spinning wheels created so much foul-smelling smoke that the beast was hidden from view.

Doc said, "Warm-blooded metabolism requires tremendous amounts of food, but I did not think that—"

Another blast from the laser cannon gouged the orangetop between the coach and the tyrannosaur. The twenty-foot-tall monster spat out a mouthful of plastic parts. As soon as the volcanic eruption subsided, the tyrannosaur leaped fearlessly across the puddle of molten road surface and dashed madly after the careening coach.

"Sandy! Get up in that turret." Sam fought to keep the vehicle under control. He headed straight for the rising drawbridge. "You gotta blow up the guard shack and demolish the hydraulic system."

Sandra clambered up the tube in a flash. "What about the flyer?"

Preceded by its long shadow, the tyrannosaur galloped along the highway right behind the still-accelerating coach. Rows of rapacious teeth chomped the air. Sam did not dare slow down. "It can take care of itself."

"Undoubtedly full of administrators escaping the city. The dearth of pilots—"

Doc was again cut off by a laser blast, this one uncomfortably close to the starboard side. The windows blew in, and the bulkhead dented, but held.

"In the future, Rusty, I shall keep my thoughts to myself. Dragon methods of negative reinforcement are much stronger than yours."

Sandra blasted away at the bottom of the saucer. Power cones blew into pieces from her accurate fire, dissuading the flyer from following too close. Then she redirected her rotating barrels at the armed and armored guardhouse coming into range. Bright flashes of light attested to enemy alertness. The green bolts of energy seared the roof of the coach and melted one side of the turret. The blockhouse laser cannon was akin to a shotgun: it was intended to fight off encroaching carnosaurs, so its beam was spread for maximum close-range coverage. At a distance, its effect was lost in the scatter.

Sandra kept her finger pressed tightly on the trigger. The gatling gun emitted burst after burst of high-powered, pinpoint energy. Sam steered the coach without deviation. Every bit of speed and forward motion was necessary to stay ahead of the rampaging tyrannosaur. Sandra poured a deadly hail of fire into the guard shack. Excess energy poured into the blockade wall behind it, causing the plastic to sag like a collapsing mud bank.

The drawbridge's upward motion halted when the platform was raised a third of the way. It jerked up and down as if it were slipping a cog.

"Hit it, Sandy! Hit it!"

Between shots the black hole of the laser cannon's barrel was clearly visible. Sandra put an energy bolt right down the tube. In an instant the blockhouse, guard shack, and dragon soldiers were converted into molecular particles as a titanic explosion ripped outward from the supercharged battery packs. The orange ball of expanding gases created such intense heat that nearby trees were stripped of their leaves and left as smoldering, blackened sticks of charcoal. The grass was turned to cinder.

Flames billowed into the sky and across the road, completely obscuring the drawbridge from view. Sam's hand never wavered from its position on the throttle. The coach hurtled headlong into the seething cauldron, passing so quickly through the conflagration that, except for a brief finger of flame that darted in through the windshield slit, the heat did not have time to penetrate the cab.

The coach lurched sharply when the front axle hit the angled platform. Scott felt his stomach drop as he was launched out of his seat. Only a death grip on the backrest of the seat in front of him kept him from crashing into the roof. All he saw out the bubbled windshield was the purpling sky. The silence was palpable. The coach seemed to hover in the air on gossamer wings. Time was frozen.

Scott was several feet about his seat when the crash came. An instant later he was slammed against the floor and wrapped into a ball under the next seat forward. He floated through the bounce, then hit hard again when the coach contacted the earth for the second time. The vehicle went into an uncontrolled skid, left the road, and dug up the lawn for a hundred feet before sliding sideways to a stop. The cab was full of dust.

Scott blinked in the eerie silence that followed. His ears were ringing. He inhaled deeply, gratified that he was still alive. But every muscle in his body was battered and bruised. He moved slowly. A long while passed before he could focus his good eye. Then he saw Jane crumpled on the floor next to him. She was limp and unresponsive.

In a daze, Scott pulled her head onto his lap. Long golden hair flowed around his legs like strands of silk. He tried to talk, but the lump in his throat prevented his vocal chords from working. A tear rolled down one cheek as he brushed her hair back from her face. She looked so lost, so forlorn. They had gone through so much together that he could not bear to lose her now. He would rather die himself. He bent down and barely brushed his lips across hers.

Jane's eyelashes fluttered. She blinked, but did not otherwise move. Then she twisted her head suddenly and gazed into Scott's eyes. She snaked her hand out of the wreckage and placed it against his cheek; she wiped away the lone tear. "We are alive?" Her voice was soft and mellifluous.

"Oh, Jane." Scott hugged her tight. Her bare chest felt so good against his.

Jane returned his embrace, lingered in his arms for a moment, then pushed him away. "The others?"

Scott coughed. The cab was filling with smoke. "Doc! Rusty!" Both companions lay prone under a blanket of dirt, plastic, windowpanes, and ceiling insulation. He pulled Doc out from under the debris. His face was white with powder. "Doc."

Death Wind rose up out of the wreckage like the mythological phoenix and brushed himself off. "Sandra."

The turret seat had torn free from its mounts and lodged in the access tube. Sandra hung onto the gun by the breech. She kicked out wildly, gained purchase with her feet, and climbed back onto the turret shelf. "I'm okay."

The Nomad turned his attention to Rusty, who was pinned under a broken bench seat. Death Wind tore the seat off its one remaining stanchion and shoved it aside. The redhead blinked his eyes and spit out a clot of mucus. As the Nomad hauled him to an upright position, Rusty went into a coughing spasm that did not end until he emptied his nose of inhaled grit.

In Scott's arms Doc finally started breathing. Acrid fumes wafted up through the floorboards. Scott clamped his hand over Doc's mouth and dragged him toward where the windshield used to be. Sam lay on the grass twenty feet away. "Help me, Death Wind." Scott lay Doc on the floor, climbed out the opening, and reached in. The Nomad picked up the doctor and handed him to Scott, who carried the limp form to where Sam lay motionless.

Carrying her always present handbag, Jane helped Rusty out of the coach, then went immediately to Sam's aid. She placed her hands on his forehead. "Sam. Sam."

Sandra screamed at Death Wind. "Lemme go. I said I'm okay."

Death Wind struggled with the jammed seat. "Coach on fire."

Scott could hardly see the Nomad through the smoke and rising flames. "Get out of there before it blows." He turned his attention to Jane. "Come on, let's get them farther away." He dragged Doc across the grass while Jane and Rusty did the same for Sam.

"Leave me alone." Sandra undogged the seals, leaned back, and kicked open the upper hatch. "I'm clear."

Still wearing his quiver and bow and carrying his long-shafted spear, Death Wind ducked and jumped through the windshield opening. He dashed across the lawn to where the others scrabbled away with their charges. "We have trouble."

Scott looked where Death Wind pointed. The flames of the blockhouse explosion had nearly died out. Out of the smoke stalked the angry tyrannosaur, its head darting pigeonlike as it lumbered along the partially raised drawbridge. It balanced skillfully on the upper edge, tilted his head, and without hesitation leaped across the gap to the inboard platform.

A laser gun fired explosively. Scott nearly jumped out of his moccasins until he realized that Sandra was the shooter. The dazzling laser bolts seared rectilinear paths through the air—not at the storming tyrannosaur, but upward at the descending flyer.

The enemy flying machine veered away from the landing pad adjacent to the brightly glowing time transport structure. The thrumming of the saucer's power cones filled the air in concatenation with the electrical crackling of the time portal focusing nodes. Scott's hair stood on end from the static charge in the air.

The flyer's laser cannon fired at the smoldering coach and succeeded in demolishing the driver's compartment. Sandra nipped away at the saucer with smaller blasts that did no major structural damage, but which chewed up the undercarriage with telling effect. The flyer gradually lost altitude.

"What an unfortunate time to be deprived of one's faculties." Doc shook the gravel out of his snowy white hair and rubbed the back of his head.

"Doc!" Scott yelled. "I thought you were—are you hurt?"

"Abrasions and contusions, but nothing serious. I seem to have misplaced my cane. Could you help an old man—"

"Dragons! Up there." Jane indicated the technicians piling out of their vehicle, next to the transport dome.

"They're headed for the control bunker," Rusty shouted.

Sandra redirected the gatling gun long enough to stitch a line of laser beams through the waddling horde. Then she spun around as fast as the turret would rotate and zapped the tyrannosaur in the fattest part of the abdomen. The befuddled creature stopped in its tracks. Shriveled, two-clawed paws clutched at the site of sudden pain.

"Hell, I've lost turret power." Sandra climbed out of the hatch and onto the roof of the coach. The compartment below her was a mass of flames. She reached into the turret, removed the trunion clamps, and lifted the heavy gatling gun off its mount. Resting the muzzle on the lip of the turret, she fired again at the settling flyer just as it let out another blast that tore a long blazing furrow in the grass.

Jane implored to Doc with one outstretched hand. "Sam is hurt."

The tyrannosaur's scales smoked. Instinctively, the huge head tried to bite the hole that was causing such internal distress. Its attention was diverted for only a moment. Then the great coal-black eyes locked on the struggling humans on the lawn. Primitive mental associations racked its prehistoric brain. It screeched like a speeding freight train with its wheels locked on steel rails.

Scott's hackles rose as he jumped up and ran waving his hands. "Here! Over here." Nimbly, he darted across the grass and ran a zigzag pattern up the hill toward the hovering flyer.

His ruse worked, and the dim-witted carnosaur charged after him.

Doc knelt by Sam's stationary form. He placed his ear against his son-in-law's chest. "His heart beats weakly."

Sandra danced from foot to foot as the plastic heated up. She picked up the gatling gun and held it in both arms and carried it as far away from the smoke-filled turret hatch as the power cable would let her. She poured a deadly stream of fire into the flyer's extended pedestal. With the saucer now practically on the ground, her laser beams enfiladed the undercarriage and blasted through the forest of power cones. The flyer wobbled as it struggled to maintain a level attitude for landing. The pedestal was still ten feet above the nonmelt orangetop when the flyer, deprived of most of its force field channelers, dropped suddenly.

Because of the uneven destruction of its power cones, the flyer was listing considerably when it contacted the ground. The impact of the crash sheered off the cylindrical pedestal where it periscoped out of the base of the saucer. The flyer pivoted; one edge banged hard against the landing pad. The power ceased, and the whole weight of the flyer collapsed on the side of the displaced landing pedestal, crushing it.

Sandra immediately pirouetted and aimed at the dragon technicians who had been convinced to steer clear of the control bunker. Now they were making good their escape by converging on the dome. "Oh, no, you don't." She fired a controlled burst into their ranks, then kept a solid line of deadly beams between them and the portal entrance. The focusing nodes glowed with spectacular brilliance, ready at a moments' notice to discharge their pent-up energy and disrupt the space-time continuum.

Scott nearly collided with the caped dragons emerging from the wreckage of the flyer. They descended from the central opening, where the saucer was supported by the flattened pedestal, and crawled along the landing pad on all fours. Scott brazenly kicked the lead dragon in the chin, heard the resounding clack of breaking teeth, and slipped past it under the edge of the flyer. A solider clambered out behind the stunned administrator, gun in hand.

With a terrific bound the tyrannosaur leaped into the fracas, chomped off the caped dragon's head, and swallowed it like a mint. The soldier fired point-blank into the carnosaur's mouth.

The laser burned a hole through the thick jaw, but it served only to enrage the beast. The tyrannosaur stretched its neck under the flyer and took such a huge chunk out of the soldier's body that all was left was four limbs and a curved backbone.

Leaving the tyrannosaur to complete its carnage, Scott dashed back to where Death Wind guarded his companions huddled on the lawn.

Jane pulled the strap over her shoulder and laid the gadget bag on the ground. A whiskered, furry head poked out of the end folds. The antediluvian rodent wrinkled its nose and sniffed the grass with innocent curiosity. Jane dumped the bag. Eight baby rodents the size of thimbles tumbled out behind their mother; the newborns lay in a mass kicking silently.

"Where'd they come from?" Scott asked incredulously.

Jane stroked the mother as it nibbled at the young and corraled them into a hollow next to a small rock. "Here." She indicated the birth canal. "They are strong. They will survive."

Sam twitched.

Doc quickly ran his hands along Sam's arms and legs, feeling for broken bones. "Yes, and they will bring after them a new order of life to the face of the earth—an order that will dominate the next era just as the dinosaurs dominated this. Their descendants may very well— Sam. Sam. Can you hear me?"

Sam rocked his head and struggled to open his eyes. "Where am I? When am I?" He groaned as he sat up, and grabbed his neck. "Oh, do I hurt."

"Likely a case of whiplash. That was quite a pitch you took," Doc examined Sam's pupil response by swaying in and out of the light of the setting sun. "There are no breaks or apparent concussion. Do you think you can move? It is imperative."

Sandra let out a yell. "Damn. Just when I was having fun." She pulled the trigger several more times, but the laser gun refused to fire. She thrust it aside and leapt off the roof as it sagged from the heat and jumped ten feet to the ground. She landed on her feet, went into a roll, and came up running. "Clear the decks!"

The electrical wiring short-circuited, detonating the batteries. The resultant explosion blew apart the coach and sent flames and debris a hundred feet in the air. The rebels covered their faces as shrapnel and burning chunks of plastic fell like hot hail. When Scott uncovered his eye, the ground was littered with flaming debris: a graphic restoration of Hell.

Death Wind was the first to stand. "We hurry. Dragons make for dome."

As the tyrannosaur gobbled down the lizards struggling to escape from one side of the flyer, a pair of armed soldiers led their superior officer out the other side. What remained of the technical crew that had survived Sandra's withering fire gave up on their previous objective of attaining the control bunker; now they waddled as fast as their lizard legs would carry them to the top of the hill toward the shimmering blue curtain at the center of the time transport structure. The sky was a blaze of red: the pageant of early twilight.

"Hey, they're gonna go through," Sandra bellowed.

Rusty clambered up on hands and knees. "There's no more juice coming in. Once the capacitors are discharged, there's no way to recharge them."

"Come on, DW." Sandra charged the technicians approaching the dome's entrance portal. She was completely weaponless. "Let's get 'em."

Death Wind was right behind her, and Scott behind him. The Nomad tossed the spear to Scott in a running lateral pass, then in one smooth motion drew an arrow from its quiver and notched it on the string. He shot the arrow past Sandra's head and into the back of a vested dragon. The lizard let out a hiss as it clutched at the shaft stuck deeply in its flesh.

"Way to go, DW." Sandra swooped up behind another technician, grabbed its tail, and kept running. Caught unawares, the dragon was twisted around and yanked off its legs. It no sooner hit the plastic then Death Wind leaped on its chest and buried his knife in the snakelike throat.

Scott passed the skirmish and buried the spear tip in the hindquarters of another dragon. The powerful beast turned so quickly that Scott, still holding onto the spear, was swept aside like a fly. He maintained his grip on the shaft. The dragon kept turning, but Scott dug in his heels, found his footing, pulled out the spear, and quickly plunged it into a more vulnerable spot. Blood spouted like a geyser as the spear sliced into the chambers of the heart. The dragon collapsed like a puppet with its strings cut.

"Good going, Scott." Sandra patted him on the derriere as she brushed by him. "Now, how do we take down those soldiers when all we have are sticks?" The question in the air did not slow her charge.

The only technicians left were sorely wounded and no longer a problem. But the oncoming soldiers had their guns drawn. A laser bolt whipped past Scott and exploded in the control bunker bulkhead.

"Don't let them damage the transmitting station," Rusty called out as he and Jane dragged Sam, too injured to move on his own, up the hill and onto the orangetop. Doc limped along painfully on his bad leg.

Scott, having to dodge another laser blast, angled to where the bunker was no longer behind him. Sandra and Death Wind spread out in the other direction, thus dividing the fire of the enemy soldiers.

"It's *him*!" Sandra screamed. "The one with the gold cape." The cape was a mere shred, singed black; the dragon's scales were charred.

The moment of inattention nearly cost her life as one of the soldiers zapped her. The searing bolt went through her vest and left an ugly black furrow across her rib cage. She fell to the ground clawing at the smoldering material. Death Wind loosed a bolt that ricocheted harmlessly off the offending soldier's backpack.

The Tyrannosaurus rex licked bulging, bloodstained lips. Having devoured all the lizards within reach, it looked for other prey to feed its voracious appetite. It did not take long to discover the battle between dragons and humans.

The tyrannosaur bounded away from the flyer. Tusk-sized talons gouged the plastic surface, affording perfect traction. In the time it took Scott to gasp, the creature reached the caped dragon and with swift retribution chomped down on its sloping back. The tyrannosaur stood up like a derrick two stories tall. The dragon squirmed and hissed in its mouth. Massive jaws crushed the morsel while sharp, lancelike teeth rended effortlessly through flesh and bone. As the monster munched what was little more than a tidbit, it eyed the next course. The long tail lashed from side to side, knocking down first one then the other soldier.

"Time to leave." Scott stood his ground, holding the spear menacingly as Death Wind helped Sandra to her feet and whisked her toward the time transport structure. In the gathering darkness the dome glowed with awesome brilliance; the focusing nodes crackled with stored energy. With one last look at the towering tyrannosaur, Scott turned and ran. "Hey, wait for me."

Doc and Rusty dragged Sam through the dome's arched portal. Despite Sandra's burden, Death Wind paused to help.

"I'm all out," Doc said, resting.

Jane stood resolutely and waved. "Hurry, Scott."

Scott took only one step when the world jumped up and hit him in the face. For a time interminable he saw nothing but blackness. When he again opened his good eye and sucked in the breath of life, he felt the ground shaking violently. His body bounced like that of an acrobat on a trampoline. He struggled to get on his hands and knees, to crawl across the heaving orangetop toward the time transport structure.

The clear plastic dome vibrated shrilly, the focusing nodes spat static overcharges. Rusty dragged Sam out of sight through the ethereal blue curtain. Sandra fell to the floor, groaning and clutching her wounded side. Death Wind scooped her up and plunged out of sight.

With a tremendous zap the focusing nodes channeled their energy into the stasis field, rupturing the fabric of space-time. In a split second the time transport structure was as dark and silent as a tomb. The control switch had been tripped prematurely by the quake.

The earth continued to rumble, gaining in vehemence. It shook the very foundations of the dome. Fracture lines appeared in the sleek, curved plastic. The ground rippled.

Jane appeared out of Scott's blind side. Crying, she dropped to her knees and threw her arms around him. "Oh, Scott."

As Scott buried his face in her neck, he saw a sight that was beyond his comprehension: where the sun had but recently set, there now rose a furious fiery sphere.

Somehow, Doc managed to make his way along the quaking ground. Above the roar of noise, he said, "The others got through safely."

Scott stared openmouthed. Then he heard a savage screech that made him weak with fear. He broke Jane's embrace and twisted sharply. The tyrannosaur towered overhead, switching its tail and glaring down with bloodthirsty eyes. The lips curled in anticipation of a meal that could prove to be the last supper.

CHAPTER 30

It was when the tyrannosaur reached out with its hind leg that the shock wave reached them. The blast of air from the thermonuclear explosion knocked the carnosaur off balance. Its tiny arms flailed as it crashed through the plastic structure and rolled across the floor where once had stood the blue containment curtain. Tornadolike winds whipped across the top of the hill and lashed the tall dome.

Scott was lifted off the ground, and Jane with him. Doc was bowled over like a tenpin. All three lay flat and clutched the ground.

The defunct transport structure shuddered under the tempestuous impact. Plastic already fractured snapped loudly as tiny splinters grew off the major cracks. The focusing nodes ripped out of their mounting brackets and, like giant spears, crashed to the floor and splintered into pieces. Then the entire dome collapsed of its own weight and fell in on itself. The tyrannosaur was crushed under tons of plastic and steel.

"Hang on," Doc yelled above the rush of air. "It will pass."

The ball of light on the horizon was already double the apparent diameter of the sun. Scott allowed himself only a brief glimpse of the nuclear fire. The trees in the swamp forest were bowed like saplings; many had broken off. Scott realized that they were experiencing only the forefront of the shock wave: as the gases expanded from the point of detonation, they pushed before them the earth's entire atmosphere. The intense heat and radiation could not be far behind.

He held onto the ground, and to Jane, for what seemed like an eternity before the pressure wave subsided to gale force. Then he dared to pick up his head. The pain under his chest was the thick shaft of the spear. He rolled off it and sat up. He hunched over with his back to the wind. The sky was as bright as noontime. "It's over. It's all over."

Doc, too, picked himself up. "Our friends at least have been saved. We can be thankful for that."

Jane rubbed her hand over Scott's back. Her hair whipped about her face. "We are alive."

Scott scowled. "And about to become extinct."

"There is always hope for the living," said Doc.

"Tell it to the dinosaurs."

The wind continued to howl. The orangetop was a sliding conveyor belt of dirt, sand, sticks and leaves, and plastic parts, all rasping in discordant strains. The ground moved again: a long sliding motion, as if the entire land mass was rolling on greased runners. The rubble of the time transport structure settled raucously—except for a section of cables, batteries, charging generators, and broken focusing nodes that rose up against the force of gravity.

The tyrannosaur shrugged off tons of debris like a dog shaking water off its back. It seemed not to notice the raging storm. It took but a moment for the beast to see the three people sitting on the ground.

Jane screamed. Scott jumped up and pulled Doc and Jane with him. "Quick! Into the control bunk—" Nothing but a pile of disjointed plastic remained where the building had once stood.

Doc limped off with Jane in tow. "Perhaps we can hide in the rubble."

The tyrannosaur did not pause dramatically to weigh the situation. Its primitive brain did not house thoughts of tactics— it acted merely on instinct. It crouched low, bunched its leg muscles, and with a froglike jump cleared the wreckage and landed on the orangetop. It hunched over and charged.

Scott fumbled for the only weapon he had—Death Wind's spear. Knowing that the five-ton battering ram would simply knock it out of his hands before the tip managed to penetrate the thick scaled hide, he jammed the butt into the ground. With one eye bandaged, it was difficult for him to judge distance—it seemed as if the twenty-foot-tall monster was on top of him instantly. Scott raised the shaft at the exact moment that the tyrannosaur hunched for the bite; he tried to aim it perpendicular to the bulging abdomen.

The speed and momentum of the descending body forced the spear through the hide like a straw piercing a potato in the famous parlor trick. If the tyrannosaur realized its heart had been punctured, such knowledge did not slow it down. The Volkswagen-sized head split across the middle to reveal rows of teeth that put railroad spikes to shame.

Scott ducked under the drooling mouth and without even thinking ran out between the tyrannosaur's columnar legs. He hid for a moment beside the massive hindquarters, watching the swing of the tail, before dashing away. The tyrannosaur pivoted and lashed out. Scott leaped. The sticky tongue caught him in midair, wrapped around his leg, and halted his flight with a jerk. He was sucked into the tyrannosaur's mouth upside down, swinging like a pendulum. He felt an awful pain in his foot. Then, at the opposite end of the swing, he was flung clear of the carnosaur's muzzle. Scott's body crashed into the orangetop with a wallop. He lay insensate.

His next sense of awareness was Jane's high-pitched scream. As he rolled over onto his back he saw only a few feet away a dragon soldier lying battered and broken where it had been swiped by the tyrannosaur's tail. The dragon made a dying effort to aim its laser gun at Scott's chest. Jane slid between the two adversaries and fired her stun gun at point-blank range into the dragon's face. The dazzling coruscation wrapped around the reptilian head and down along its neck. It went limp without a hiss.

The tyrannosaur, still impaled on the spear, staggered in circles as it tried futilely to break off the shaft with its feeble forelegs. It reeled toward Scott, tottered drunkenly, then stumbled the other way.

Doc dropped by Scott's side. Quickly he shed his vest and wrapped it around Scott's injured leg. "You will be all right, but I need to stem the flow of blood."

Scott was becoming drowsy, his senses were leaving him. Doc and Jane were fuzzy shapes acting in pantomime. They made a cradle by interlocking their arms and picked him up. "What good—" He felt a curious numbness all over his body.

"Let us wait in the wreckage of the dome. It will be a while yet, but we must be ready."

Scott had no concept of the passage of time. When he lapsed into the pleasant void of mental blankness, he knew that his life in this world had ended.

* * *

Voices.

In his head.

Distant and far away.

He wanted to open his eyes, and slowly came to the realization that they were already open. He seemed to be looking through a thin diaphanous veil. Everything was so fuzzy.

"—be coming out of it, my dear. Perhaps you should be here when he awakens."

"I'll go tell the others, Doc." Rusty?

An amorphous shape swam into view—a giant blur that gradually coalesced into the face of an angel wearing a halo of blond, silken hair. His mouth worked, but no sound came out. He felt a soft touch upon his forehead.

"He is—conscious?" Jane. The voice was Jane's.

"I believe so."

She leaned close to him. "Scott? You are awake?"

Scott contracted his neck muscles into what he hoped would be interpreted an an affirmative nod.

The diamond pendant sparkled. "I love you." Jane kissed him tenderly on the lips—his first kiss in ages.

He must be in heaven. He regained control of his muscles and formed his lips into words. "I—love—you—Jane." The voice was craggy and hardly recognizable as his own.

"Ease him up a bit, my dear, while I put this pillow under his head."

Jane applied even pressure to his shoulders.

Doc tucked in the pillow. "Now, we don't want you sitting up yet. The rush of blood will likely knock you out, so just lie quietly."

Scott got used to the elevated position. He saw that he was in a room formed of orange walls. Diffused light entered through a window opening. He breathed deeply. "So—what—happened?"

"I guess I lost that bet. I said you would ask 'Where am I.' "

"It's that—emotional—response—that keeps them—off balance."

Doc's face split into a broad grin. He looked so clean and neat. "And you have proved the worth of that."

He forced himself to wink. "Was that—Rusty's voice?"

"It was, and he should be back anon."

"How did—he get—here?"

"The question you should be asking is, how did we get here. Or put more properly, how did we get back to now?"

Jane sat by his side and held his hand. "We are home time."

Scott was beginning to feel better. His words came more quickly. "Thanks for the clarification."

"It is Rusty's story, and—let him tell you himself. Here he is now."

The redhead appeared in front of Scott. He was smiling and full of energy. He squeezed his friend's arm. "Hey, old buddy. How's it feel to be back among the living?"

"I'm not sure. I feel kind of—numb."

"A medication that Jane supplied," Doc interjected. "Distilled from local vegetation. You've been out for three days."

"A lot's happened while you've been sleeping off a hangover," said Rusty. "The dragons are gone, the city is ours—"

"Whoa, whoa, whoa. One thing at a time. First of all, how did we get back if the time transporter was demolished?"

Doc and Rusty exchanged conspiratorial smiles. "The system wasn't demolished—only the transfer structure in the Cretaceous. Everything on this end was fully operational. Remember, once the dragons established themselves in this city, they engineered the push-pull system so they could send and receive at the same time with an economical expenditure of energy. After we came through, I set up the force field for reception only—a one-way transmission. Of course, most of what we got was the junk from the collapsed dome, but Doc and Jane had carried you into the perimeter of the force field—then sat down and waited."

"I knew he would not let us down," Doc explained. "It was just a matter of time. Naturally, I could not be sure that we would not come back into dragon paws, but I figured that a prisoner at this time had benefits not available to one in the Cretaceous." He shrugged.

Scott said to Rusty, "What did the dragons do—just hand you the controls?"

Rusty slowly shook his head. "There weren't any dragons left."

"You mean—Windy rallied the troops to revolt?"

"No. I mean, yes. He did rally the troops—at least, those who'd been captured from the outside. But they didn't take over the city until most of the dragons had already gone—of their own volition."

"But—where did they go?"

"We figure they went into the past, to try to reconstruct their civilization from the technology that already existed. You remember they were sending back technicians by the busload. They—hey, Windy, you tell him."

Windy looked as ragged as ever, but he strutted into the room with newfound pride. "Hello there, fellar. Heard tell you was up 'n about. How's it feel ta be back inna present?"

"I'm not sure yet. My thoughts are still in the past. I guess I'm still lacking presence of mind."

Rusty groaned and rolled his eyes. "Now I know he's getting better."

"Windy, Rusty was just about to tell me how you got the dragons to chase their tails."

"Di'n't do it. Oh, we was ready fer the big fight, a few of us was. But little by little the dragons skipped out on us. Left a skeleton crew behind, never thinkin' we had the guts to mutiny. Soon's we had the upper hand, we slipped inna their beds at night an' knifed 'em with plastic needles. Once we had weapons, we done in the techs an' capers. Then we sat by the dome and did 'em in as they came through. Damn near killed your lot before we recognized 'em. Hell, we give up on you weeks ago."

"What about the natives? How are they making out?"

Windy scrunched up his face. "We lost a lot of 'em. The dragons took 'em away—an' a bunch o' corpses, too. Guess they're gone for good, now. But the rest're doin' okay. We're teachin' 'em to be independent. With Jane here as 'terpretor we're makin' a lot more headway."

Death Wind and Sandra slipped into the room. Sandra threw her arms around Scott and gave him a restrained hug. "I'm still sore from that laser shot."

"From it, or about it."

Sandra tilted her head. "Both."

Death Wind placed a firm hand on Scott's arm; Scott returned the Nomad arm shake. "You killed Tyrannosaurus rex. You are greatest brave of all."

Scott's spine tingled, and an intense heat flowed through his body. He knew that he was blushing. Death Wind's pronouncement was the most noteworthy praise Scott could imagine. It was his proudest moment.

Rusty added, "You're the only man in history to ever kill a tyrannosaur."

"I'm only one of seven who've ever *seen* one. Besides, what killed the tyrannosaur was Death Wind's spear, tipped with a tooth out of its own mouth. When you think about it, it actually bit itself to death." His gaze shifted. "But Doc, here, is the real hero: a past master who moved more than mountains—he moved continents." He winked. "If you get my drift."

Doc grinned sheepishly. "I have tried to do my part in shaping history. But it is not something that I could have done alone."

"I've got something I couldn't have done alone, too," Sandra said proudly. She hooked her arm around her husband's. "I'm going to have a brave little brave."

Scott's eyes widened. "You mean—you're pregnant?"

Sandra wagged a finger at Jane. "You'd better watch this man. He catches on quick."

"Quickly," Jane said.

"Whatever."

Scott thought for a moment. "Do you realize that you must be carrying the oldest human being in the world? A sixty-million-year pregnancy. The mind boggles."

Sandra shook her fist in mock anger. "I'll boggle your mind, buddy, if you keep up the jokes. I think I liked you better unconscious."

"You wouldn't strike an invalid, would you?"

"Don't press your luck."

"Hey, what's this? A fight in the infirmary?" The voice was unmistakably Sam's. His face came into view over Jane's shoulder. He kissed her hair, and pressed his cheeks against hers.

"Sam! It sure is good to see you're all right."

"We all got a bit battered, but you took the cake."

Rusty groaned again.

"How do you like my bride? Isn't she prettier and younger than ever?"

Scott looked at Jane, who was smiling, and his heart sank. He gulped, unable to command his voice.

"Move over, honey." Sam sidestepped and pulled another woman into view. At first, she was too far back for Scott's distorted vision to make out. Then she came closer.

"Helen!"

"Hello, Scott. It's been a long time."

Scott's jaw fell open. He was too stunned to make a wise-crack.

"I kept her on ice so she wouldn't get any older while we were away," Sam said. "It was the freezers, Scott. None of those people in there were dead, they were in hibernation, or suspended animation. Another dragon technological achievement. Usually, they reserved the treatment for their own dignitaries—those that've been injured. You see, the body continues to metabolize, but at a very slow pace. One of the side effects is that the natural healing process is not hampered. So, you take a wounded caper, stick him in the icebox, and melt him down a couple months later completely healed."

"The only good dragon is a heeled dragon," said Sandra.

"Quiet, Toad. Anyway, they got the bright idea of freezing people so they'd have slaves on hand when they needed 'em. Now I understand why all of us POWs 'arrived' about the same time. We'd been captured months before and refrigerated till needed. After the dragon slaves died off, people suddenly became a valuable commodity. Helen was in the spring thaw."

Scott managed to find his voice. "But, why the pens?"

"The freezing process heals, it does not cure," Doc explained. He placed his hand on Scott's forearm and squeezed gently, fatherly. "Neither can it replace."

"What—what do you mean?"

Doc sighed deeply. "Your right foot, my boy, was bitten off. I amputated the stump just above the ankle. It was a sacrifice that undoubtedly saved your life, but not an easy one to live with. I'm sorry."

Scott held his breath as he rose slowly off the pillow. He bent his knee to bring his leg into view. The thick bandages wrapped in a ball did not hide the fact that nothing extended beyond the lower calf. He choked back his tears. Triumph was so quickly followed by tragedy.

Jane bent down and laid her bare chest against his. Her silent tears fell on his parched skin like the soft petals of a rose.

Life would never be the same. Life was never the same. Change was the definition of life. And one could not move forward without leaving the past behind.

Scott's strength gave out. He sank back, but Jane held him

firmly and eased him down onto the pillow. He would never have to worry about falling, for his friends, and his love, would always be there to catch him. He swallowed hard. There was a brand-new world out there. He made up his mind to greet it—and to go on with no regrets.

CLASSIC SCIENCE FICTION
AND FANTASY

THE FINEST THE UNIVERSE HAS TO OFFER